Praise for *Terra*

"Prepare to be swept away by a unique and captivating fated mates romance that will enthrall you from start to finish. A fresh and imaginative take on the genre that is sure to leave you spellbound."

Judy Corry, USA Today
Bestselling Author
of Sweet Contemporary Romances

"With a Twilight feel, readers looking for a young adult urban fantasy will enjoy the hidden Elemental world of Terra. Excellent series for teen and up."

Morgan L. Busse, award-winning
author of the Ravenwood Saga,
Skyworld series, and the Nordic Wars

"Terra was a delightful surprise and kept me hungry for more. Weaving a tale of intrigue, romance, and danger, Sofia Simpson masterfully tugs on the heartstrings and crafts a tale of hope and redemption. A story to savor and an author to watch!"

Tara Johnson, Author of
To Speak His Name

Operation Jewels

Also by Sofia

Dream Weaver

An Elemental Series
Terra
Torch
Tempest
Tidal

Operation Kane Novella Bk 2.5
Operation Jewels Bk 5

AN ELEMENTAL SERIES
BOOK FIVE

Operation Jewels

SOFIA SIMPSON

OPERATION JEWELS

Sofia Simpson
Copyright © 2026
Published by Starlight Books
First Edition

ISBN: 979-8-9993845-2-2 (ebook)

ISBN: 979-8-9993845-3-9 (paperback)

Cover Design by: EAH Creative

Editing by: Jessica Gwyn

Formatted by: Sofia Simpson

To any reader who suffers from a chronic illness, my hope is you trust in our Almighty Savior Who can give you peace.

Contents

1. Jewels

What the heck did I just see? That cannot be right.

I sit in stunned disbelief. From my perch on the porch swing, I swear I just saw the craziest thing. The guy mowing my neighbor's lawn just moved a bush with a wave of his hand. He somehow parted the ten-foot long row of bushes like a conductor waves his baton. I pinch my arm to be sure I'm not dreaming.

Ouch. Nope, not dreaming.

I can't peel my eyes away. The man looks around to see if anyone's watching, then he closes the gap, *doing it again.*

That's just not possible.

I'm pretty well hidden behind my mother's eclectic art that decorates the porch with wild abandon. I always thought she was the most off the wall person I've ever known, but this guy beats her by a mile. My homework drops to the porch, my fingers numb and lifeless. The movement makes him look up and spot me peeking at him from behind a tall orange pot.

My mouth is in an O. My eyes open as wide as they can while I shake my head in shock. The man's face twists when he sees my expression.

I wish I hadn't dropped my book. I mourn my anonymity.

He frowns deeply and walks toward me, abandoning his work, dropping a shovel. I jump, wrestling my forearm crutches into position. Maybe I can use them as weapons. He looks upset, menacing almost.

If I were capable of magic, I would seriously disappear right now.

Tearing myself out of my thoughts, I lurch for the front door. Most days, I'm as slow as molasses, but I can be quick when I want to be. I'm halfway to my goal when he says behind me, "Miss? Might I have a word?"

No. Absolutely not.

Fear closes my throat and freezes my muscles. It gives him the moment he needs to jump up the stairs and is to my side before I can respond. I look up at him. He's middle-aged, normal looking with brown curling hair, a little silver at the temples. He looks at me with concern, his big brown eyes studying me. His grimace is gone; he looks harmless. But I know better. *I know what I saw.*

"Um, I'm sorry, I have to go," I choke out. Turning, I reach for the doorknob.

He reaches his hand out to stop me. "Miss? I really need to talk to you. Please wait."

I pause, curiosity winning, wondering if he's going to explain how he moved those bushes. I turn to face him.

"So, uh, I need to just ask. What did you see?" He searches my face for clues.

"Nothing. I didn't see anything weird," I say in a rush, frozen in shock and fear.

He frowns. "Nothing *weird*? So, you saw something?"

I splutter. "I don't know what I saw! I have a vivid imagination, anyway. What do you think I saw?"

He cracks a smile. "I have a good guess." He looks so friendly. Maybe I have nothing to worry about.

"Well, whatever it was, you don't have to worry. Like I said, I have a great imagination." I snap my lips together and clench my crutches, my knuckles white with strain.

My heart is beating so hard, I'm surprised it hasn't jumped out of my chest. Really, did I imagine what I saw? If I didn't, then why is he here questioning me?

"Miss, I can explain what you saw...please, what's your name?"

Why does he want to know my name? Is he going to report me?

"I don't want to tell you my name."

He huffs a sigh and runs his hand through his hair. "This will really be easier if you just give me your name."

"Well, I'm sorry, I won't." I'm determined not to give him any information about me. Who knows what he'll do with it? I've heard of stranger cases of stolen identities.

He studies me, and I stand in stubborn silence. Finally, taking one last look at me, he turns and leaves as quickly as he came. I watch him go and see that he doesn't continue his yard work. In fact, he packs up his equipment in jerky movements and leaves within minutes.

I'm staring down the road in a stupefied state, watching him drive away when I hear my mom behind me in the open front door.

"Well, have you decided to come inside?"

I turn to look at her, stunned by what I saw and the interaction with the magic man.

Her amused look turns to concern, and she comes out on the porch and bends down to look me in the eye. She's two inches taller than me, but the way I lean into my crutches makes me appear much smaller than her. She has on her customary overalls with bright spots of paint all over them. A bright red kerchief covers her wild, curly hair.

"Julia, what's wrong, honey?" She grips my upper arms and steers me inside.

I follow her dumbly because my lips are numb. *What can I tell her?* I usually share everything with her, because it's best if I'm open and honest about how I'm feeling, especially with my condition. Sometimes medication gives me wild side effects.

Maybe that's what this is. One of my meds has taken over my mind and made me see things.

I decide to go with that.

"Um, well, Mom, is it possible one of my new pain meds could make me hallucinate?"

Mom looks at me, her eyes pinched with concern. "You think you're seeing things?" She leads me to a bright floral armchair, which I sit in gratefully. I set aside my crutches. Her tone gets all businesslike. "What color eyes do I have?"

"Blue."

"What's my middle name?"

"Helen."

"How old am I?"

"Forty."

She caresses my face, her warm blue eyes lovingly holding mine. "I would have accepted thirty-five, but I think you're okay."

Even though I answered all of her questions correctly, a wave of paranoia hits me. *Did I imagine the whole thing? Even the conversation?*

"Mom, did you see me talking to someone?" I ask quickly.

She nods, and I slump in the seat in relief. "Well then, what exactly happened?" I put my hand on my head.

Mom squats in front of me. "Honey, what are you talking about? Now, you're worrying me."

I bark a laugh. "I'm worrying myself! I could swear I saw something, but it's impossible."

"What did you see?"

I straighten. Even though I have spina bifida, my spine allows me to do that. I look my mom in the eye. "Mom, I could swear I saw a man move a bush with the wave of his hand."

Mom studies me for a second before she worriedly looks away. She shakes her head. "That's not possible. It looked like he waved them apart?"

"Like the Red Sea."

She blows out a breath and squeezes my hands.

"I know it sounds crazy! But when he noticed me, he came up to ask me what I saw."

Her forehead furrows. "That's weird."

"I know! Do you think he can do magic?"

Mom shakes her head, but says, "There's no explanation for that, but maybe he had a tool in his hand that moved it?" She looks at me, her eyebrows raised.

"I didn't see one. He asked for my name."

"You didn't give it to him, did you?" she asks quickly.

"No! Of course not. But I would do anything to find out how he did it. Maybe he's telepathic?"

"Telepathy is the ability to read minds, honey. You mean telekinesis."

"Yeah." I brighten and squirm. "Could that be what happened?"

She bites her lip. "I don't think so, baby."

We sit and think for a minute when the doorbell rings. We both look at each other with wide-eyed expressions.

"Do you think it's the same man?" she whispers to me, still crouching down. She hunches further.

We're in full view of the door window, so her attempt to hide is not working. I look through the window and see it's not the magic man, but a younger guy.

"Who is that?" I ask with a frown.

"Let me take care of this," my mom says in a no-nonsense tone. She stands up in one smooth motion and walks to the door. I've always envied her easy grace. I could never do that. I don't resent her, though, not anymore.

She cracks open the door and asks, "How can I help you?"

I don't hear what he says, but after a few moments, Mom allows a handsome twenty-something-year-old guy into the house. My eyes widen at his easy admittance.

What did he say to her to gain entrance so easily?

"Julia, we have a visitor. He says his name is Drew. He'd like to ask us a few things about questionable activity in the neighborhood." She says the last part with her eyebrows raised and a meaningful look in her eye.

I breathe through my mouth, attempting to control my galloping heart.

Maybe he can give me some answers. Wait, what if this guy is part of the magical police?

He looks at me with a grim smile, projecting a confidence you don't learn overnight. It's easy to see that he is very comfortable in his own skin. It's taken me my whole life to even start doing that, while he seems to have mastered it ages ago.

"Can I help you?" I ask, glad my voice doesn't waver.

"Actually, yes." He folds his hands in front of him. His dark wavy hair is long enough to hang in his eyes and is down to his shoulders, but it doesn't take away from his attractive gray gaze. It's like he can see right into my soul.

I slam those thoughts down and break eye contact. I will not allow myself to drown in his stunning eyes. So, I continue an unbiased assessment of him. He's wearing a blue polo shirt and khakis. If he were part of a magical organization, wouldn't he be wearing, oh, I don't know, like leather pants or even a suit? My imagination goes wild, and I can't wait to hear what he has to say. The fact that he's here so soon after what I just witnessed cannot be a coincidence.

"May I ask you your name?" He turns to face me after he looks around the room.

"Wait a minute," my mom interjects, pushing her way in between us. "Why do you need her name?" She folds her arms in front of her like she does when she means business.

"I'm just being polite. I'd like to know who I'm speaking with," he answers easily.

Mom is planted in front of me, so I lean to see around her. "Well, we don't want to tell you our names."

"But you have witnessed strange behavior in your neighborhood recently?"

"Well, yes," Mom says with some hesitation. "But I don't see why we'd have to tell you anything more."

"That's fine." He peeks around her to look at me. "You said at the door that your daughter witnessed something?"

My patience is waning. I want an explanation of what I saw, and it seems I can get my answers from this guy. It will help me figure out if my medicine is doing its job or something extra unpleasant.

"If I tell you what I saw, will you explain it?" I ask in a steely voice.

He takes a step to the right of my mom, who hasn't moved an inch. "It really depends on what you saw."

Sweat dots my forehead and makes my hands clammy. "Look, am I in some kind of trouble here? If so, I know my rights." And I do. I'm planning on getting a law degree. My interest in justice for the oppressed and the long days I've spent researching the law have gifted me with that kind of knowledge. But he isn't a cop. At least, I don't think he is.

"Are you a cop?" I decide to ask.

He smirks. "No. I'm not a police officer. I'm just here to investigate what you may have seen today."

"Why only you? Are you part of the Concerned Citizens' Committee or something?" I ask.

He huffs a laugh. "Something like that. Now, would you mind describing what you saw?"

If I want an explanation, I'm going to have to say something about what I saw. I take a controlled breath and say, "Well, I noticed the man next door from a lawn care company... walk through bushes like they weren't even there."

He lifts an eyebrow. "Can you go into more detail?"

I throw out my hands. "It's like he parted them with a wave of his hands. There's no way anyone can do that though, unless he's Moses with a magical staff...or even Harry Potter."

"I see," he says with a small smirk. "How many bushes are we talking about?"

He didn't seem even remotely surprised or shocked by this. Encouraged, I answer, "About ten feet of them, I would say."

"I see," he says again. He looks down, studying his shoes.

"What? What do you see? Can you tell me if I imagined that?"

He looks up at me through the locks of his hair. His eyes are arresting. I've never seen that shade of gray before. What I just said makes them almost silver. They hold me so still, I'm surprised when my mouth moves. "Please," I ask. "I think I'm going crazy."

He gives me a sympathetic look, and I unclench my hands in my lap. "You're not going crazy. You're perfectly normal." He pauses before he glances at my mom, then back at me. "I promise you answers, but first, I'm sorry. I believe this is necessary."

At that cryptic comment, he reaches into his pocket and draws out his hand in a clenched fist. Before I can blink, he tosses powder in my mom's direction, then spinning to me, throws the rest in my face.

We both cough violently when we can't help but breathe in the powder.

I try to stop breathing, but I've already sucked in too much of the noxious substance. *He just drugged us?*

In horror, I watch my mom drop onto the floor. My limbs go limp, and I can't help but fall back in my chair.

My mind feels numb, and I watch with glazed eyes as Drew picks Mom up easily, carries her over to the couch, and sets her down gently. He bends over her, and I'm struck with the horrifying knowledge that we are at his mercy. *Is he going to hurt us?*

I'm hit with a violent fear, but I can only look on as Drew seems to take my mom's vitals. He's holding her wrist and looking at his watch.

He straightens, looking satisfied.

My mouth is just as lifeless as the rest of me. I want to scream and rail, demanding answers, but I can't seem to get my tongue to form the words.

"Well," he says, "this is the only time when I can be fully honest with you."

What? That you're a psychotic murderer?

As limp as my limbs are, I'm also frozen in fear. What is he going to do to us?

"The truth is, I'm the only one who can give you the explanation you're looking for. You won't find answers anywhere else."

What is this cosmic explanation that we've just sacrificed our health for?

"Now, I'm a man of my word, but the truth is you won't remember any of this conversation. In moments, you will forget everything you've witnessed and done today."

I try to move my arms, to do *something*, but I'm powerless.

His eyes are twin orbs full of concern and sympathy. "You witnessed an Elemental using his ability to move the bushes. There's a whole group of humans in this world who have elevated gifts. We can do many things, and today I'll use some of my gift to make this experience somewhat easier on you and your mom. I'll try to ease what I can. And the only reason I'm even telling you this is to absolve myself of some of the guilt I have for putting you through this experience."

Ease what? What's going to happen to my mom and me?

As if in answer, my body starts spasming. Where my arms and legs were once boneless, now they're painfully stiff, and I can't stop convulsing.

Drew bends over me and runs his hands over my arms and legs, and the resulting warmth relaxes some of my rock-hard muscles into a softer, more pliant condition.

I barely notice my mom experiencing the same symptoms. Drew moves over to the couch and does the same magical treatment to her.

Time moves slowly as I go through periods of spasms that are especially painful because of my condition. My back has always been stiff and difficult to move without pain, but the way the convulsions are quaking my body makes me cry out in pain and torment.

"I'm sorry. I really am. Hang in there. You'll get through this." His voice is warm and comforting. As angry as I am at him for inflicting me with this, I soak his words in like water. Drew seems especially compassionate with me, and he spends more time healing me than my mom.

"You're doing great. In just a few more minutes, you're going to completely forget about this experience."

That's where he's wrong. Even if I forget this traumatizing experience, my body won't. I dread what I'm going to feel tomorrow. I've taken meds in the past that caused seizures, and the aftermath was always worse than the actual convulsions.

I find I have my voice back and I yell at him, "You don't know what you've done!"

He looks at me, his gray gaze peeling back layers of defense I've woven tight over the years. "I think I understand. And I'm sorry. I'll try to help if I can."

He sweeps me up and lays me on another couch, turning me over onto my stomach. His hands cover my misshapen back with searing heat that makes me arch under his touch. I gasp. "What are you doing?"

"Give it a minute," he says softly.

In moments, the heat cools into a pleasant warmth, and I find I can move in a way I've never been able to before. I'm not healed by any stretch of the imagination, but he's just improved my back more than years of intensive therapy could ever do.

I slump down flat, completely exhausted. He moves his hands over the muscles in my legs and arms, and the same wonderful warmth soaks through the punishment that the toxic powder caused.

I relax.

Satisfied with my progress, he moves over to my mom and gives her the same treatment.

When he's treated us both several more times, he straightens, his shoulders slumped, and his face drawn in exhaustion.

Rubbing his hands together, he looks at us and says in a weary tone, "Tomorrow morning, you'll wake up feeling like you've forgotten something, but that's it. You will remember nothing from today. It's really for the best, and for the record,

I'm sorry for what you went through. It's always painful, but your condition made it worse for you. For that, I'm genuinely sorry. I assure you, what I gave you both is harmless. It's nothing to worry about, more like a vitamin, completely natural. It's made from poppy seeds."

I can only look on numbly, too exhausted to respond in any way.

"For what it's worth, I think you're incredibly strong for a human. I wish you all the best in the world."

And with that, he lets himself out of the house. He's gone before I know it.

What? Strong for a human? *What did he just do? Apparently, by tomorrow, I won't remember.*

2. Drew

♥

I leave the home of the unknown girl and her mother with intensely mixed feelings. My stomach is in knots after watching the poppy seed formula brutally punish her body. I have never seen a human react so badly to the formula. It's not an easy experience for anyone. But watching her endure that kind of punishment was hard, especially because I caused it.

As I make my way to my car, my mind is full of the traumatic experience. I tried to make my penance by easing her pain and even healing some of her condition, but I hope and pray she doesn't have residual effects tomorrow. I'm thankful I'm more gifted than most Elementals in healing or I would have had to just watch her go through all of that.

Knowing a little about her condition helped me to ease her pain for the next couple of days, too. I hope it was enough.

I drive home, and my mind runs. Knowing what I do about spina bifida, I know that she experiences horrible stiffness, and I'm actually amazed to see her with crutches. That she can walk shows that she's incredibly blessed. Her spine was affected lower down, giving her the incredible opportunity for mobility. But it's clearly not easy.

I wince as I remember the state of her muscles in her back and legs. She was as tight as a drum. She suffers every day. But her face carries a strong resilience, and her eyes are so full of bright determination that I can't help but admire her.

When she cried out that I didn't know what I did, it tore my heart into shreds. I felt horrible. If I could, I would have argued that I did have an idea. As a pre-med major, I've studied enough to know that the poppy seed formula is a hundred times worse for her than for a healthy person. She cried out in pain only a few times, when I know she felt more than that. Administering the poppy seed formula is always hard to witness. In fact, I don't know how the other clans can make humans take it without the gift of healing.

I shudder at the thought of inducing so much pain just to make a human forget about us, but we haven't come up with anything better to erase a human's memories. I know we're working on other remedies, but so far nothing has been as effective as what we already use.

Thinking back to the girl, I recall her soft beauty. I can't help but remember. Her short dark hair and petite facial features remind me of a pixie. As if those exist, I laugh inwardly. I have a feeling that if they did, she would be one of them. Despite her condition, it's almost magical how strong she is.

I chuckle when I remember the questions she fired at me. She's intelligent, which I admire even more than her beauty. She looks eighteen or older, if I had to guess. But she wouldn't give any information about herself. With her address, I'll be able to get the facts about her and her mother and whoever else may live in the home soon enough.

She's a force to be reckoned with, and if there's anything I respect more than her natural intelligence, it's her strength of character. I pray she won't suffer for what I just put her through. Muscles have long memories, though I tried my best to ease the trauma. I'm more exhausted than I've ever been after administering the formula. But I would gladly heal her again. It was worth it if this is all behind her.

One thing is certain: I'll carry the memory of her for some time to come. I shake my head. I need to forget her. She's human and therefore could never be a part of my world. Well, my real world. Though I live and work among humans, I shouldn't have such feelings for one. I resign myself to remembering her with fondness.

3. Jewels

O ne year later.

I'm walking toward the bus stop at my university when I hear a message come through on my phone. I stop to take it out of my pocket.

For the thousandth time, I hope to see Vela's name, but she's been gone for over a year, and I don't know where she is. She was such a good friend, I can only hope she'll be a part of my life again soon. At least I have Elia. I can thank Vela for introducing us. Elia's a bright light I love basking in. She's full of optimism. You can say I'm optimistic, too, but in a more controlled way.

I glance at the screen and see it's Mom.

Mom: Hey honey, good news! Our insurance approved the new treatment we talked about! You can start this week! I made an appointment!

I groan. I'm not very hopeful that this new treatment will help me any more than the other ones did. Some of them eased symptoms a bit, but nothing is going to cure me of my condition. The best I can hope for is a little more mobility. That's what this new intensive program promises.

I take a deep breath.

Jewels: Great. Can't wait.
Mom: No need to get testy.
Jewels: Who said I'm testy? I have high hopes, really.

Mom: Sure, you do. Let's stay positive, okay?
Jewels: Sure, Mom. I'll try.
Mom: You will. Period.
Jewels: :)
Mom: That's my girl.

I turn off the notifications and drop my phone into my bag. Suddenly, I don't feel like talking to anyone. When I get like this, I just want to crawl into a hole and stay there for a good, long while. When this black mold of emotion takes over my mood, I'm terrible company. I fight it as best as I can, but sometimes I can't help but give in to it.

I try not to feel too sorry for myself and the condition God's allowed me to have. It's as much a part of me as the nose on my face. While I can't change my circumstances, I can change my attitude.

But sometimes it's really hard. Looking around me, I see everyone else walking around upright and with easy steps. I was born with spina bifida, where my spinal cord didn't form correctly. I am lucky, though; I can still walk with the aid of crutches. It's not easy or smooth. I have to twist my body to drag my legs forward one at a time.

I'm one of the lucky ones. There are many others with my condition who are unable to walk at all. I have to force myself to remember that from time to time. Like anyone else, I need an extra dose of hope to fuel my day. And what I need to do when this mood hits me is remember Scripture.

I whisper the words as they come, "*My grace is sufficient for you, for my power is made perfect in weakness.*" *2 Corinthians 12:9 NIV.*

I think about my weaknesses. My physical impairment is not all I am. I am a normal person who struggles to do what's right. God gives me grace because I'm not a perfect human being. I have flaws that I work on every day.

Like my attitude.

As I make my way to the waiting bus, I take a deep breath, push away the dark emotions, and bask in the uplifting that the

Scripture did for my bruised heart. Stopping, I lift my hand, raising my pinkie, forefinger, and thumb in the sign of I love you. I point it at the sky, thanking God for His constant encouragement through His Word. I do this when I need to remind myself that I'm thankful.

One dragging step after another, I carefully walk up the bus steps and list everything I'm thankful for. I have a future. I'm one year into my political science degree at Denver University, and I intend to follow that up by going to law school. As a lawyer, I hope to spearhead efforts to help patients like me. Those with lifelong conditions often face battles with insurance companies that won't allow the much-needed care they deserve. I plan to help change that.

I find a seat on the bus, and when I look out the window; I take a deep breath. A student sitting with her back against a tree is playing with a flowering weed that grows next to her. I dimly wonder if she's the one who grew the flower.

Ever since a year ago when I saw a man move bushes with his mind, I've become more aware of strange things I never would have noticed before the incident. I've seen a couple more inexplicable things.

A man who thought he was alone opened a hole in the ground with just his mind. On vacation, I saw an unnatural breeze cool off a woman who didn't think anyone was watching.

Drew told me I wouldn't remember what had happened on that fateful day. But though he erased my mom's memories, I remembered everything. When I brought it up to her the next day, she had looked at me like I had lost my ever-loving mind. I started to think I *had* lost it, but the memories were still there, fresh as a daisy.

When I saw that man open the soil with a wave of his hand a couple of months later, I knew what I remembered was real. And so was the excruciating experience after breathing in that foul powder. I haven't had pain like that for years, since I was a child. I was shocked it hadn't affected me for the next few days.

Drew did something to me that not only eased the pain in my back but slightly improved my walking.

So, for the sake of not going through that kind of torture again, I didn't breathe a word about my experiences with what seems like magic. I've kept my sightings to myself. I've also never seen Drew again. He disappeared into the abyss of mystery that will always surround my memory of him.

He's kept his gift a secret. And if a human like me witnesses him performing his magic, they'll be treated the same way my mother and I were. Their memories will be wiped clean. My poor mom didn't even see anything, but because I told her what I witnessed, she was put through the same horrible experience.

I want to ask Drew why I didn't forget like he promised I would. He was so certain my memory of the incident would vanish once he left.

Why did I remember?

Is there something wrong with me that makes me resistant to the powerful effects of that powder?

Now that my suspicions have been confirmed, I can't go back to how it was before. It's like my mind has been blown open and tantalizing possibilities have now become believable. I've read my share of paranormal books. If magic exists, do werewolves? Vampires? Are the magic people really fae or elves?

I smile at myself. I'm letting my imagination run away with me. Drew said his people were human, just with elevated gifts. But I can't help but wonder who else is full of magic like Drew? It's made me look at those around me in a new light. I'm constantly alert, trying to discern who might have these wondrous gifts.

It's obvious Drew can do more than just move bushes or dirt. He can heal with his hands. I would do anything to have another five minutes under his hands. I'll never forget the tantalizing warmth on my back, legs, and arms. I've had plenty of massages where the masseur's hands were warm, hot even. But Drew's touch was different. It's like he fed heat deep into my body, into my muscles and even bones.

I think about this new treatment. The only reason I agreed to try one more thing is I'm searching for an elusive touch like Drew's. Surely there are more like him out there. I just might get lucky enough to encounter a gift like his.

I crinkle my nose at my next thought. He thought I wouldn't remember his healing ability. So, I doubt I will ever experience it again. He hides his gift, so it would make sense that anyone else like him would do the same.

Maybe he only healed me like that because he felt sorry for me.

That's a definite possibility. If our world knew about people with powers like this, they would be greatly sought after, even exploited. I'm sure they've kept themselves hidden for their own protection.

No, I don't blame them for staying hidden. I certainly won't say anything. I learned my lesson the last time.

As the bus approaches my stop, I get up early to give myself more time to make my way to the door. When I step off the bus, I notice the sky getting dark. Taking a deep breath, I put a little more speed into my gait. I'll have to be quick to stay dry. I feel my phone vibrate, since I turned the ringer off, but I ignore it, hoping I get home before I'm soaked.

Thunder rumbles, and I pray God holds the rain off for a bit longer. I could crow in relief when I make it onto my porch ten minutes later, nice and dry. The skies open a few seconds after I walk in the door, and I kiss my fingers and hold them up.

"Julia, is that you?" Mom calls from the kitchen.

"Yes, Mom, it's me," I answer, slumping into one of the comfy chairs in the living room. Mom has the most comfortable seats for me, and I couldn't be more grateful. I rest my back against the soft cushions and lay my head back, sighing.

"You just missed the rain," she says when she walks into the living room, wiping her hands with a towel. She skirts the Saran-wrapped sculpture that's taken temporary residence by the TV. It's a piece she's just finished and must be waiting for the shippers to come and pick it up. She too looks wrapped up in a kind of sarong and bright pink tank top to go with it.

"I know," I say tiredly, closing my eyes to her brightness.

"I wish you'd let me pick you up from school."

I peek at her through one eye. "You know I like to do things myself."

She frowns and crosses her arms. "Yes, but you could have gotten wet and stuck in the rain. What would you have done if you had caught pneumonia?"

"I would have gotten over it, like always. Let me be, Mother. I love you, but stop fussing over me."

She clicks her tongue at me. "I wish you'd let me fuss more."

I pick my head up. "When is my appointment?" I would specify, but she already knows. I have so many doctor appointments, it's a miracle I can go to school at all. Between neurologists, physical therapy, and my amazing GP, my schedule is chock-full of time with doctors and specialists.

"In two days. I can't believe I got you in so soon. I've heard great things about this place," she says with a bright smile.

I return her smile. "I hope it's as great as they say."

"How were classes today?" She flicks open a fan and waves it in front of her face like it's ninety degrees in here. It's not. She's just perimenopausal. Going through this phase of her life so early has really thrown her for a loop.

I wave my hand. "Like usual. My general classes are fine, though not that thrilling. And my one poly-sci class only covers cases I've studied before. I'm looking forward to more difficult ones."

"You and your ambitions."

"I might have a bum back, but my mind is perfectly fine, and I like to use it."

She laughs. "It's one of my favorites of your many wonderful qualities."

"Thanks, Mom."

She walks away to finish the dinner I smelled when I walked into the house. As well as being a talented sculptor, she's a wonderful cook. She's tried to teach me her kitchen secrets, but it's useless. I can't move as quickly as she does, and grabbing a boiling over pot or spinning from the cutting board to lift vegetables into a skillet is not easy for me.

But I try. I always will.

Just then, I remember my phone had gone off when I was trying to beat the rain. I fish it out of my bag and smile when I see Elia texted me.

Elia: Hey Jewels! Wanna have a movie night?

I think before I answer her. I have about an hour's worth of homework to do tonight. I think I can fit in a movie.

Jewels: Sure. But it better not be another cheesy rom-com!

Elia: Hey, those are the ones Kane refuses to watch with me. Who can I enjoy them with if not you?

I smile sadly. She misses Vela fiercely, but I'm a fair substitute. I'm just happy Elia is my friend. Oh, the things I do for her.

Jewels: Fine. Which one are you going to torment me with tonight?

Elia: Oooooo, there's an oldie goldie called *The Princess Bride* that is amazing! Tell me you haven't seen it?

I have not seen this movie for a very good reason. I don't typically like movies like this one. Where the guy gets the girl and blah, blah, blah. I let my head fall back on the chair. This has a long night written all over it. She's going to want to gush about every facet of the storyline after we watch it. I don't mind watching these movies with her, but must I be tortured by re-living it over and over?

Elia: Hello?

Jewels: If I say yes, you have to bring my favorite ice cream over. That's the only way I'm going to survive this tonight.

Elia: It's too good! You'll love it, I promise!

Jewels: Only for you, bestie.

Elia: Take one for the team, sister.

Jewels: How did Kane get out of this one, anyway?

Elia: He said he would rather die than subject himself to this movie. So dramatic!

I know just how he feels. I can easily relate to his wisdom. Since he's a guy, he can get away with it. But my stupid gender makes me much more qualified to endure these movies with my high-spirited friend. According to Elia.

Elia: I really don't understand why you don't like rom-coms. ???

Jewels: Because love doesn't exist like that.

She doesn't respond for a few minutes, but when she does, it guts me.

Elia: You don't know it yet, but you're going to feel love so wide it will have no measure.

This time I'm quiet for a while. Finally, I respond.

Jewels: I sincerely hope so. Until then, I'll watch your stupid movie.

Elia: I sincerely promise you'll love it.

We figure out a time that will work, and I extract myself from the chair to enjoy dinner after Mom calls me in.

After dinner, Elia shows up, her hands full of ice cream and a gazillion toppings.

"Did you bring the entire grocery store with you?" I ask, laughing.

She carries her huge bundle by me and walks into the kitchen, saying over her shoulder, "You know the ice cream you like is no good without extra stuff in it."

"What? Cookie dough ice cream isn't flavorful enough?" I follow her into the kitchen, and count at least ten toppings she spreads on the island.

"No, absolutely not. It's way too boring. You need to liven it up, Bestie." She grabs two bowls and the ice cream scooper, which she promptly uses to dish several large scoops into both bowls. I look on with horror as she slathers hers with all ten toppings. When she moves to do the same with mine, I cry out, "Hey! No way! Don't desecrate mine with all that stuff. I'll take mine simple, thank you very much."

I move next to her and reach to pinch the lip of the bowl with my thumb and forefinger. Satisfied I can hold it and walk, I go into the living room. She follows me grumbling, "You're no fun."

"I'm actually a lot of fun, or you wouldn't be here. You can't be in the same room as someone who's a dead bore."

"True," she says, scrunching her nose. "Is that a bad quality?"

I laugh, careful to tip my bowl down on the coffee table without spilling. "No. I'm actually honored to be among the few who can handle your manic positivity in large doses."

She narrows her eyes at me. "I feel like you just insulted me in the middle of a compliment."

I smile, sit down, and lean my crutches on the chair next to me. "It's one of my many impressive talents."

Throwing a pillow at me, she cries, "You admit it! You did insult me!"

"And complimented you, remember?"

She snorts. "I guess you're forgiven then."

We settle into our spots, her on the teal couch, me on my mom's bright orange armchair. My mom is eclectic in her furniture choices, that's for sure. But I wouldn't change her for anything. Elia locates the movie on one of the streaming services, and I find myself surprisingly drawn into an impossible adventure/romance.

After a couple of hours, and a lot of squealing from Elia, we finish the movie and I have to admit, it was really well done.

Just as I expected, Elia turns to me and starts her commentary. "Oh my gosh, can you believe he loved her the whole time when he was her farm boy, and she didn't know it? How did she not know it?" She falls back on the couch and looks dreamily at the ceiling. "And every time he said, 'As you wish,' he was saying he loved her!" She jumps up, her eyes wide. "Then! Just when she realized she did love him, he left to get his fortune only to be attacked and assumed dead."

Elia's hair is a wild curtain all around her. She flings it around as she smiles. Her hair is almost waist-length. I could never keep up with hair like that, but it looks great on her. "And then the prince wants to marry her, which she basically has to agree to, since her Wesley is dead."

I shrug. I don't really need to give her my opinion unless she demands it. I just let her ramble until she exhausts herself and the topic. You can't hold Elia back; you just have to let her run with it.

So, she continues, "And then! Wesley is alive after all and finds her after she's kidnapped but then hides his identity? Swoon!" She dramatically falls back again. I groan.

She's going to keep this up for a while. "Elia, please. I beg you. Can we talk about this tomorrow?"

She turns burning eyes to me. "Jewels, you know I need to get this out of my system before it makes me crazy. I'll die if I don't have anyone to talk to about this."

And just like that, she continues on for a full half hour.

"And then he gets use of his limbs again and fools the prince into thinking he's dangerous only to..."

Finally, I stop her mid-sentence. "Elia," I say tiredly. "I have homework to finish before it's too late. You know my medicine makes me sleep for a full eight hours. I have to get started on my work."

She blinks at me and purses her lips. "Okay, I guess. You did like it, though?"

I smile because it's the first time she's checked on my feelings. This movie really captured her imagination. "Yeah, I liked it. It was pretty good."

She nods decisively. "Okay, from you, pretty good means really good. You hate all the so-so ones I pick out." Standing up, she turns to the kitchen. "I need to pack up all my glorious additions to the boring ice cream you picked. I know you won't enjoy them, or I'd leave them for you."

"You're welcome to them all. Cookie dough is a perfectly fine addition to vanilla ice cream. Although I wonder what it would taste like with chocolate ice cream?" I muse, tapping my lip with my finger.

She spins. "See? You admit it! It needed something more. You could have had all that goodness with hot fudge or chocolate sauce. You missed out, girl."

I snort and hang my head. "Next time, I'll allow you to add chocolate to my dish."

She squeals. "I'm going to rub off on you one of these days."

I smile softly. "You already have." And she really has. No one is as positive as Elia. It's easy to see why Vela chose her as her best friend. I count myself blessed Elia turned to me when Vela moved away. I've always been friendly with people who mattered, but Elia has shown me the bright and beautiful side of life I didn't see as well before. And I've found myself with a lot more friends because I look for people's better qualities and try not to make my first impression my only one.

I walk Elia to the door and see her off, making sure she gets to her car safely. My neighborhood is safe enough, but my bestie is tiny, so I worry about her sometimes. But if there's anything I know about her, she can fend for herself. I would feel sorry for anyone who tried to mess with her.

Using my crutches, I make my way to my room and settle down with my laptop. For a second, I have an urge to do an online search for sightings of magical people, but I have a dismal history of pointless online searches. I've gotten nothing but headaches looking for answers.

I'm sure this is also one of those topics I could never rely on online searches to answer. So, I focus on my homework.

Maybe one day I'll find someone who can answer my questions. I don't hold out much hope, though.

4. Drew

♥

I'm having a crazy busy day. So busy that I don't even have time to do a thorough check of my schedule. Usually, I look over all my patients' backgrounds and medical histories. But today I'm lucky to keep up with my hectic schedule. As a licensed massage therapist, I'm hoping this experience will add to my growing resume for medical school I'm applying to. I'm not sure if it's because I'm an Elemental and it's my nature to heal that I enjoy massage therapy so much or if it's just a bonus. Either way, I love my job.

I'm washing my hands in the clinic sink when Betty, the clinic assistant, comes into the room. "Your next client is ready."

I look up at her and take note of the time. I've been able to keep my hour-long appointments on track so far. It's amazing I'm not running late today. Usually when I get like this, I lose track of time, too.

I need to catch up, but first, it's time to focus on my next client. Their experience is what matters, not me and the clumsy handling of my day.

The door opens, and Betty stands in front of two people. Betty's average in height, so whoever is behind her must be on the shorter side. I notice one of them has crutches, but that's not unusual for this clinic.

A woman speaks, and it stops me completely in my tracks. "See, honey? This place is so nice!"

I know that voice. I haven't heard it in over a year, but when the patient answers, my heart stops. "It *is* nice, Mom. I have full use of my eyeballs."

When she labors into the room, heavily leaning on her crutches, I clamp my mouth closed.

It's her.

Careful not to show any sign of recognition, I note that though it requires much more energy for her to walk than most people, her deep concentration doesn't mar the beauty of her face.

Just then, she looks up at me. Her mouth drops open, and she blurts, "It's *you*!"

My mind spins. There's no way she remembers me. The poppy seed formula works too well for that to happen. I look at her in confusion, and her face transforms from delighted surprise to a blank slate. She twists her mouth as she looks away.

"I mean, it, it's the doctor who's helping me. How nice," she stumbles over her words, her face flushing a bright shade of red.

Is it possible she remembers me?

Now I stumble over my words. "I'm...not a doctor. Not yet. But I'm working on it." I smile at her. My usual professional smile is strained. I never thought I'd see her again. "My name is Drew Ashcroft, and it's a pleasure to meet you."

Her forehead furrows. "Ashcroft? Do you happen to have a sister or relative named Vela?"

I truly smile at her in surprise. "Yes, that's my sister. How do you know her?"

Beaming, she looks at me in awe. "We went to school together. I never knew she had two brothers. She mentioned one, Kane, right? He's dating Elia."

I fold my arms, tucking my clipboard under my arm. "Yes, that's my brother. So, you know Elia, too? That's Vela's best friend."

Her face goes through a wash of emotion, like she's just realized something. She says with distraction, "Yes, well, now that Vela has been gone, I've tried to fill that role. But no one can truly fill Vela's shoes." She looks up at me, wiping the confused expression off her face. "I haven't heard from her in a long time. How is she?"

I don't hear from Vela that often, and I wish that were different. Ever since she married a Festan Grand Elder's son, she's been blissfully happy, so I hope she's truly doing well. Plus, she has a lot going on. "She's good, she's married, which is kind of young."

Her eyes widen. "She's *married*?"

I shift uncomfortably. This should be Vela telling her this news, not me, so I say gently, "I'm sorry, but for the sake of time, we need to continue with our examination. I don't have much time with you. Can we continue on?"

She blushes. "Oh, I'm sorry. Of course."

As I direct her to sit down, I look for fear in her eyes of me, but I can't find a trace of it. Surely if she remembered me, she would recall vivid memories of what she went through that day. It was awful and pure torture. But I don't see anything to raise concern when she finally looks back up at me.

She's smiling politely, but I can see her eyes burning like she wants to ask me a million questions. I'm not sure if they have to do with my sister and her unexpected marriage or what we do here for services. We are an intensive-therapy clinic that specializes in patients much like her. People who need more fluidity in movement, more mobility.

"Well," her mom, who doesn't have a shred of reaction to me, starts talking like she's never seen me before. It's clear the poppy seed formula worked on her, but did it work on her daughter? "We've heard so many good things about this place. We're hoping it can help Julia here. Especially now that she's walking around so much for her college classes."

Julia, that's right. I looked up their names after my fateful interaction with them. And she would be in college by now.

But for some reason when I looked her up on social media, I couldn't find a Julia Patterson anywhere. Does she not have any accounts? That's unusual for a young person.

Shaken, I make a point of looking down at the clipboard Betty handed to me. I force myself to pay attention to what I'm reading while I fight frustration. *Does she remember me?*

I quietly focus and review her case and her long history with spina bifida. As a massage therapist, I usually can't look at all her records, but the clinic has given me special access with all my medical experience. I've been a paramedic and have a nursing degree. Plus, I double-majored and received a biology degree. I review the bloodwork she had done before this visit and see her numbers are kind of high in some areas, but that's not unusual with how much medicine she's taking. Looking at that list too, I try not to wince when I then review her extensive time spent under the knife.

She had surgery for spina bifida cystica, the worst type, when she was three days old. Soon after, she had hydrocephalus, fluid on the brain, which required draining. That's pretty common for babies born with this condition. She's had three more surgeries, and it remains to be seen if they've been successful. Her time spent in physical therapy is just as extensive. She's worked hard to get here, and I decide I won't be one who is of no use to her at all. I resolve to help her.

But I can't help her too much.

Blowing out a breath, I put her file down. It's time I did my exam. I put on nitrile gloves because she's allergic to latex. Most patients with spina bifida are. I clear my throat and find her studying me.

"So, Julia. Let's start with some basic flexibility movements."

"It's Jewels," she says softly, looking down at the floor after watching to make sure I don't grab the latex gloves.

I want her to look at me. Her eyes are stunning. They're dark, almost black, but so expressive. I can see her mind working as she sits. I've always appreciated a bright woman. I belatedly recognize her correction. "Oh. Did I get your name wrong?" I look back down at the clipboard.

"No," she says, her face flushing again. "My name is Julia, but I prefer Jewels."

So, that's why I couldn't find her on social media.

"Oh, okay. So, Jewels, I should ask. Do you have questions for me first?"

She directs her gaze at me, and I find I'm holding my breath. I almost wish she did remember our first meeting. I wonder what it would be like to really know this young woman. I noticed on her chart that she's nineteen. I almost breathe in relief. She's not too young to think about as a woman.

"I'm always full of questions, but what kind of time do you have?"

I smile and laugh softly. She's direct.

I like that.

"Well, we have an hour together. I'd like to make the best use of your time. How about we save the questions for later? I'd like to see what we have to work with."

She studies me for a moment, then exchanges a glance with her mom. Her mom's face is full of optimism, but Jewels's is more reserved. I'm sure she's seen her fair share of help from practitioners that did little to nothing. Most treatments for spina bifida provide temporary relief of symptoms at best.

My patience is rewarded when she finally turns to me and asks, "Well, first I'd like to know your background. How qualified are you?"

I find it interesting that it's her asking these questions and not her mother, but I don't question it; I just answer. Holding the clipboard down, I say, "I'm not a doctor, not yet. But I do have a nursing and biology degree. I've been a paramedic, and currently I'm a licensed massage therapist. I've been doing this for close to a year while I study for my MCATs, the entrance test for medical school."

Studying me with her expressive eyes, she nods and pushes down on one arm to help her stand up, then balances herself with the other. "Okay, where do you want me, Doc?"

I smile. "Like I said, not a doc yet, but hope one day I will be." I tear my gaze away from her eyes. I keep getting drawn into them.

She nods. "Then I'm all yours, Doc." She smiles and waits for my instruction, her dark orbs twinkling.

I am filled with a fierce desire to really help her. With my gift, I mean. I'm not often pushed with this kind of intention, but I can't seem to avoid it. She has a way about her that I can't help but respect, and I really want to be a part of her recovery.

I wonder if I could heal her? Is that within my capabilities as a Gyan?

I resolve to look up cases in the Gyan medical reports I have access to thanks to my parents, who are Gyan Elders. If we can heal Gyans with this disability, then shouldn't I be capable of healing Jewels? We're as human as the rest, just with a special gifts. We've been tasked by God to take care of the Earth; with elements and the gifts he provided. I'm an Earth Elemental and possess the ability to control nature and heal.

The question is, could I heal this amazing young woman?

I instantly shut that thought down. We are not to use our gifts on humans. The only exception is when we administer the memory-erasing poppy seed formula. They won't remember our gifted handling of their seizures, so we're allowed to help them. Clamping my lips, I refocus on Jewels, who has moved to stand in front of me. She spends the rest of the hour bending, stretching, testing her reflexes. I need to see the extent of her condition, and by the end of our time, I have a good idea of what I have to work with.

Our clinic is becoming well known for groundbreaking treatments for muscle stiffness and pain. We use a combination of heat therapy and computer diagnostics to find the best treatments for our patients.

By the end of the appointment, I'm more than impressed with Jewels's stellar attitude and resilience. I want to help her, at least as much as the clinic can. I might not be able to help her like I want, but I know we can ease some of her discomfort.

I try not to feel too badly that I've completely exhausted Jewels. She slumps onto the clinic's bed and rubs her lower back.

"I'm very sorry for putting you through the paces like that," I say, looking into her tired eyes.

She half-smiles at me. "It's nothing I haven't done before. When will we start the good stuff, Doc?"

I smile at her nickname for me. "Well, now that I have a better idea of your specific condition, I think you'll see some relief by the end of your next visit."

She definitely will. I'll be sure of it. Not with my gift, but with my massage.

Her eyes twinkle at me. "You seem awfully confident."

I laugh, not able to help it. "I am pretty good at what I do. I'm just sorry that we couldn't do any of the fun stuff today."

She twists her lips. "Yeah, the first visits are always the worst. I wish I could just imprint my mind on yours so you could see my issues, instead of me doing gymnastics to find out."

"I wish that too, believe me."

"Have you ever seen a case like mine work with this new treatment?"

I nod. "I have. Everyone is different, so we adjust as needed. By this time next week, I promise you, you'll be feeling better."

She smiles more widely at me. Her white teeth show, and I take a breath, because she just short-circuited my brain. I'm amazed at how her smile transforms her whole face. "I'm looking forward to it," she says.

I am too.

I train my gaze on anything other than her beautiful face. I've never met anyone as strong as she is. She put up with the exam like a trooper, not complaining once, not even when I stretched her past her limits. She just gritted her teeth and allowed me to do what I needed to do. I'm awed at her positive attitude. Even the poppyseed formula didn't diminish her strength. She's a bright gem, and she literally sparkles. Especially her eyes.

"I'll see you next week," I say.

"See you next time, Doc."

Her mom thanks me, her eyes shining, full of hope and happiness. She has great faith in me. I won't let her down either. In fact, I vow it.

5. Jewels

❤

I *cannot believe I just had an entire hour exam with Drew!!*
And he's Vela's brother!

I try to hide my excitement from my mom, but she's a blood-hound right now, sniffing out any positivity I have about my appointment.

"He's great, isn't he?" she gushes. "I just know he'll be able to help you. Julia, this is going to be life changing. I just know it."

And the fact is, she's right. He does have the ability to help me. But the question is, will he use it? His *real* abilities? I stuff down my hopes and concentrate on what he said during our appointment. I can't let my mom know that he has anything other than human skills that can aid my progress.

I do not want her to ever go through that mind-altering powder experience again.

"Yes, I really think this is going to be amazing," I say.

She looks sharply at me. "You really agree?"

I laugh as I settle into my seat, putting my crutches in the back. "Yes, Mom, I'm serious. He seems very capable, and he thinks he can help, so I choose to believe him."

"That's just wonderful. You're usually more reserved after an initial visit. He must have really made an impression on you."

Oh, he made an impression all right.

I grimace. "I know I've been an unbeliever, but I think you're right about this clinic. I'm really happy you found it, Mom. Thank you."

She looks at me with some surprise. "Of course, honey. You know I would do anything for you."

"I know you will, Momma. I'm blessed to have you."

She sighs. "Sometimes I think I did something during my pregnancy to cause this whole thing. But..."

"Stop right there, Mom. There is no proof of that."

She looks away, but not before I see a tear trail down her cheek.

"Mom, don't do that." I say, putting my hand on her arm.

She sniffs. "I know, honey. I just wish...that you didn't have to deal with all of this."

"I do too, but Mom, we can't change this. Just make the best of it. And that's what I'll always do. I won't ever let this thing get me down. You've taught me that. To keep my head up."

Wiping her cheek, she laughs tearfully. "Well, if that's one good thing I've done, I'm grateful."

"We have a lot to be grateful for."

She nods.

We drive in quiet, comfortable silence. I think back to my missing father. The one who abandoned my mom once he learned of my condition. Mom never talks about him. He tore a piece out of her I'm not sure will ever be replaced. If he couldn't stand by her side when she needed him, then she definitely doesn't need him in her life. Nor do I.

But I've come to terms with his absence. And any father figure, really. Mom is very careful about who she dates. It's so rare for her to go on a date, I think I can count on one hand all the times she has.

We've done fine without anyone else in our lives, though. Mom makes an income from her sculptures and art. She's made a name for herself in the art world, and I'm so proud of her. God is my Father, Heavenly and otherwise. He is everything I need. I'm thankful to have my faith. It's helped me more than anything.

When we make it home, I walk slowly inside, my thoughts returning to Drew. He's just as handsome now as he was a year ago. It's very clear after his exam with me today that, unlike me, he's in very good physical condition. I was up close and personal with his biceps a couple of times, and I couldn't help but notice. I'm just sorry I didn't know him from when Vela and I would hang out at her house. He must have been away at college doing those double majors he mentioned.

Remembering his eyes, though... those were what got to me the most. How can such a boring color show such emotion? Several times today, I had to drop my gaze from his. It was too piercing, too knowing, too understanding. He took one look at my medical chart and did not, for one second, treat me any differently. But he had a look of respect and admiration that moved me.

I've seen every kind of reaction, from disinterest to worse, pity, that I can't help but admit, I melted a little when Drew put the clipboard down and saw me for who I am, who I really am. When he didn't reach for latex gloves, I knew he would take good care of me.

It does not surprise me at all that he wants to be a doctor. After his exam with me today, it's clear he's gentle and compassionate enough to take care of patients. He exhibited patience and care that not all practitioners have. I honestly feel honored to be one of his patients.

What I've signed up for is intensive therapy. I fully anticipate being as exhausted after each session as I am today. Drew seemed to regret putting me through such hard exercises. I appreciate that. In a way, it's like we're already friends.

I would very much like to be his friend.

Thinking of friends, Elia pops into my thoughts. Kane and Drew are brothers. So, that means Elia *has* to know about this whole world. Is *she* magical, too? I've never seen her do anything remotely out of the ordinary. She's extraordinary, that's for sure.

I mean, I've always thought her zest for life was otherworldly. But I never saw her do anything not human. Now, I have to know. How do I ask her and not make her suspect I know things I shouldn't? I decide to call her. Even though I can't tell her what really happened today, I can maybe tease answers out of her.

I get comfy in a bright armchair and dial her up. Within a few rings, her breathless voice comes on the phone.

"Hey Dragon Girl, how's it goin'?"

I sigh at her nickname. She teases me for loving the band Imagine Dragons. "Hey, I have some yummy news."

"You got your first kiss?"

"No. But I had a veeerrry interesting day today."

"Does it involve a guy you can possibly kiss? Please say yes."

"Why does kissing have to be a part of this conversation?"

She giggles. "Because of my yummy history of kissing Kane. You need that kind of excitement in your life. Trust me."

"Talking about Kane, I met his brother today."

"Oh, really? How did you meet Drew?"

"First of all, why haven't you told me how *hot* he is? That seems like very important information."

She laughs. "I'm sorry. He's a few years older than you, so maybe that's why I never mentioned him. Although I digress. How did you meet him? He's really busy."

"You know, I'm remembering now Vela talking about her brother who's going to become a doctor, but I always assumed she was talking about Kane. Anyway, I'm going to a new clinic where they have specialized heat therapy. Drew's the therapist overseeing my treatment. I'm a little confused, though. Why does he look nothing like Vela?" Drew has dark hair, and Vela's is bright gold.

"Remember, Vela found out like a year ago that she was adopted?"

"Oooooohhh! Right, I remember that now," I say, remembering when Vela found out about that, how shocked she was.

"Yep. You should totally ask for a best-friend discount."

I mull over that for a moment. While I'm thinking about how to get her to say something about his abilities, Elia's suspiciously quiet.

"Elia? What are you thinking about over there?"

After a pause, she said, "Did you say he was hot? You never comment on things like that."

"Yes, does he have a girlfriend or something?"

She laughs nervously. "No, no girlfriend. Although there are plenty of willing candidates."

My stomach clenches uncomfortably at that thought.

"Then what is it?"

"Nothing! I'm just surprised, is all. Is he any good?" she asks carefully.

My heart picks up speed. Is she insinuating that he's magically gifted, like he's too good? "Yeah, he's amazing. It's almost inhuman," I say carefully.

She goes silent for a beat before she says, "Well, Vela has always raved about how talented he is. So, that doesn't surprise me."

"And he's trying to get into medical school, so I'm lucky I got in with him before he got in one."

"You're lucky alright."

"What does that mean?" I ask quickly.

"You do have eyes, don't you?" she answers. Like she's covering her tracks or something. She's hiding her comment behind his good looks. I won't let her.

"What do you know about him, Elia? Spill."

"I have nothing to say other than he's a really, really good guy. Go easy on him, girl."

I'm quiet for a moment, frustrated she won't take the bait. I understand, though. She's not allowed to talk about her real world. I scoff. "Like I'm at all threatening."

"You might not be threatening, but you have a good, loud bark sometimes."

"Hey, I need to stick up for myself sometimes. Anyway, how did this become about me? I want to know what you know about Drew."

"I don't have anything to say except that you are in very good hands. And before you ask, I know very little about his dating history."

"Believe me, I *know* I'm in good hands." Especially because he can use magic to help me. I don't tell her that, but I wish I could. I'm strangely relieved, though, that she doesn't have any dirt to bring up from Drew's romantic past.

After a few more minutes of chitchat, I hang up with Elia, giving up digging up any truth about my new therapist, and rest my head on the back of the chair, consumed in thought.

Is Vela magical, too? Maybe not, since Vela is adopted. Is that kind of thing inherited? I'm dying to really talk to Elia about these things. But it's clear she won't talk about what she really knows.

I'm not supposed to know anything. So, I'll keep quiet.

But I want to know Drew's secrets. Will I ever catch him at magic, like I did the others? I scoff. I doubt he'd ever be careless enough to let anyone like me see him performing impossible acts. He's too...I don't have a word for it, but careful is one I can be satisfied with. I just don't see him making a mistake. But if he does, I'll be onto him.

I don't think for one second he'd let me remember what I saw. The question is, can I ever tell him that the mysterious powder doesn't work on me like it's supposed to? What would he do with that information? Would he try to administer it again and again until it worked?

I shudder.

I can never tell him that my memory from that day is intact. I can't help but mourn at that thought, though. I'd like to be let into his world, like I let him into mine today. It takes a certain kind of trust for me to allow someone to work on me like he did. He instantly put me at ease, which made the whole thing much easier than usual. I wish I could do the same for him.

Maybe one day I will.

I'll just have to hold on to that hope and pray I'll be allowed into a world so foreign I can't help but be drawn to it.

What more do I not know? I know I've only seen a tiny fraction of what's actually out there. Well, if I know myself, I'll dig until I find the answers I need. If I'm anything, it's tenacious. Drew won't know what hit him after he's done with me.

Why does that make me so sad?

6. Drew

After Jewels left, I'm ashamed to say I spent the rest of the day just going through the motions. I wasn't running late. It was more than that. It's like when she left, she took the best part of my day with her. Like a cloud formed over me when she was gone. One thing I pride myself on is the quality of the attention and care I give my patients. They each deserve my best, and I'm ashamed to say that I was nearly neglectful to some today.

I tried to shake Jewels from my thoughts, but it's clear she's made an impression. That is a very dangerous admission. I keep reminding myself that she's human. She can be a friend, and that is all.

Those thoughts I had of really helping her? I have to banish them. I can't risk the exposure of my world because of one human. Even one with as captivating eyes as Jewels Patterson.

Did she feel our connection like I did? It was hard to read her. As much as I could look into her eyes, they contained mysteries I'm itching to solve.

I've never had such a visceral reaction with a human or Elemental. From the first time I met her, when she endured the horrid effects of the poppy seed formula, she's surprised me at every turn. That's not an easy thing to do. As someone in the medical field, I've seen a lot. Even in this clinic, I've met every kind of personality.

But Jewels is completely unforgettable.

Does she know she's had such an impression on me? I'll have to be very careful to keep that under wraps. For one thing, she's my patient. That makes her automatically off-limits. Two, she's a human. Two strikes that are fatal in my world. There's no outcome for us other than a professional relationship.

Even a friendship is risky.

When I finally leave, my spirits sink. Thankfully, no one at work seemed to notice my mood. But I did. I have plans to eat dinner with my parents, and I find I'm really looking forward to it. I need to be around my people, my family.

I park in my parents' driveway and sit for a second, allowing the day I had to sink in. I can't believe two of the humans I had to administer the poppy seed formula to actually walked into the clinic. What are the odds? Very slim. My parents usually have the uncomfortable job of erasing memories, but they asked me to take care of it that day. I'm a good alternative since I'm trying to get a medical degree. But really, any Gyan could help humans with the terrible side effects. But I've been blessed with an especially strong gift of healing that made me the perfect candidate to do it.

When I finally leave my car and walk into the house, I smell my mom's homemade apple spice bread. I take a deep breath, salivating at the thought of having two or three thick slices. I hope it's ready to eat.

"Mom? Dad?" I call out. I pocket my keys and look in the kitchen, hoping to see the bread cooling on the counter.

Score! It's already sliced, and when I reach for a piece, it's even warm.

There's nothing better for my day than a few slices of Mom's homemade bread.

I'm on my second piece when my mom's voice behind me makes me jump.

"Couldn't wait until after dinner, could you?"

I turn my mouth full, and I'm pretty sure a guilty expression on my face.

She laughs and hugs me. I squeeze her slight frame and swallow the bite in my mouth. "Sorry, Mom, I couldn't wait. It was just sitting there."

Her body shakes as she laughs again. "It's okay. I made it especially for you."

She leans back and looks at me with a big smile, but when she sees my face, her face morphs into concern. "What's the matter?"

I sigh, pushing her gently away. "I'm fine, Mom, just had something unexpected happen today."

I reach for the rest of the slice I hadn't devoured yet. Holding the sweet bread in my hand, I brush the brown sugar topping off my shirt with my other hand. I look down, frowning.

"What ruffled the immovable Drew Ashcroft? Now, I'm curious."

"Do you remember Julia and Clarissa Patterson from a year ago?"

This time, she frowns. "Yes. I remember every human we force the poppy seed formula on. Why? Did you run into them?"

I sigh. "Yeah, you can say that. The daughter, Julia, or Jewels, as she goes by, is now one of my patients."

Mom gasps, putting her hand to her mouth. "Well, there's no chance she recognized you, but what a small world!"

I nod. Scrunching my eyebrows, I say with some hesitation, "I don't know. I think a part of her remembers. She acted like she knew me when she first saw me. But that's impossible."

"It *is* impossible," Mom says firmly. "Maybe her subconscious reacted to you."

I smile crookedly at her. "That's one way of looking at it." Flicking her nose, I chuckle. "Her subconscious unconsciously knew me?"

She blushes. "You know what I mean."

I pop the last bite of bread into my mouth and lean on the counter with both hands. Hanging my head, I'm comforted when Mom rubs my back.

"This really got to you, didn't it? Can you give her case to someone else?"

Popping my head up, I recoil at the thought. I shake my head and finish swallowing the bread. "No. I can do it. She needs my care. I don't trust anyone else to do her treatment right."

Mom's eyebrows lift. "She needs *your* care? Drew, you're sounding a little too attached."

I grimace. "I'm not. She's special, Mom. She's been through a lot and deserves to feel better."

"This is the high schooler with spina bifida?"

I straighten and nod. "She's actually in college now. And it's not as bad as some cases, but she's been through a lot to get to our clinic. I want to help her."

Mom reads my face perfectly. She frowns deeply and crosses her arms. "You can't *really* help her, Drew. You know that."

Dad walks in and, reading the room right, asks, "What's the matter?"

Mom looks over at him and says, "Drew is tempted to heal a human."

I open my mouth to argue when Mom stops me. "Drew, you are my firstborn. I know you. Don't try to talk yourself out of this."

Dad gives me a sympathetic look when he reaches for a piece of bread. "I'm sure it is tempting, son, but you know you can't."

Mom slaps his hand away from the bread. "We're about to eat dinner, and you boys are stuffing your faces!"

I stifle a grin at her outraged face. "Sorry, Mom. And I'll be careful. But I really feel led to be in this young woman's life."

Mom turns to her husband. "He gave this girl and her mother the poppy seed formula." She turns to me. "A year ago, right?"

When I nod, Dad's eyebrows rise, and he looks thoughtful. "Are you talking about the Pattersons?"

I nod. It doesn't surprise me they remember them. My parents are diligent when it comes to the humans who scratch the surface of our world. They take erasing people's memories very seriously.

I wish again that we could find something else to give them. If I were any better at chemistry, I would go into research to discover another remedy. But my gifts run more toward patient care. I'm better with one-on-one treatment, not a chemistry lab.

Can I remain distant emotionally and still be hands-on with Jewels?

Yes, she needs my help. I will help her. God help me, I will help her with her mobility.

After studying my face for a moment, Dad says, "Son, it's clear you're conflicted about this girl. Maybe it's best if you leave her in someone else's care."

I surprise even myself when my voice rises. "No! I can do this!" I temper my voice. "I have full confidence that I can help her."

"Yes, but should you?" Mom asks gently. "The more time you spend with her, the more you'll want to help."

I turn away, frustrated she could see into me so clearly. I wall up my emotions, the dangerous ones that care so much for a girl I've barely met twice.

But both times were so profound. I can't help but be drawn to her.

Again, I force those feelings aside. With my mouth in a thin line, I look at both my parents, resolve firming in my veins. "I'm positive I can do this; I'm a professional. There's nothing I would do for her that anyone else in my clinic couldn't. I won't heal her. I don't even know if I could. You don't need to worry."

My parents exchange a glance before Mom says, "Okay, how about some dinner? I'm sure David is famished, even if you're not. Why did you spoil your dinner, anyway?"

And just like that, the tense moment lifts. That's what I love about my family. We get the hard things out of the way and go forward. I've learned that skill from the best. It's no surprise to me that my parents were chosen as Elders in our Gyan community. They do what needs to be done, say what needs to be said.

I can only wish to be a version of myself that will make them proud. I can't let them or myself down. But one more thing is clear. I can't leave Jewels to face her illness alone, either.

So, I decide to help her as much as I can, within the bounds of the clinic's treatments. She'll benefit greatly, even without my extra help.

I'll restrain myself, even if it kills me to do it.

7. Jewels

♥

I'm so nervous going into my next appointment with Drew that I keep wiping my hands on my pants to dry the ever-present moisture.

Mom isn't with me this time. She had an important commission meeting she couldn't miss. It's actually better this way. I'd like to test Drew a little, and I don't want my mom around to question me about it later.

The office assistant calls me back, and I make my way to the chair, settling into it instead of the examination table. They've placed the table lower than the usual hospital beds, but it's still hard to get into it.

Folding my hands in my lap, I wait for Drew to come into the room.

Why did such a hot magic guy come into my life? I can't even admit I've met him before. It's just my luck.

Forcing myself not to think about his hotness, I consider the questions I have for him that might give me a little more insight into the magical world.

After a few moments, when I worry he's going to be late and therefore cut our session short, the door opens. Drew, in all his masculine perfection, walks into the room. He's looking down at some papers, but when he looks up and sees me, a warm smile breaks out on his face.

My mouth goes dry, and I forget every single question I had just gone over in my mind.

Poof. Mind blank, I panic, and my hands sweat again.

Drew had resumed studying his papers, but glances at me when he asks, "Hello Ruby, how's your day going?"

I squeak, "Fine," before clearing my throat and trying again. "It's Jewels, remember? And my day is fine. How's yours?"

Did he really forget my name? And that was not one of my questions.

He smiles. "I figured if you were going to give me a nickname, I'd give you one, too."

I blush and look down, my heart thumping wildly in my chest.

"Today is better than on your last visit. If you noticed I was a little frazzled, please forgive me. I wasn't having the best day."

Shoot. That was one of my questions. I remember now. Did he recognize me from somewhere? Well, it's not all lost. I can still ask that question.

"Oh, umm, I don't think I noticed. But I did wonder something. Did you recognize me by chance? It seemed like I'd seen you before." I pay close attention to his face and am rewarded with startling him.

He smooths an alarmed expression quickly. But he answers my question with one of his own. "Why? Did you recognize me?"

I scramble for an answer that won't be seen as suspicious. "I don't know if you have a face that resembles someone I know, but it does feel like I have seen you before."

He frowns and turns away.

Okay, is that a bad reaction? Does he suspect I remember the whole sordid experience he put me through?

He studies his papers and says, "Have you lived in this area a long time?"

"I have. My whole life."

"Well, we must have crossed paths at some point. Because I don't remember meeting you before." He says it in such a flat voice, my suspicions spike. I *know* he knows me, but he doesn't want *me* to know it.

I hum. "Maybe that's it."

He turns to face me, putting his papers down. "So, any more questions? About your treatment, anyway? Did you have a chance to review all the papers we sent home with you last time?"

I nod, gripping my knees. "I did."

On to my next question.

"Will there be a lot of massage involved? And will you be doing it?"

Please say yes. If I can feel that amazing heat again, I'll die and go to Heaven.

Half of his mouth quirks up in a smile. "Yes, that's one of the therapies we'll use. But first, you'll have a treatment that will prepare your muscles for the hard work they'll go through later."

"The deep tissue massage?"

"Yes. The table will pulse heated magnetic waves into your body, stimulating them for relaxation. We want you to feel really good after each session. You will feel relief immediately."

"You did promise I would feel better."

"And I meant it," he says in a sure tone. He then strides to the door. "I'll leave you to get into your gown."

I nod, and then he closes the door. I put the gown on, leaving on my underwear and bra. He didn't specify, but I'm pretty sure I can keep them on. I blush when I think of my crush seeing me in this, but I'll have the gown on, so it'll be fine. I use my walking aids to get myself off the chair. After he knocks to be sure I'm decent, he directs me to follow him to another room.

The room's dark, and when my eyes adjust, I see a table hooked up to a machine with lots of red lights flicking on and off. I'm not sure which way to lie on it, so I wait for Drew to give me instructions.

He's talking to a tech who's behind a glass wall, so I lean on my crutches and wait for him to finish. He does quickly and walks back to me. Holding out his arm, he asks, "Can you come this way? Wait and see how great this feels. You'll love it."

I approach, still unsure which way to face. "Are you going to make me guess, Doc?" I ask, giving up on figuring out my dilemma.

"Guess what?" he asks, his eyes questioning me. His gaze is so direct I lose my train of thought for a second.

I finally admit, my cheeks red, "I have no idea which part my head is supposed to be on."

"Oh, right," he says. He walks to the far end of the table. "Your head goes here." He eyes my crutches. "The table should be low enough for you to get on easily, but if you need help, I'm happy to assist."

After studying the table for a moment, I shake my head. "I should be able to do it myself."

Respect, and a glimmer of what looks like regret, gleam in his eyes.

Wait, did he want to help me?

Before I can decide, he backs up, giving me room to maneuver. I get over to the table and find I can sit on it. Now, it's not exactly pretty watching me swing my legs up on the table, but, to my relief, Drew turns to talk to the tech, presenting his back to me, almost as if he can sense my unease of him watching me.

I slide my crutches off my forearms and lean them on the table so I can reach for them later. Taking a deep breath, I maneuver myself completely onto the table, which is a little harder than I thought. I'm tired after walking to my classes all day. I didn't realize how much until now.

I'm lying down, sweating, when Drew appears above me, smiling gently. "All set?"

I nod and try inconspicuously to wipe my forehead off.

"You're trembling," Drew says softly. He puts his hand on my arm, and I gasp when I feel warmth seeping into me. Instantly, my muscles relax.

It's just like last time! He's giving me a little of his magic. It's not as much as last time, but I recognize the feeling.

He yanks his hand off my arm, his lips in a thin line. "Sorry," he says gruffly. "My hands run hot."

That's not a normal hot.

Instead of calling him out on it and telling him I feel better than I've ever felt, I smile and say, "It's okay. Warm hands are much better than cold."

He turns, his forehead furrowed and a frown on his face. I wish we could get the warm moment we just had back. His shoulders are stiff, and he looks decidedly unhappy with himself.

Did he not mean to do that? Was it a knee-jerk reaction?

If I hadn't experienced what he can really do a year ago, I wouldn't have thought twice about it. It's easy to believe he just runs hot. But I know better. I need to be more careful not to react if he does it again.

I hope he does. So much.

The tech takes over at that point, telling me her name is Mary and asking me questions as she hooks me up with patches all over my legs, arms and back.

Drew seems to shake off the weird moment because he steps in to supervise where the tech puts the little sticker things. He points to my hips. I blush when Mary raises my gown to add the stickers where he wants them. She allows me to be modest, keeping me covered while she applies the sensors.

Drew saves me from embarrassment by filling the air with chatter. "The nodes are put in optimal positions to stimulate and encourage mobility." His face is a professional mask.

I blush when I realize he will see a lot of me during the massage. I remind myself he's a medical professional and he'll only be touching my back, arms and legs.

He walks behind the glass wall, and soon I hear his voice pipe into the room. "Are you comfortable? Just nod, I'll see you."

I do and he says, "Okay, we're going to get started. Let us know if the heat is too much, okay? Wave your hand and we'll adjust the temperature. Though it needs to be as hot as possible to be the most effective. So, try to take as much heat as possible."

The machine starts whirring and flashing more red lights. Suddenly, I feel little pulses radiating into my muscles. It's incredibly soothing, and I relax onto the table. I actually love heat on my muscles, so I don't complain once about the temperature. Drew's voice continues to talk me through the treatment, and I fall into the rhythm of heat and Drew's deep voice. I'm lulled into such a feeling of relaxation I almost fall asleep.

When I feel someone shake my shoulder, I realize, with some embarrassment, I actually did fall asleep. "Jewels? How do you feel?" Drew asks. He's leaning over the treatment table, and I take a moment to appreciate his dark good looks. I have to admit, I get a little lost in his penetrating gray eyes, too.

Shaking my thoughts free of his magnetism, I take stock of how I'm feeling physically. I'm languid and more relaxed than I've been in a long time. "I'm really good," I say with a smile.

Drew nods and says, "Just wait until after the massage. You'll be feeling like a million bucks."

"I can't wait," I say breathlessly. Because let's face it, who wouldn't want a tall, dark and handsome guy massaging them?

My blissful thoughts are dashed when he leans back and says, "I will warn you, though, it's deep tissue, so..."

"Yeah," I say, sighing, "I've had those before." My spirits sink. He's saying it's going to hurt. But I comfort myself with the thought that I'll feel better afterward. And maybe he'll send some of his mojo heat into me, too.

It's easier to get off the table than on, so when I do, I follow Drew out of the room and into another one. This time, there's just a table and a sheet.

"Please take the gown and bra off and get under the sheet. We'll get started as soon as you're ready," he instructs. "On your back, please."

I nod awkwardly, and he leaves the room.

My face is bright red at taking off my clothes, but I'll be under a sheet, so it'll be fine. It takes some work to get situated on the table, and I'm thankful he gives me a few extra minutes. Once I'm positioned, a short knock tells me he's ready to come in.

I answer, and once he's in the room, he makes short work of getting started. He starts with my arms, and I try not to wince at his strong hands digging into my muscles, but it's hard. I don't want him to feel bad for doing his job.

He's quiet as he works, and for that I'm glad. I'm desperately trying to ignore the fact that his hands are all over me. After about ten minutes of going over my arms, legs and upper shoulders, he asks me to turn over, which I have to get off the table to do. He again leaves, and I wish I were more mobile than I am, but I work with what I have. Drew doesn't even bat an eyelash when he comes back in the room and starts working on my back.

As much as I don't mind his hands on me, I'm disappointed when he only uses traditional massage techniques. It seems the time earlier when I felt a warmth in his hands was a mistake on his part. Is using his powers based on emotion? He reacted to me when I overexerted myself. Should I do that again? No, I won't manipulate him into helping me. It has to come from him.

I'll give him this. He's excellent at finding all my tense muscles and forcing them into a submission. There's no arguing he's talented at what he does. I just wish it were a softer massage so I could enjoy it more. And I am trying to ignore the fact that I find him so attractive.

He's an ugly old man. Not a young, wildly beautiful one.

Soon, he stops his work, and I immediately miss his hands working my muscles. Even though he was tough on them, it's nice to feel his caring touch.

"Time to sit up, Jewels. When you're ready, come back into the first exam room, okay?"

I nod jerkily, disturbed that I'm so sad he's finished. I'm soon becoming very attached to this guy, and that's dangerous. When he leaves the room, I lie there a minute, evaluating my muscles. They're so relaxed, I'm not sure I can pick myself up off the table. After a good pep talk, I haul myself up, don the gown, and allow a minute to rest before I slide on my forearm crutches. Feeling relaxed, I make my way back to the first room.

"Are you feeling okay?" Drew asks once I enter, concern on the edge of his voice.

I pick my head up and smile faintly, feeling so much better. "Yes, I'm fine. Just getting my bearings."

"Sorry if I was a little too tough on you today. You had a lot of knots to work out."

I wave my hand. "I should be used to it by now. It's fine. Don't worry."

I just wish he had infused more of that healing power of his.

"I'd like to see how you walk after your first treatment." He sounds nervous and excited, like he's invested in my recovery.

I smile and can't help but feel all warm and fuzzy inside. His enthusiasm is contagious. I take three steps. I'm feeling looser than I've ever felt before. I raise my eyes to his and can't help a huge grin stretching across my face.

He returns it. "Better?" His eyes are so bright and hopeful, I laugh.

"I really am. Thank you," I say with all the sincerity I can infuse into my voice.

He grins and says, "I'm just happy this has been a successful treatment."

"Why? Do you have unsuccessful ones?" I tease.

Surprise lights up his eyes at my teasing. "Sometimes," he admits. "Everybody is different, and usually there's some trial and error before we find the right treatment plan for each person. I'm really happy that we got it right on the first try with you."

I want to ask him why he seems to care so much, but I stifle the question. I don't want to scare away his good intentions, because I'm sure that's all this is. He wants all his patients to feel better.

I'm nobody special. Just someone he forced to forget about him. Well, tried to anyway.

I try to ignore the sudden sadness I feel that he wanted me to forget that part of his life.

Well, it's not like I'm part of his real life. Only his professional one.

And that's all I'll ever be. One of his patients.

I have to be okay with that.

Thinking back to my questions, I try one out on him. "Do you have any other jobs?"

He quirks an eyebrow, his eyes twinkling. "Do you think I'm a workaholic?"

"No! I'm just curious, that's all."

He turns and looks full on at me. "No. This job and studying for the MCAT are all I have time for. Don't worry, I won't allow anything to get in the way of your treatment."

"I'm not worried about my treatment. I'm really just trying to get to know you."

And figure out who sent you to my house a year ago.

"You really don't have any other jobs?" I ask, desperate for answers to my many questions about the magical world he's a part of.

He shakes his head and looks at me quizzically. I decide to stop my questions before he gets suspicious.

"Well, I'm afraid that's all we have time for today. I hope you have a wonderful rest of your day, Emerald," he says smoothly as he opens the door for me.

I huff a laugh, enjoying my nicknames. "Right, Doc. I'll see you next time." As I leave, I'm impressed with how much more limber I am. It's not as painful to walk, and for that I'm supremely grateful. Even without his magic, Drew helped me a lot today. I turn around to tell him, "You really made a big difference. Thank you."

He smiles softly at me, but I notice him clenching and un-clenching his fists at his sides. I take that as my cue to leave.

Drew Ashcroft, I will get to the bottom of your secrets. Just see if I don't.

8. Drew

♥

I shake my hands out when Jewels leaves, because it took everything in me to contain my healing gift. There was a small plant in the room that nearly exploded into growth at my excess energy, but I managed to rein it in, barely.

I blow out my breath and look at the computer and my next patient's stats in an attempt to distract myself. There's something so intriguing about Jewels, and I have to remind myself she is now my patient, so any extra thoughts besides professional ones are out of the question.

There's no denying it, though. She does something to me. All morning, I looked forward to seeing her, and when I treated her, I was again impressed with her grace and determination to do all she can to be well. She has an inner strength and light I find addictive to be around.

I can appreciate her attitude, and that's it. My day flies by after I force that last thought into my mind, and I'm driving to the gym before I know it.

Parking in the first spot I come to, I reach in the back for my gym bag. Walking briskly in, I'm ready for a good hard workout. Whenever my gift is on the surface like it has been ever since I treated Jewels, I find that if I throw myself into cardio and weights, I can repress the urges better. Another way is obviously to go to my parents' house and work for an hour in the thriving garden in the backyard.

But today, I'm ready to sweat and forget.

That seems to be my mantra lately. I have not been able to get my new patient out of my mind, and today is no exception. When I felt how tense and knotted she was on the massage table, my heart went out to her. The pain she deals with daily is no joke. I had to grit my teeth the entire time to keep from infusing her with healing.

But what amazed me the most was how she hid her reaction to my deep massage. I didn't hear one moan, one cry. She's one of the toughest people I know. I can't help but respect her. I also had to force myself to keep my interest in her muscles strictly professional. It wasn't easy, though; I have to admit.

Okay, man. Stop it with the admiration.

I change quickly and hit the treadmill at full speed. I'm streaming sweat after running for a good half hour, and it eases the compulsion to heal or grow something. By the time I step off, I'm feeling a measure of relief. I wipe my forehead with a towel and redirect my attention to the weights. I know I'm not done when Jewels pops into my head again.

Growling, I head straight for the 50-pound dumbbells. I need a good burn, and I intend to get it. An hour later, I'm breathing hard, and my mind is blessedly clear. I've got music pounding in my ears, so that helps too. I leave the gym feeling a little better.

Forcing myself to focus on my next thing, homework, I get to work. I have to get some studying done, but I appreciate what that does for my headspace. After I make it through the door of my apartment, I lose myself in anatomical facts and figures.

After a couple of hours, I decide a break is in order. Grabbing my keys, I head over to the local coffee shop and take one of my books with me. I'll spend the evening getting some studying in.

I park in front of the coffee shop and, after shutting my car door, I look up to see the object of my attention in front of the coffee shop.

As pleased as I am to see her walking a little easier, I can't help but be frustrated. I'm trying to get her out of my thoughts, and who shows up? *Her.*

Pasting a smile on my face, I approach her. If her reaction is any indication, she's as shocked to run into me as I am to run into her.

"*Doc?* What are you doing here?" Her bright yet dark eyes open wide at finding me here.

"Is it possible I'm looking for a quiet place to have coffee?" I tease.

She snorts, laughing.

That's too cute. Okay, stop that.

"So, Sapphire, are you here for the same reason?" I enjoy the flustered look on her face far too much. It's like I caught her doing something she shouldn't. She seems to like my nicknames if her blush is any indication.

What secrets are you hiding, Jewels Patterson?

That reminds me to check her social media accounts now that I know the name she goes by.

Stalking much, Drew?

Shaking my head to rid it of those thoughts, I hold the door open for her.

"Yep, you caught me," she says brightly. "I've got a serious coffee addiction. The paperwork at your clinic said for me to watch my diet, but I didn't see that I couldn't have coffee."

"That's just for foods that naturally cause inflammation, like pasta and bread. Gluten. Don't worry, coffee, thankfully, is off that list."

"Do you follow that strict diet, too, then?" She studies me with her dark eyes, and I have to look away. They are too piercing, like she can see all my secrets.

If only she knew. Then, I look at her curiously. *Does she know?* No, there's no way.

We walk up the line to the cashier. "Yes, and no. I find it's healthier to stay away from all that stuff. And it's easier to tell others to follow that diet when you're doing it yourself. I fall off the wagon occasionally, though."

"Ah, I see. So, scones aren't on the menu for you today?"

I look at her curiously. "What is a scone? I feel like I've heard about those in a movie somewhere, but I have no idea what they are."

She laughs, and it generates a warm glow in my heart.

Get a grip, Drew. You've made a girl laugh before.

But her tinkling laugh perfectly fits the pixie reference I felt when I first laid eyes on her.

She stops laughing and, holding her stomach, says, "I find it hard to believe you don't know what a scone is."

Her eyes are sparkling, so I know she's messing with me, and I find that I like it. Too much. I'm surprised to find her frankly irresistible, refreshing and confident. If I were in her position, would I be the same way? She's had so many hard knocks in her life, but she hasn't allowed them to get her down. She just rises above it.

"I really don't. Enlighten me."

She smiles. "It's a pastry. It's really good. If you're not counting calories, anyway. And it's most definitely on the gluten list."

"I think the hour and a half workout I did today should allow me one tiny little scone."

She gives me an appreciative look.

I like that way too much.

"Okay," she says, "but don't tell me I didn't warn you that you'll be hooked on them forever after."

As we follow the line to the cashier, I'm not really paying attention to the floor, but Jewels stops suddenly. She skirts a small wet spot I never would have noticed and makes the I love you sign with her hand, kisses it and points it at the sky.

When her hand drops back to her crutch, I have to ask, "What was that?"

She flushes and says, "Oh, it's something I do when I want to tell God I'm thankful for a blessing."

I look back down at the wet spot on the floor and can see why she's thankful to have avoided it and the injury that could have resulted. "So, you're a Believer then?"

She smiles and nods. "Are you?" she asks quietly.

"I am. I just have a hard time understanding God's motives sometimes."

"What do you mean?"

I motion my chin at her crutches. "Like, why does He allow bad things to happen to good people?"

She smiles again but doesn't take her eyes off me. "I believe that God wants us to rely on Him always and give Him credit for every good thing in our life. It's not providence or chance that things happen."

I look at her in awe that her tiny little body houses such a strong, indomitable spirit.

Then she recites softly as she looks away, *"That is why, for Christ's sake, I delight in weaknesses, in insults, in hardships, in persecutions, in difficulties. For when I am weak, then I am strong. 2 Corinthians 12:10."*

I can only stand in stunned silence as her strength shines through. Here she is struggling to walk, and yet the words out of her mouth are ones of hope and life. This is not a young woman who has given up on anything. She shines and thrives despite her condition.

She turns to me, her face so serene, I want to rub my shoulder against hers to see if her amazing outlook and faith would rub off on me. "I've never seen a faith like yours," I say.

Her eyes are shining when she replies, "You can, though. You don't need to walk in my shoes to believe that God can do anything, be everything for you."

I'm silent again, rendered speechless. *When will this girl stop amazing me?* "I don't think I would be as positive as you are if I were in your shoes."

"You'd be surprised what you can do," she says quietly.

"I certainly am surprised."

I can't help but find my heart is sore. I not only feel bad for her, I want to help her. It's not fair I can't use my gift to heal humans. They deserve it as much as Elementals do. She certainly does. If she were an Elemental, she would be treated or possibly healed. And I could ask her out on a date.

But even in a best-case scenario, I'm not even sure I could heal her. I resolve to look up cases when I get to my parents' house next time. For now, I try to concentrate on our conversation.

It wouldn't usually be so hard. She makes me think and feel everything.

What is it about this girl? I don't know, but one thing I didn't expect is to have my heart yanked out of my chest today as I find out.

9. Jewels

♥

I study the floor, suddenly feeling self-conscious. I've never shared my faith like that before. Drew's gone quiet, and I wouldn't say the silence is bad, just intense.

"I have a feeling I could learn a lot from you," he finally says.

"Like my knowledge of scones?" I tease as we move forward again.

He smiles, and I have to look away. It only makes him better looking when he does that. "You know, now I'm curious. How good could they be?"

I laugh. "You'll see when you try it. I recommend the blueberry one."

"Hmmm, got it." By this time, we've made it to the cashier, and he motions with his hand for me to order first, which I do quickly, pay, then move over.

Drew places his order. "I don't think I've been this excited to try something new in a long time. I'm so hungry, I wonder if I should have ordered two."

"You'll love it," I assure him, excited for him to try my recommendation. Some guys would never even consider ordering a scone, claiming it's too girly. I like that Drew is taking my advice.

I like it a little too much.

The barista hands him a paper package, and he turns to me, holding it out. "Want some?"

"Oh no, this is the one and only time I'll turn down that offer just to watch your face while you eat the whole thing." I say it smiling, and I have to look away again because he seems to be studying me.

Do I have something on my face?

"Okay, here goes," he says and reaches into the bag.

"Stop!" I cry, holding out my hand. "You have to take a sip of your coffee first, then take a bite."

Drew looks like he's trying not to grin. He fails miserably. "What? Why?"

"Just trust me. You do want the whole experience, right?" I raise my eyebrows at him.

"Fine. I'll wait until I've gotten my coffee."

"You didn't get one of those sugary ones, did you?" I grill him. "I wasn't paying attention to what you ordered."

"No, why?"

"Because the scone is sugary enough and not too sugary at the same time. If you had a sugar-filled coffee, you would have ruined your first taste."

"Please tell me what you're studying at college. You're so passionate about something as simple as a scone. I have to say, I'm dying to try it now."

I smirk. *Cute.* "As it happens, I'm a political science major, planning to attend law school next."

"Ah," he says, laughing. "So, you're very well suited to convince someone of just about anything."

I hide a smile, turning my head. "Only when I'm speaking the truth. And the fact is, scones are amazing. Although," I say with a cheeky grin. "I'm sad that this place doesn't have clotted cream. Then, it would be heaven on a plate."

"What kind of law do you want to practice?" he asks, turning to face me fully.

When the barista calls my name, Drew jumps into action when I move to get my drink. "I can grab your drink for you if you'd like," he offers.

Looking at him to see if he's pitying me, I really don't like to see that expression on people's faces. It's like my pet peeve. I can't help but be disappointed when there is some of that in his eyes. So, I say, "That's okay. I can manage it. They know me here and give me my drink a certain way."

His gaze is so direct, I can't help but squirm. My attitude must have bled through because he says in a low tone, "I'm sorry. I didn't mean to offend you, Ruby."

I lower my eyes. "No," I breathe, feeling guilty. "If I catch a whiff of someone feeling sorry for me, I get a little ornery. It's one of my worst traits. I'm sorry. You were just being nice."

"There's nothing wrong with wanting to be independent. All is forgiven. And for the record, I don't pity you. I only admire you."

I blush under his intent gaze.

Wait, am I blushing at his compliment or because of this new look in his eyes?

I decide it must be a compliment and not to read too much into it. I'm sure he agrees that the fact I'm his patient makes me as off-limits to him as he is to me.

The barista holds my coffee out in a large cup that's only half-full. I grab the lip, and Drew turns to one of the tables once he accepts his own coffee.

I turn too, and I'm surprised when he asks, "Want to drink our coffee together? You can see me try the scone and answer my question that way."

I look down at the book he's holding. "Were you going to study something, Doc?"

"Yes, I was. But it can wait. If you'd like to sit with me, I can put off studying for a while."

Pleasantly surprised, I say, "Then I'd be honored."

"I'm not taking a quiet evening away from you, am I?" he asks.

I think about my wild, impetuous mother and wonder if I should share with him why I come here so often. Finally, I admit, "I come here to get away from my mom's crazy projects.

I usually get lost listening to music. I wouldn't mind hanging out with you instead."

"Great," he says, and chooses a table close by. He looks down at my tilted drink and says with begging eyes, "Hey, let me take that from you. Please."

It seems I can't deny him anything, because I find myself handing it over reluctantly, a blush coloring my cheeks. I stuff my argument down and allow him to be the gentleman.

We sit down, and he sets down both cups of coffee. He takes the lid off his and asks, "So, what kind of law do you want to go into?"

"I actually want to be a health insurance lawyer," I say, getting comfortable in my chair, sliding my crutches off my arms and setting them beside me. Rubbing the impressions the crutches left on my arms, I add, "I hate that insurance companies won't cover certain treatments for patients. I want to help put a stop to that."

He flicks his gaze at my arms, then gives me an admiring look, and I drop my eyes to his hands. Reaching into the paper bag, he pulls out the triangular pastry. He pinches it between his fingers and is just about to dip it in the coffee when I put my hand over his cup.

"What are you doing?"

He looks up through his hair to say, "Isn't it obvious? I'm dunking."

I giggle. "Okay, I did not expect you to embrace this that fully. I meant for you to just take a sip of your coffee and then take a bite."

"I'm not allowed to dunk?"

"Please do! I just didn't peg you for a dunker."

"Well, I guess I am. I dunk my donuts, too. Does that surprise you?"

I laugh again. "Yes, it does. Okay, stop stalling. Try it already!"

He has a look like he wants to remind me I'm the one who stopped him and dunks the scone. Lifting it to his lips, I'm distracted by how soft his lips look. I bite my lip in response.

His eyes bulge when he notices, and suddenly he coughs violently. He must have breathed in crumbs.

With my heart in my throat, I rush to put my crutches on. I push myself up, get over to him and pound his back. "Are you okay?"

He reaches blindly for his coffee, and after a few careful sips, the coughing lessens. He looks up at me with watery eyes.

I'm leaning over him and inhale a whiff of his cologne that makes my mouth water. My eyes are drawn to his lips since he's so close to my face.

What would it be like to kiss him?

Shoving that thought out of my mind, I straighten up.

He says in a slightly choked voice, "I'm good now. Sorry to scare you there."

"Really, are you okay? I'm so sorry. What happened?" Satisfied he's not dying, I return to my seat.

"I inhaled some crumbs before I could enjoy my first bite." He wipes his watery eyes.

"Well?" I ask.

He looks around. "What?"

"How was it?"

"I honestly have no idea. I was trying to breathe. Should I try again?"

"If you have the courage," I say with a grin, eyeing him while I take my crutches off again and lean them on the table.

"I do," he says and takes a bite after dunking it, of course. He pauses, tasting the delightful combination of flavors I know and love. After he's completely chewed and allowed time for dramatic effect. He shrugs and says, "It's alright."

I cry out so loud that almost every table looks in our direction. I can't help it.

He bursts out laughing.

I reach over and smack his arm. "You were just messing with me, right? It was amazing. Pure perfection."

After he gets his breath back from laughing so hard, he says with a big smile, "Yeah, it was pretty good. I'm a fan."

"Yes!" I cry and wiggle around in my seat. "I knew you'd love it. Now, we just need to find a place that serves the cream, and then you'll really get the full experience."

He lets that sentence hang there because I just implied we'll meet somewhere else *on purpose, like on a date,* another time. After I realize what I said, I squirm in my seat, my face a brilliant shade of red.

I splutter, "I mean... next time you see scones on the menu, see if they have clotted cream."

He just looks at me expectantly, and I want to be anywhere on this planet but here.

Humiliated that I put my foot in my mouth like that, and even though I've barely drunk any of my coffee, I cram my crutches on my arms so hard; I leave scratches. I heave myself up out of the chair and reach for my cup when he stops me with his hand.

"Hey, wait. Where are you going?"

"Well," I say, wanting to be a million miles away, "Uh, I have to go. It was nice to see you."

When I reach for my drink again, he puts his hand over it. "Are you going to carry this all the way home?"

I shake my head hard. "No. I was just going to throw it away."

"Please. Allow me," he says, his face twisting in that hated expression, pity. Or is it regret?

I'll examine that question later. I wish we could return to the easy moment we had just a second ago, but it's gone.

I escape the coffee shop as fast as my legs will carry me away. How I wish I had two good legs and a spine that would let me run. I would sprint if I could, which is sad to think about because that's an experience I'll never know.

Oh, to let my hair blow in the wind as I get the heck out of this coffee shop. I've not been this embarrassed in a long time. How could I assume that Drew and I would meet again, like on a date?

As I leave the coffee shop and walk toward the bus stop, I'm mortified. He looked at me with such surprise; I could have died right there and then.

What was I thinking?

Oh, yeah, in another world, where I wasn't me and he wasn't my doctor, or therapist, or whatever he is, we would meet up somewhere and spend time together. The facts, though, glare at me that I am in his care, and therefore, he is totally off limits.

And apparently, so am I.

As I walk to my bus stop, I wonder what I saw on his face earlier...did he regret I was leaving? Or pity me like I feared?

Now because of my fear, I'll never know.

10. Drew

After two long days of working in the clinic, and what seemed like months of studying, I finally make it to my parents' house. I plan on getting to the bottom of my insatiable curiosity. I need to know whether Gyans can heal spina bifida cases.

Not that I'm going to do anything about it. I'm just satisfying my curiosity, I assure myself. My conscience pricks me I'm not being entirely truthful, but I ignore it.

I won't heal Jewels. I won't. This is just research, data collection. With that thought firmly in mind, I ask my dad for access to the medical files on his computer.

He doesn't even blink at the request. He's used to my researching everything I can get my hands on regarding the Gyan gift of healing, knowing how much I love it. I won't disappoint him or make him regret giving me access to these files.

So, I settle down for a long night of research. My thoughts drift to my last meeting with Jewels and how she rushed from the room because of a harmless comment. I wanted to assure her I would absolutely see her again...but then I know that's not entirely true. There's nowhere in my world for her, a human.

I focus my attention to my research when my spirits plummet. I'm honestly not sure what I'll find. Gyans have sometimes healed difficult illnesses like cancer and otherwise incurable diseases. But I've never looked up paralysis or cases like it. I know that there are things that are beyond our scope to heal. We're making headway on even the most difficult cases, but what about spina bifida?

Jewels's case happened during the first 28 days of pregnancy. Her spinal cord didn't develop properly, leaving an opening where a portion of her spine protruded from her body, forming a sac. When Jewels was younger, she had surgery to close the open part of the spine. Thankfully, it was located low on her back, close to her hips, allowing her the chance to walk, albeit with crutches. If she had been born with the opening closer to her head, she'd most likely be paralyzed for life.

The question is, have any Gyans been cured of this condition? I'm sure there are cases; there must be. One in 3,000 births results in this condition, so I'm sure we've seen this happen with our people. We're human too, after all.

After reading for some time, I hit the jackpot when I find answers. I lean back, running my hand over my mouth. The results aren't what I expected. I thought that since this condition is from birth, there would be no chance of healing.

But I'm proven wrong. Gyans who've been born with less severe cases of spina bifida have been healed. It took time and multiple healings. Some have documented full healing that required more than ten sessions.

I let my mind run. Is Jewels's case similar to this one? Would it take that many healings? Could she possibly walk unhindered? My professional mind works out details of her anatomy that would take a specialized healer to treat. Could I do it? I'm more gifted in healing than most Gyans, if anyone could do it, it's me.

And I can't help but desperately want to. It's always been my dream to be a doctor, and I've been working toward it for five years. I want to tackle the challenge of healing such an all-encompassing condition, one that other Gyan healers have struggled to resolve.

I turn off my professional brain and just think about Jewels. Her dark, sparkling eyes, her smile. I must admit, I'm drawn to her fire, her drive. It doesn't surprise me she wants to be a lawyer to help others with debilitating conditions. She is exceptionally driven, and I can't help but admire her for it.

I think about the level of pain she lives with daily. My own hands felt the state of her muscles. Stiffness and pain are constant factors in her life. Walking with crutches all day causes her massive suffering. Yet she pushes through and has a great attitude.

I imagine her healed. She'd be even more unstoppable than she is already.

I laugh, despite myself. She'd be the US Attorney General, I'm sure of it. She'll probably achieve that without any of my intervention. Mainly, I just want her to be free of pain. I see the pain she tries to hide when moving.

Leaning over, resting my elbows on my knees, I run my hands through my hair.

I have to stop thinking like this. I can't heal her. I just can't.

Not even the poppy seed formula would make her forget multiple cases of healing. I'm guessing with my gifted ability, it would take at least five sessions with me. Why did my mind automatically go there? It seems that no matter how much I know I cannot heal her; my heart has other ideas.

Stop that, Drew.

What about Jewels has me in such a state, ready to consider using my gifts on a human and violating an ironclad Elemental law?

Using the resources of the clinic will have to suffice. I cannot risk exposing the Gyans.

I hear my mom's soft footsteps and snap my head up. "Drew? Everything okay?" She's looking at me with such concern, I wipe all my tormenting thoughts off my face.

"Yeah, I'm fine. What's up?"

"Oh, nothing. I was just passing the office and saw you holding your head in your hands. Are you sure you're alright?"

I wince, wishing she hadn't seen that. "I'm fine. Just going over some research that I can't wrap my head around."

She leans over the desk and spins the computer to face her.

My stomach plummets.

In the light of the computer screen, she lifts her eyes to mine. "Drew?" she asks quietly.

I try to play dumb. "Yeah?"

"You're looking into spina bifida cases with Gyans? Doesn't the girl you met last year, who's now your patient, have this condition?"

I shrug. "Yes."

She straightens and folds her arms. "Please tell me you're not thinking what I suspect."

I answer in as firm a voice as I can, "No. I'm not going to attempt to heal her. I was just curious, is all."

"And the fact that there have been documented cases of Gyans being healed of her condition tells you what, exactly?"

I look away. "Nothing that I can do anything about," I say faintly.

Mom blows out her breath and moves to the back of my seat. She massages my tense shoulder muscles, and I relax when she infuses me with a healing warmth. "You don't have to do this to yourself, you know."

I pull away and swivel in my seat so I can see her. "I'm not doing anything but satisfying my curiosity. You never know when a Gyan baby will be born with this condition."

"And you don't want to practice on this girl?"

"Woman," I correct.

She lifts an eyebrow.

"She *is* a young woman," I say, throwing my hands up.

"Drew, you don't just *say* anything. Everything out of your mouth has a purpose."

I cock my head, wondering what she's implying.

She soon enlightens me. "Drew, she's off limits."

I sigh heavily. "I know that, Mom."

"And there's no future where you can heal her...or date her."

I give her a dark look. "I can help her at the clinic," I growl, frustrated she's read me so well.

"That's not what I mean, and you know it, Andrew Ashcroft."

I lean back in my chair. "I know that, Mom. But haven't you ever been frustrated that you could heal someone, but *can't*? To have your hands tied?"

"Drew, it's the law that every Elemental across the world follows. Do you realize the pandemonium that would ensue if humans found out about our abilities? It would cause massive unrest for our people."

"Yeah, I know." I run my hand over my face. "But it's not exactly fair that we get all the benefits of our gifts and humans get nothing."

She frowns. "We take care of the Earth so they can live in a healthy world. That doesn't benefit them?"

I stand not answering. Snapping the computer's screen down, I say quietly, "It's like a surgeon never going into surgery. I'm going against my nature by not healing her."

"Drew," she says softly, her eyes full of pity.

Wanting her to understand, I say with heat, "If you only knew this girl. There is *no human* more deserving of having a full life. She's already full of spunk, full of fire. If her body were healthy and whole, there would be no stopping her. She could be pain free, Mom."

"And what makes this human more deserving than, say, a cancer patient?"

I hang my head and clench my hands. "I don't have an answer for that," I finally say.

"You would be ostracized from our community," she says in a hard voice. "Drew, you have no idea how far the Gyan Grand Elder will go to keep our world secret."

"It's not a matter of me exposing our world, Mother. I'm not stupid enough to do that. I could do it in a way that looks natural."

She looks askance at me, her eyes full of doubt. "A woman born with spina bifida suddenly being completely healed would make national news, son. Think about that. It's impossible. No matter how special this girl, sorry, young woman may be, it sounds like she's found a way to live with this condition. Leave this alone."

She's right. There's no way I can heal Jewels without attracting a lot of attention.

I finally nod. "Don't worry, Mother. I know my place."

"Really?"

I hold my hand up. "I get it, Mom. Believe me, I do. Sorry, but I have work to do."

I quit the room, my insides churning. One thing is certain. I'm conflicted. That much, I admit. It's what I'm going to do about it that has me worried because Jewels is pulling me in a direction I never thought I would go.

I need to keep my distance from this girl, that much I know. It's the only way.

11. Jewels

♥

When I walk into the clinic's exam room, I find Drew's already there. He glances up at me but then resumes reading his clipboard, his brow furrowed in concentration. "Hello," he says in a distracted tone.

"Hiya, Doc, any good news in there?"

He studies the paper and says, "Eventually, there will be. I think I already see progress from your initial reports."

I smile. "That's good."

He doesn't say anything, doesn't even look at me. When he continues to read his report and does not speak to me, the air sits silent, thick and heavy. My smile drops.

What's the matter?

He finally puts the clipboard down and asks me, "Are you ready to get started?" His voice is so monotone and dead that my chest constricts. He doesn't smile and just turns to the door, opening it. "I'll let you get changed."

I can only nod when he leaves. Dumbly, I dress in a gown, wondering how to draw him out of the shell he seems to be in. He knocks on the door, escorts me out of the room, and I can't help but wonder what happened to the friendly Drew I've known? Well, besides when he grimly attempted to erase my mind.

He leads me into the treatment room, and I wrack my brain for what I've done to warrant this change in him.

I don't trust people easily, which makes new friendships hard. Also, I have a strangely optimistic personality, which people don't know what to do with. And when I shy away from people's pitying looks, I detract invitations instead of inviting them. But Drew's cold treatment is so strange. We had a fledgling friendship, and right now, he's making me feel as if I've lost what could have been a good friend.

When he comes back into the room, I attempt to catch his eye and smile at him, but he only presses his lips together in a grimace and averts his gaze.

I'm relieved when Mary comes in to apply the sticker things. Because of the change in Drew, my nerves are frazzled.

Can he somehow suspect I know about his magic? Is he plotting to administer that terrible powder again?

Worried, I bite my lip and try to relax as the machine blinks and whirs.

The pulses of heat do their magic, and I can't help but moan in relief at how good it feels. My back muscles have always been particularly tense and stiff, so I appreciate the treatment immensely.

Once it stops, though, I realize I'm going to have to endure Drew's painful silence while he massages me to finish up the day.

I don't think I can handle that.

Going from our playful conversation in the coffee shop to this cold indifference is excruciating. Then I realize. *He's distancing himself from me because he thought I was coming on to him.*

I thought I was embarrassed before, but this! This takes the cake. I make a decision that isn't pleasant but must be done. I'm going to request another masseuse. I have rights as a patient, and I don't have to put up with a frosty attitude. Especially after I've completely embarrassed myself.

I don't know how much good this heat therapy is doing now with how tense my body is anticipating this conversation. The treatment is over too quickly. Mary comes in and removes all the nodes and leads me into a darkened room. The massage room wasn't dark the last time, but I appreciate the lack of light.

I don't want to see Drew's expression when I basically fire him.

Debating internally, I backtrack. I'd rather never see him again than deal with an unfriendly version of Drew. My heart crashes at that thought.

Can I ask him what's wrong? Do we know each other well enough for that?

He makes my decision for me when he enters the room, wiping his hands off with a paper towel. He never once looks in my direction as he briskly instructs me, "There's a sheet on the table. Get under it, and I'll return to give you your massage."

He's so perfunctory that I just sit in stunned silence. I already know what's wrong. He's disgusted at the thought of me asking him on a date. It doesn't matter that I only implied it.

And this is his response. He's icing me out. Well, I can return the favor. "Actually, no," I say in a strong tone, my chin up. "I would prefer another therapist."

Even in the darkened room, I can see his surprise when he turns around and finally looks at me. "Excuse me?"

"I don't want you to massage me. I'd like to request someone else. Anyone else, really."

His mouth turns down in a deep frown. "Are you sure?"

"Quite. It's what I prefer."

He looks *guilty* and full of regret. Eventually, he wipes his face smooth and nods like this is an acceptable conversation between two people who, just three days ago, shared coffee together like old friends.

Well, I didn't start this.

"I'm sorry you feel this way," he says quietly, looking down. But then I can't help but notice a shadow of relief cross his face. I wish I hadn't seen it.

"I am, too," I manage to say, my throat dry. I keep my chin up, and when it quivers, I turn away so he can't see it.

He excuses himself from the room, and when I'm left alone, I sink down on the massage table, taking off my crutches and setting them next to me.

Am I really so disgusting that one little comment warrants such a change in someone?

I don't really want the answer to that question. Besides, I've basically gotten it with today's events.

Blinking back tears, I get myself onto the low table. A knock on the door announces the new masseuse, and I call out that I'm ready.

A woman walks in and introduces herself as Kathy. I politely say hello but wonder what she must be thinking about me turning down a massage from an extremely capable, and handsome, guy. I don't really care what she thinks. I just want to get this over with.

I am relieved Drew won't see the scars on my lower back or anything else, though.

Now, I've got a masseuse who probably doesn't have an ounce of magic in her, and I'll miss out on the heavenly heat only Drew's hands can offer. As Kathy works a deep massage into my muscles, I ignore the tears slipping down my cheeks.

Am I so disgusting and repulsive?

I'm bereft as I'm left with no answers.

12. Drew

I ignore my aching chest when I enclose myself in my office. Leaning on my desk, I hang my head and ask myself how I could hurt someone so badly. It was clear I did when Jewels requested another practitioner.

I don't blame her. I basically turned a cold shoulder to her from the minute she stepped into the exam room. Cursing, I straighten, wiping my mouth with my hand.

I made the decision yesterday to be nothing more than professional and courteous, but instead, I was rude. I'm kinder to patients who yell at me than I was to Jewels today.

It was all so I could distance myself, so I wouldn't be tempted to heal her.

Right now, Kathy is doing my job because I couldn't even so much as return Jewels's smile.

I've been so wracked with guilt over my urge to heal her I became an indifferent monster. It required enormous restraint to keep myself from placing a healing hand on her back and attempting the process of repairing the nerve damage on her spine.

I had it all worked out, but my conversation with my mom repeated in my mind. There are risks for me if I heal a human. Am I prepared to face those risks to heal Jewels?

I decided to follow the law of my clan, to listen to logic instead of to my heart. I forced myself to believe that Jewels was a friend, nothing more. That I had to keep her at a distance to avoid my feelings.

But one thing is painfully clear. It's too late because I already care for her. I admire her too much to bear the thought of what happened today.

How could I turn on her like that?

I know that one more conversation like we had in the coffee shop would push me over the edge. She's ensnared me, and I am deeply invested in her healing.

Not that I proved that today.

What must she think of my behavior?

I'm ashamed I felt relieved when she requested another therapist. I felt like I had just dodged a bullet. But after I saw her chin tremble, I felt like the biggest jerk alive.

No woman has affected me like Jewels, and I have a feeling I'll never be the same again. Then the last of our conversation in the coffee shop hits me, and I reel back like I've been struck.

She assumed we'd spend more time together, that we might go on a date. It was pretty sweet. But then she ran out of the coffee shop as fast as her legs would carry her. I felt bad that she was embarrassed by her remark.

Now that I've treated Jewels like a stranger, she must think I'm disgusted at the thought of spending more time with her. I spin and yank open the door, running to the massage room. I have to fix this. I can't let her leave thinking badly of herself because of my conflicted feelings.

I open the door only to find the room empty of Jewels. Kathy is putting away the oils and turns to look at me in question. "Where's Jewels?" I ask, my heart racing.

"You mean Julia? She left after I finished the massage..."

I don't even wait to hear the end of her sentence when I rush to catch Jewels.

Bypassing the reception desk when I don't see her, I throw open the front door only to see her pulling away in a car with her mom at the wheel.

Leaning over my knees, I resist screaming in frustration. I notice a plant responding to my wild emotions and spontaneously combust in growth.

Fisting my hands, I look all around to make sure no one saw my lapse of control. I haven't done that in a very long time.

Straightening up, I plan to get Jewels's phone number from her records.

No, that would be a huge abuse of my position.

How can I make this up to her? Thinking furiously, I wonder if I could show up at her house again?

No, same problem.

She would think I got her address from her file. I'm left with only one option. I will make this day up to her. And I have an idea how.

13. Jewels

I walk around with a bruised heart all week. I can't help but feel like something really great was taken from me before I really had the chance to enjoy it.

Drew's friendship had come to mean something to me, though I tried to deny it at first. I mean, he's in a world that glitters so brightly, I can't help but want to shine in it. And the truth is I've only had four interactions with him. One that he believes I don't even remember, so according to him, we've had three.

Each moment together did something to me. It made me hope that I could mean more —be more to someone than just that girl with crutches.

I've never even had my first kiss and look where trying to be *friends* with someone got me.

Alone.

I've had opportunities—well, a few—but each time, I put a stop to it. I want my first kiss to be special, with someone I care about. The guys I could have kissed were nice, but I didn't feel strongly enough about any of them to trust them with the privilege of being my very first kiss.

In my best-laid plans, I only hoped for a friendship with Drew. But I swear I felt something in that coffee shop. Maybe that's why I blurted out that we could spend time together again, because it felt so natural. Like it was the obvious next step.

The only thing that has kept me walking and with my head held high is my time in the Word. God has gently reminded me, as He does all the time, that I have value. I go over a Scripture that gave me hope just this morning. *Charm is deceitful, and beauty is vain, but a woman who fears the Lord is to be praised. Proverbs 31:30.*

I don't need to be what this world calls beautiful, for that's just vanity. It's my heart that sets me apart.

For I'm to do what Matthew 5:16 tells me: *Let your light shine before men in such a way that they may see your good works and glorify your Father who is in heaven.*

So, even though my heart throbs, I have hope that my life is worth more than my imperfect back. I can shine with God's holy light, so that He burns through me. That's an awesome response that's real, and I want to bask in that, not this pain that keeps dragging me down.

I'm a prime example of the hope God can give. I might struggle physically, but my heart and spirit have been given over to a Savior who encourages and replenishes me daily.

I'm not going to let this situation with Drew steal my purpose or my joy. I might feel hurt, but whatever the reason Drew treated me like he did the other day, I forgive him. I wish we could be friends, but if that isn't meant to be, I'll be okay with it.

Eventually.

In the meantime, I give myself time to grieve and mourn what could have been. I know I didn't imagine our easy camaraderie, but Drew ended a friendship before it even began.

I'm walking out of the library on Saturday when my phone rings. When I pull it out of my bag, I nearly drop it. Fumbling, I hurry to answer.

"Vela?!"

"Hey," she says, laughing. "Long time no hear, friend!"

"You're telling me! Oh my gosh, what the heck? I don't hear from you in over a year, and you call me now? I thought you'd dropped off the face of the earth!"

She laughs again. "I kind of did. But a little birdie told me to give you a call."

I clamp my lips shut. Did Drew ask her to call me?

She interprets my silence correctly. "He says he's sorry. I'm to give you that message."

I can't help but blink tears away. Wiping my cheek, I can't believe he went to this much effort to have Vela deliver an apology message.

I clear my throat and take a second before I say, "Well, he certainly knows how to get someone's attention."

She asks quietly, "What happened, Jewels? Can you tell me? He said the story should come from you."

I bark a laugh and say, "Vels, I don't want to go into my problems. I want to hear how you've been, where you've been!"

"Oh, you know, I got married and all of that, but come on, Jewels, you can't keep me in suspense! I've never seen Drew this upset over a girl."

"I can't *believe* you and Linc got married!" I say, ignoring her plea.

She sighs dreamily. "Yeah, it's been magical. But hey, you're killing me. Please tell me what's going on with my brother."

I sit in stunned silence that I'm finally talking to Vela but say, "Believe me, he's not interested. I'm just his patient."

"He sure went to a lot of effort to reach you."

"Hey, why is it so hard to get ahold of you, anyway?"

"Oh," she sighs heavily. "I'm involved in something I can't talk about...not yet."

"Sounds mysterious."

"Sorry, but it has to be."

It must have to do with Drew's magical world. Even though she's adopted, she has to know what Drew can do. There's no way someone could grow up with a brother and not know about his abilities. That's why she can't talk to me about what she's doing. I'm not supposed to have any knowledge of their mystical world.

I'm blown away by that thought. I've unknowingly been friends with someone magical for years.

"Jewels? Are you there?"

"Yeah, sorry. Are you anywhere close by? Can I see you at least?"

"No, sorry. I'm not. I'm to give you this message, and I'm sorry it has to be so short, but I can't be on for long."

"Okay." My heart sinks that I won't get to talk to her more.

"I have enough time for you to tell me what happened with Drew, though."

So, I give her a condensed version of the more recent interactions, not mentioning our first one. She would tell Drew if I relayed our first real encounter.

"I don't know, Vela; it's like we had a moment together, something real and surprising... then he ghosted me. Well, iced up, anyway. He was like a completely different person. I appreciate his apology, though. It does my heart good."

"It sounds like you two made an impression on each other," she says, a smile in her voice.

"Well, he made one with me, that's for sure. I don't know his side of it."

"So, what's stopping you from making a move on my brother?"

I laugh outright. "You are kidding, right?"

"I couldn't be more serious. You're perfect for him. I'd love for you and Drew to get together."

"Vela! He's like my doctor! There are rules and laws against that kind of relationship."

"So, fire him. Make it so he's not your doctor."

I blink. I'm so surprised at what she just said that I blurt out, "I kind of already did."

"You fired him? You're not at his clinic anymore?"

"No, I am at the clinic, but I asked to work with someone else."

"Hmmm, Jewels, I have to go. But before I do, listen to me very carefully. Drew doesn't go out of his way like this for just anyone. Remember that. Do what you have to do, but don't throw away something like what you could have with my brother. Make sure that's what you want. I love you, friend. I'm really sorry, but I have to go."

I say goodbye and then stare at my phone after Vela hangs up. I marvel at talking with a friend I haven't seen or heard from in a year. Then, I can't help but giggle. Is Vela right? Does Drew care more for me than just a patient? There's no way of knowing unless I spend more time with him. And the only way to do that is to see him at the clinic.

Do I re-hire him just to see him again?

Or can I ask him for his number? Do what I suggested at the coffee shop and go get scones with cream somewhere?

I abandon that thought immediately. I could never ask him for his number; I'm way too shy for that. So, it looks like I'm going to be his patient again.

I tense at the thought, suddenly very nervous to see him again. Will this guy ever stop surprising me?

Shaking my head, I can't help but enjoy those surprises. Especially this one. He's made my day having Vela call me. I can't wait to thank him.

14. Drew

Dad catches me by surprise as I'm leaving his office. I went to their house on my lunch break to do some more research on Gyans with spina bifida. I didn't expect to see him there during the day.

Dad's eyes twinkle as he says, "Glad I can still sneak up on my son at my age."

"What? You're still a young chicken. I'm not surprised at all."

"Will I be surprised when I check the search history on my computer?"

I'm taken back to when I'm nine-years-old and he caught me red-handed stealing quarters out of my mom's purse to use at the old arcade. I smooth my face to be sure guilt doesn't show and say, "Depends on what would surprise you, Dad. You know I've got a curious mind and research all kinds of things."

He lifts an eyebrow. "Even cases of spina bifida among Gyans when there's a certain young lady in your care with that same condition?" His voice slices through any paper-thin argument.

I try the most honest tactic. "She's not actually in my care anymore," I say, sticking my chin out.

Dad's my height, so we're standing eye to eye. He responds smoothly, "But you will see her again?"

"Yes, she's still a patient at my clinic. Dad, she's raised a professional curiosity in me about our history with those who have her condition. I had to scratch it, if you will, that's all."

I'm hiding my real motives, even from myself, and I want to believe the words I've just spoken. But I can see how flimsy my argument is. He'll see right through me.

He does.

"Drew, you know I'm beyond proud of the man and Gyan you've become. God has gifted you with an extraordinary healing ability. One of the best I've ever seen. I mean this as high praise, to say the least. I don't want to see your skills go to waste."

"Why are my skills in danger of being wasted?"

His face hardens, and he reaches up to squeeze my shoulder. "I believe your mother warned you about the consequences of healing a human."

"She said I'd be ostracized and in trouble with the Grand Elder."

He nods grimly. "You don't know how far he will go to ensure our way of life remains a secret, son. Please think carefully about your next steps."

I look down at the floor and reveal a side of myself I don't always show people. "Dad, what happens if I fall in love with a human?"

His eyes widen, and he reflexively squeezes my shoulder. "Has it come to that? Are you in love with her?"

I laugh, throwing my hands up. "I barely know her. I, I, I don't know." I step back from him, and his arm drops. I half turn and run my hands through my hair. "I only know that she consumes all my thoughts, and I'm...honored to be in her presence. She's like this bright light, and I just want to stand in her warmth."

His look of surprise isn't lost on me.

"Dad, I know I can't have a relationship — a romantic one — with a human. But surely it's been done in the past? I can't imagine that in the history of our world, not one Elemental has fallen for a human."

He crosses his arms and clears his throat, looking away. "It has happened, yes. It's a regular practice among some indigenous peoples. But, son, have you thought that these feelings for this girl could be a byproduct of your interest in her medical case? She's unlike anyone you've known, so..."

"Of course she's unlike anyone I've ever known," I say in a hoarse voice. "She faces life with a smile on her face. When anyone else would be cursing God, she's praising Him. She's got a will to live that's so strong, I can see her doing amazing things with her life. I don't know. I just want to help her. Ease her pain."

Dad's look hardens even further. He turns to me. "Have you thought this through?"

"No." I spin around. "I don't know." I clench my hands, trying to control my gift. Just the thought of healing her sends hot energy racing through my veins.

Dad sighs heavily. "Look," he says in a deep voice. "Your mother and I are deeply concerned. We want only what's best for you. Being involved with a human isn't part of those plans. We don't see how it could work. But you are in charge of your own destiny. Think very carefully about your decisions. As your parents and your Elders, we must warn you of the consequences of doing anything rash. I can't tell you much more, just that you need to be careful."

I look him in the eye and nod. "I accept that."

He shakes his head and turns away but then looks back. "Why don't you bring this girl to dinner? Would it help you if your mother and I met her?"

Relieved more than anything, I say, "Yeah, that would be great. But first I have to see if she's accepted my apology and still wants anything to do with me."

"You're already apologizing to this girl? What on earth did you do?"

I grimace. "I tried to distance myself from her and treated her pretty terribly."

"Well, if she feels something for you, she'll forgive you for that. Too bad you can't explain to her why you did it."

Then it hits me what I'm even contemplating. I'm considering bringing a human into my life. "Dad, do you think I could hide my gift from her?"

"Forever? No." He shakes his head. He gives a half chuckle. "You don't do things in half measures, do you, son?"

"It seems not."

"Well, invite her over, and your mother and I will try to see what has you so captivated."

I cringe at my next thought. "Should I ask her over when we haven't even had an official date?" I don't count the coffee shop.

"That's up to you. This is all very unconventional, so it would make sense that it's so backward."

"I don't know. I'll have to feel her out. I'll let you know."

Dad turns away, and I leave the house, checking my watch. I have thirty minutes before I have to get back. I took a long lunch today, but I don't regret it. I needed to talk to my dad. He's a fount of wisdom, and his offer to have Jewels over for dinner is much appreciated. I could use their opinions.

But how would Jewels take that invitation?

I back out of the driveway and chuckle at the idea of introducing a girl to my parents before we've even had a date. The woman would ask the man to meet her parents first, anyway. And that's if they've been dating for a while.

It hasn't escaped me that I might scare her away before I know if she feels the same way I do. I will need to tread very carefully in her treatment. I'll try to see how she feels about me the next time I see her.

I can't risk my entire way of life on just anyone. And I don't want to secretly heal her. I want my family's full support. I can see my brother, Kane, hiding a thing like that from my parents, but I'm not built like that.

As I drive to work, I can't help the excitement that builds in me at the thought of talking with Jewels again.

What did she think of Vela calling her?

I hope it made the desired impression on Jewels. It took forever to get ahold of her. It was a miracle that I did. She's not the easiest person to reach nowadays. She's got a very full life as our Chosen One, prophesied thousands of years ago to heal and unite our world. I didn't want to bother her, but this was important.

So, what do I say to Jewels now? That I care about her, and I really am sorry. I have a lot to make up to her. Eventually, I come to my senses and pray. I ask God for favor and wisdom about how to handle these crazy new feelings of mine. I can only thank Him that my dad didn't freak out at the idea of me falling for a human.

Well, if I have to be honest with myself, I am kind of freaking out. My dad is right. I don't do things by half measures. I jump in with both feet. Always have. But the image of Jewels laughing in the coffee shop is burned in my brain.

She looked so happy, so real. Like she would take life by the horns and not let go until she got what she wanted.

But the question is, would she want me? The only way to find the answer to that is to ask. I hold my breath and work up the courage I'm going to need to do just that.

15. Jewels

♥

I'm in a daze as I go about the rest of my week. My appointments at the clinic are on Thursdays, and while I'm in my classes during the week, I throw myself into the work. I surprise myself when I finish my assignments and don't drift off into la-la land.

My time is spent in blissful anticipation of Thursday. By Wednesday night, my insides are a knotted mess, and I'm distracted as I sit at the dinner table, half listening to my mom.

"Julia? Are you paying attention?" Her pretty face is screwed up in annoyance.

I sigh and put down my fork. "I'm sorry, Momma. My brain is just full, that's all."

"Of what? School? Did something happen? Did someone do something to you?" As always, her eagle eyes read me only too well.

I incline my head as I play with the peas on my plate. "Kind of. It's a bit of a long story." I'm not sure how much to tell her about Drew. She probably won't like that he's shown interest in me since he's technically the one in charge of my treatment.

She puts down her fork and leans on her elbows to look at me. "You've been off all week. Don't think I haven't noticed. I'm your mother, not your roommate. When you were a baby, I used to stare at you, memorizing your expressions. Don't think I ever stopped."

"Creepy," I say dryly, my eyebrow lifted. One look at her face, though, and I know I'm not going anywhere without a satisfactory explanation. "Oh, fine," I say, giving her my full attention. "You know Drew?"

Her eyes brighten. "The guy at the clinic? What about him?"

I bite my lip. "Well, we kind of ran into each other the other day."

Her forehead furrows and she frowns. "Where? At the clinic?"

"No," I blow out a breath. "At my favorite coffee shop. We had a really great time."

"You mean you spent time with him there? You didn't just run into him?"

I shake my head. "No, we met by accident. But we had a connection. It's the weirdest thing. I felt like I could talk to him about anything." I'm looking off into the distance, smiling widely, when my mom groans. Snapping my head toward her, I ask, "What?"

"Julia Patterson. That man is your therapist. You can in no universe date him. Get that out of your head right now."

"He's not my therapist anymore. I requested someone else to treat me."

She puts her fork down. "Why would you do that?"

Pursing my lips, I say quickly, "Before you jump into protective mom mode, hear me out until I'm finished, okay? Promise?"

She looks at me with dark, suspicious eyes. She finally nods.

"Okay, so the next time he saw me at the clinic, he barely spoke to me. He was really aloof, making me feel like he barely knew me."

When her face turns red, I hold my hand up. "You promised, remember?"

She clamps her lips shut and nods briskly, waving her hand, asking me to finish the story.

"Well, see, he's Vela's older brother. You know my friend who moved away a year ago, and I haven't heard from since? Well, he arranged for her to call me a few days ago and give me a message."

Mom asks with gritted teeth, "What was his message?"

"An apology. Vela isn't exactly reachable, but he managed to find her, to have her call me, so he could make up for how he treated me. It was really sweet."

I let that sink in and drift off into my pretend land where it would be totally fine for me to ride off into the sunset with a handsome soon-to-be doctor.

"Let me get this straight," Mom finally says, smoothing out her napkin. "A guy you have a great time with blows you off quite rudely, mind you, and to make up for it, he gets in touch with his sister, who blew you off for a year to deliver an apology message to you?"

My mouth turns dry. When she puts it that way, it doesn't sound like such a grand gesture after all. "Yeah, I guess?"

"Julia. I don't like this. Remember when I told you that guys are dangerous? They want your complete devotion, and when they have it, they're careless and throw it away so quickly, you'll wonder what you ever saw in them in the first place."

I look at her sadly. My dad did a real number on her. My heart breaks for what she's gone through. "Mom, that doesn't have to happen to me. Drew is a really good guy."

She huffs, folding her arms over her chest, and looks away. "That's what they all want you to believe. Can't you see that?"

"Mom, I won't say that I'm experienced when it comes to guys. But why does your life translate to mine? Can't it be that Drew might genuinely care about me?"

Her face closes off, and she stands up, throwing her napkin down. "Well, let's hope that's true. I, for one, will be praying he doesn't destroy your heart in his attempt to capture it. Don't look now, but it looks like he's already gotten his hooks in deep."

I'm not going to tell her about the first time I met Drew. I wasn't going to anyway, but now it's clear how suspicious she is of his intentions, I'm going to keep that experience very close to my chest.

We clean up the dinner plates in an uncomfortable silence. I wish I could fix my mom's broken dreams. I can only hope that I've made her life somewhat bearable.

She's quiet as she bids me goodnight.

I go to my room and try to rest my mind to get ready to see Drew tomorrow.

It's not an easy task.

I'm dressed and out the door an hour and a half before my appointment at the clinic. It's only an hour from the bus, with how long it takes me to walk from the bus stop, but I go early anyway. As I ride, I'm twitching in excitement.

But then I second guess whether Drew is even interested in me. Just because he had his sister call me doesn't mean he's thinking of me romantically. He could have just been apologizing for his rude behavior. But what Vela said gave me hope that he feels more for me than friendship.

Vela's got it in my head that he likes me as in *like, likes* me. I think over what she said about keeping him fired. If he isn't my caregiver, we'd be free to date. My heart jumps into my throat and my stomach falls at the same time.

What good would I be to someone who wants a family? I don't know if I could ever have a child, and at that, my thoughts careen wildly out of control. Could I carry a child full term? What happens if I can't?

Holding my head, I force my brain to stop jumping from one crazy thought to another. I take deep breaths in through my nose and out of my mouth to calm myself down.

First things first. See Drew and get a feel for what he's thinking. Then, more questions assail me. How will I know if he does like me that way? Will I just know? Can I differentiate between flirting and normal conversations? My inexperience is sorely testing my resolve to talk to Drew openly.

And with each question firing into my brain, my heart palpitates faster. I'm sweating like I just ran a race, at least how I assume one would sweat after a race. I know that I'm not just nervous; I'm terrified.

The bus slows at my stop, and I almost stay on and avoid even going into the clinic. At the last moment, I flag the driver down and disembark as quickly as I can.

I'm no chicken. I will face this and see where God is guiding me. I might be sweating bullets, but I also have a strange kind of peace about facing Drew. Taking a deep breath, I figure God is giving me the thumbs up to do this. So, into the clinic I go.

Drew is at the front counter, bending over talking to the receptionist when I walk in. When I walk up to the front, he notices me, and his face lights up. His mouth stretches in a huge grin, and then he nods at me and points one finger in the air, asking me to wait.

I do and inconspicuously wipe my hands on my pants. When Drew stands up, he leaves the desk and comes out into the waiting room.

I can't help but smile shyly at him when he stands in front of me.

"Hi Ruby, can I talk to you for a second?"

I nod, happy he's back to giving me a nickname. He leads me to a private conference room. When we both enter and he closes the door behind me, I notice he's as nervous as I am. He's clenching and unclenching his hands before he runs his hand through his dark hair.

"Um, first I want to say, I hope you got my apology."

I nod, tucking my chin into my neck to hide my blush. "It was really nice talking to Vela. Thank you for having her call me."

"It was selfish, I know, using her like that, but I had to get an apology to you before you came in again. I couldn't use your information from this place, so...I got creative."

"I liked it." My heart palpitates in my chest.

He smiles. "Good. Now, I know that you've asked for a different therapist, but hear me out, please don't go to that extreme."

My eyes widen, but before I can comment, he continues, "I know that's asking for a lot, but I *know* I can help you. Please keep me on, and I promise you won't regret it."

I'm fighting for composure. I don't know what to think.

Does he like me or not? Does he just want to be in charge of my heat therapy?

As these questions run through my mind, he says, "I've been horribly unprofessional. But you don't have to worry about that anymore. I'll be my friendly self from here on out, I promise."

He gives me a look of anticipation so great that I couldn't refuse him anything. If he asked for the key to my heart, I'd gladly hand it over. But he's not asking for that. He only wants to continue my treatment.

What was I thinking that he could look at me in that way, anyway?

As my heart pumps brokenly in my chest, I nod and find myself saying, "Sure. You can resume my treatment. I don't mind."

I mind only that he won't ever love me. How did my heart become so involved so quickly? When they say falling in love is falling hard, they're not kidding. I feel like I'm smashed on the rocks at his feet right now.

I smooth my face, gather my emotions, and tuck them deep, deep down. "Do you want to start today?"

He claps his hands, rubbing them together. "Yes! That would be great. Let's get you in a gown, and we'll have you feeling the best you've ever felt in no time."

I'm carried along in his excitement as he leads me to the machine room. He's going on and on about upping my levels and monitoring my progress as we walk.

Barely listening, I'm fighting back tears.

Blast Vela for giving me such hope like that. What was she thinking?

I numbly go through the motions when he hands me a gown, and I put it on after he leaves the room. When I'm covered and resting on the table, Mary applies all the nodes on my back, legs, and arms. When that's done, Drew returns and I try to smile at him, but I'm pretty sure it looks like a grimace.

He looks at me twice when he sees my face, but Mary shoos him into the tech room so she can get started with the heat therapy. It looks like he reluctantly joins her, which lifts my bruised heart a little.

I should feel lucky that he wants to spearhead my treatment. He's much better than Kathy at the massage part anyway, but I can't conjure up any excitement in my current despondent state.

Settling into the heat pulses, I answer the questions Mary and Drew ask through the glass as they adjust the levels. It really is amazing what they can do in this place. Despite my jumbled thoughts, I'm feeling pliant and relaxed by the end of the treatment.

When the machine stops whirring, Drew walks briskly back into the room. "Okay, time for the massage. I'll be right back after you get off the table."

I morosely get down, working harder than I usually do. It's like all my energy seeped out, gone with my dreams. Drew comes back into the room and leads me into the massage room.

Looking at the sheet on the massage table, I realize he's going to get a good look at my scarred back. But I said he could be my therapist, so here goes.

He gives me my privacy to lie face down on the table and get under the sheet. It takes several minutes, but finally I'm ready. He knocks on the door, and when I answer that I'm ready, he comes in with a bright smile. He looks as if he's anticipating something. He glues his eyes to my back, and I can't help but tense.

When he approaches, he gets to work on my arms and he says in a low voice, "Relax, Ruby. Everything is going to be fine."

His deep voice is so soothing, I can't help but obey. He makes it easy to trust him. I focus on what his hands are doing instead of what I wish his heart would do.

After about ten minutes of his rubbing my arms and shoulders, I'm so relaxed that I barely notice when he starts working on my back. My eyes pop open when I feel a deep heat saturate my lower back. I'm glad my head is turned away from him so he can't see my shocked expression. He's using his magic on me! I know his hands are going to be warm after massaging me for so long, but this is different. This is what he did on the first day of my treatment, and that day he blew the powder in my face. He's infusing heat into my back, and it feels *wonderful*. It's the best feeling I've ever had.

I can't believe that this is what he meant when he promised earlier that I'd feel amazing. He intended to do this from the start.

Warm feelings bloom through my chest. He must care about me if he's willing to use his magic during my treatment. Why else risk being exposed?

The question is, do I say anything?

No. He'll only stop like he did that one time he put his hand on my arm, and then he'll deny everything.

Okay, so now that I'm going to keep his secret, I vow to do a good job. I won't reveal it to anyone.

But what will happen after this supposed massage? When he did this to my back the first time I met him, I found I could walk better the next day. Will the same thing happen tomorrow?

The heat is almost too hot to be comfortable, but it's going so deep, reaching my spine, it's almost like it needs to be that temperature. He continues to apply the miraculous heat to my lower back, concentrating all his attention on the area around my scar. After a good thirty minutes there, finally he moves to my legs. He just massages them normally. Even though his hands are warmer than usual, I don't feel the infusion of heat like I did on my back.

When he's done, he pauses for a moment, breathing harder than he normally does after my massage. I'm about to ask him if he's okay when he says, "All done for today. I'll be back when you're dressed." I watch him as he walks out of the room with slow steps.

I'm shocked to my core when I get up. It's not the same lurching movement I had just forty-five minutes ago. I'm up in a smooth motion, much more quickly than usual, and I can't help but gape in shock at my improvement.

Reaching around to my back, I feel the same scars as before, but I swear I can move much easier now. Feeling wildly hopeful, I bend forward and gasp when I can go further than I ever have before. Giggling, I straighten, and the pain I've felt for as long as I can remember is much less. I stretch to the right and left, and while I can't go as far as most people, the fact that I *can* leaves me gaping.

Emboldened, I try something I haven't done since I first learned to walk with crutches. In utter shock, I take a step without them. Before, I would have fallen straight on my face without a walking aid, but now I can't help but cry out when I see that I've taken a step on my own. It's not pretty, but I can support my weight.

Drew knocks on the door, speaking through the door, "Jewels, are you alright?"

I laugh, tears crowding my eyes. "I'm great. Give me a second."

I step toward my crutches, still astonished that I can move this way. Blinking back tears, I know that I won't be able to keep it up for long. But taking two steps on my own-is a miracle!

Collecting my emotions, I force myself to calm down. I have to keep his secret, and that means hiding it even from Drew. After a few moments of deep breathing, I lean on the bed, put on my clothes, and slide my crutches on my forearms with shaky hands. I call out to Drew that I'm ready.

He opens the door, looking shyly at me with a small grin on his face. "How are you feeling?"

His eyes hold a knowing look, but instead of telling him what just happened, I smile widely and say, "You're right. This is the best I've felt in a long time."

I'm afraid to call him out for what he did. I don't want to scare him away. So, I say, "The treatment left me feeling amazing!"

He nods, but I notice dark circles under his eyes that weren't there before. Did using his magic drain him completely? I'd imagine it would, though I'm resolved to keep his secret, so I keep my questions to myself. I say, "Thank you for my massage, Drew. You really are the best masseuse I've ever had."

He accepts the praise gracefully but cautions me, "Just because you're feeling good now, don't overdo it. You don't want to push your healing too fast."

Healing? Doesn't he mean treatment? Is that what he just did? Healed my back? Is this improvement permanent?

Forcing my questions back, I nod and agree. When I turn to leave, he says, "I'll see you next week, Emerald. Take care of yourself."

He leans against the wall with one shoulder, looking like a stiff breeze could blow him over, and smiles softly at me. I'm tempted to say that he should take care of himself too, but I hold myself back. Instead, I decide to be brazen. "Hey, you have a promising career ahead of you, Doc. I can say firsthand that your touch is magical."

A flash of curiosity shows in his eyes, then he chuckles. Running a hand over his neck, he says, "I'm glad you feel that way. That's high praise coming from someone who's seen her fair share of therapy."

I beam a grin at him. "Since I'm such an expert, just know that my five-star rating comes from a very qualified reviewer."

He grins. But his eyes droop, and he looks like he's ready to drop. I try to hide my concern about him.

"Well, it looks like you could use a break, so I'll see you next time. And again, thank you."

"You're very welcome. I'm just glad the clinic's treatments have you feeling better."

His *treatment, he means. I don't have any doubt it was his healing that did this; nothing else could have made such a difference.*

Smiling at Drew, I leave the room in stunned silence, shocked at how much easier it is to walk. My stride is longer and less jerky, and I'm moving with a lot less stiffness and pain.

When I glance behind me as I move down the hall, Drew is watching me go with a soft expression on his face. I can't help but give him a big smile. Then I laugh, feeling like a million dollars just rained down on me.

What Drew did today was next to miraculous. He's able to do things with his hands that no one in this world could. Well, maybe a lot of people in this world can; I just have never met them.

I think he attempted to *heal me. That's why he said healing.* I'll take it as the priceless gift that it is.

I won't tell a soul, though, keeping his secret until the day I die. He might not have confessed an undying love for me, but what he just did today shows he cares enough to risk his secret coming out.

Well, it won't be from me.

Instead of coming in today and leaving his girlfriend, I'm leaving as the captain of Drew's fan club.

That's going to have to be good enough.

16. Drew

I watch Jewels walk away, and even though I'm more exhausted after a healing than I've ever been, I swell with pride. I'm fit to bursting with how she's moving so much more easily. I hang onto the wall so I can watch her walk down the hallway.

Then she laughs. That does something to me. When she laughed before, I imagined her as a pixie. Cute and adorable with a hidden side of her, I wanted to find out more about her. Now, she's an enchantress. Just knowing that I'm responsible for her joy is addictive. I want to do that again and again.

I've never felt this way for anyone, Elemental or human. She makes me think about life differently. She's been handed a life that most people would rail against.

But not this girl.

She's unequivocally the most fascinating woman I've ever met. I can't help but want to be in her presence. Even now, I'm tempted to run down the hall and pick her up and spin her in circles.

I stop myself only because, for one, I don't think I could run if I tried, but also, I don't want any attention drawn to her. Let them think she's happy and walking better from the treatment.

Turning tiredly to my office, I walk with heavy steps to my chair. I'm going to have to go outside to replenish my energy with the plant life if I'm going to get through the day.

Dropping into my seat, I lean my elbows on my knees. I need to think over my explanation of Jewels's progress. She'll garner a lot of attention, and I need to prepare to address questions that come my way.

I'll keep it as simple as possible. She's responding excellently to her treatment plan. I'll attribute most of her success to the heat therapy. That I'm actually healing damaged nerve endings won't be revealed until they order an MRI. Even then, I'll just say that Jewels is a full-bodied miracle. There are plenty of instances when medical science just can't be explained.

Jewels will be one of those mysteries. That's if they dig for answers.

I fully intend to continue her healing. Now that I've taken the leap and begun healing her condition, I don't regret one second of it. She's worth the attention and skepticism I'll face.

Lots of Elementals have told the world that a miracle occurred when it comes to the unexplainable. This will be one of those times.

I'll just need to have my parents' support. That's one thing I'm planning on getting tonight at dinner. Which reminds me, I've got to get a message to Jewels about coming over.

I couldn't ask her while she was here because she's my patient. It would look like I'm asking her out. Technically, it seems like I'm asking her on a date, but dinner with my parents does not really count.

After firing a text to my mom, I wait for an answer before I pull up my social media account. I type in Jewels Patterson, and spot her right away. I chuckle at her expression. She's smiling at the camera in a-no-nonsense way. I click to follow her and then send her a message.

There's a chance she won't see it in time for dinner, but I have to try. I meant to do this yesterday, but I was so consumed with pouring over Gyan cases of spina bifida, I didn't have the chance.

DrewAsh279: Sapphire, sorry to stalk you here, but I have a question for you. What are your plans for tonight?

I erase that whole thing. I need to stop giving her nicknames, but I can't seem to help it.

DrewAsh279: Jewels, imagine finding you here. I hope I'm not imposing on your time, but I was wondering if you'd like to enjoy my mom's homemade lasagna tonight. It's not gluten-free, but it's incredible. Totally worth cheating on your diet.

I read the message over and over, combing it for creepiness. It sounds friendly enough.

Pushing send, I hold my breath and wait for a couple of minutes to see if she'll get the message right away.

My heart jumps when she responds.

JewelsPatterson16: Didn't I just see you? Couldn't you have asked me ten minutes ago?

I smile. She's feisty. I really like that.

DrewAsh279: Not really. It would seem like I'm asking you on a date at work.

A couple of minutes go by before she answers.

JewelsPatterson16: And that's not what this is?

I hesitate before I answer. I would love for this to be a date, but I can't have her thinking it is one. She has to understand the position I'm in.

DrewAsh279: Only because I'm your therapist. This is just a family dinner. Sorry if it seems weird. I just told my parents a lot about you. They'd love to meet you.

I hit send only because I know she's waiting for a response. I suddenly feel like I'm overstepping my friendship with someone I think a lot about.

What must she be thinking? Who asks someone to dinner with their parents as their first invitation?

Apparently, me.

Suddenly, I feel so weary, I'm going to drop if I don't get outside and replenish some of my energy. I'm feeling even more drained because my emotions are strained. Closing my laptop, I make my way outside. We have a small lawn in the back that sits against the building with some bushes.

Thankful there are no windows on the neighboring building, I look inside the back windows of our clinic. All clear. Leaning my shoulder against the building, I put one hand onto the bush growing next to it. It seems like I'm just getting a breath of fresh air, but really I suck out the life force of the plants.

Energy flies through me, giving me just the boost I need. I pull my hand away before I kill the poor plants.

They droop, but I'm satisfied they'll survive, so I walk back into the clinic feeling a hundred times better than I did five minutes ago.

Mary stops me. "I saw Jewels leave, and she looks so much better! Whatever you're doing in her treatment is just right. You're nailing it!"

This is when I have to plant the seeds of the unexplainable happening. "Well, sometimes everything in the treatment just falls into place. The heat therapy has been going really well."

She looks at me with pursed lips. "I'd say! Whatever you're doing, keep it up." She walks away before I can say anything else.

And so it begins. Jewels has already made an impression on the staff. Before we know it, everyone will be talking about her rapid recovery.

I'm going to have to slow down her healing sessions. Her improvement needs to be believable. Miraculous, but not suspicious. After healing her today, I've determined that I could complete her healing in one or two more sessions. But to keep from drawing unwanted attention to myself, I think we will have to lengthen the process.

Walking briskly back to my office, I decide I have a few more minutes to message Jewels. Did she respond to my last message? Did she say yes?

Opening up my laptop, I find a message.

JewelsPatterson16: Sure, I can come. When?

I respond with today's date, my parents' address, and the time, while my heart beats wildly in my chest.

This is it. My parents will finally meet the girl who has totally captivated me. What will they think?

JewelsPatterson16: I'm not really anyone special, Drew. I kind of feel like I'm being put on display.

DrewAsh279: I'm really sorry. I don't want you to feel that way. You are special; you don't realize how much you impress people.

JewelsPatterson16: I feel like you're just trying to get an even better review out of me than I gave you before. You don't have to do that, you know. And thanks for the compliment. I don't really deserve it.

I couldn't disagree with her more, but for the sake of not sounding like an even bigger love-sick idiot, I say that I'll see her soon and sign off.

I'm on pins and needles the rest of the day, thinking about tonight and seeing Jewels away from the clinic. Work is a place I put on a show for humans, but at home I'm completely myself. I won't be able to show her my Elemental side, which will be hard, but at least I'll be comfortable.

I just hope she will be too.

If things go well, and by well, I mean, if she feels for me what I'm starting to feel for her, maybe I can consider sharing my gifts with her. It would be amazing if she knew about my world, my family's world. I know she will at least love my mom. Everyone who's ever met her has gushed over her. But that's just not possible. It's a pipe dream.

I finish my day at the clinic and race to my parents' to talk with them before Jewels arrives. When I pull into the driveway, I jump out and bound up the steps in seconds. Throwing open the door, I call out for my parents.

They both answer from the kitchen. I inhale deeply the best smell in the world: my mom's lasagna and garlic bread. When I walk into the kitchen, Mom is stirring the sauce on the stove. Her back is to me, and I step up behind her and wrap my arms around her middle.

"Hi Mom." I breathe in her unique lavender and vanilla scent.

She stiffens and says, "Drew, don't you try to butter me up. You're putting us in a very awkward position, having that young woman here tonight."

I let her go and step up to her side, leaning on the counter. "I know that, Mom. But I need your input."

She looks at me with her eyebrows raised. She turns and puts tin foil over the finished pan of lasagna that sits on the stove. "On what? Her healing? You know more about what she needs than I do."

I sigh. "No. Not that. I've got that covered. I need your advice about *her*. I can't get her out of my head, and I could use your and Dad's impressions."

She purses her lips. "Your father told me what you said. And this isn't about us, and you know it, son."

Dad walks over and reaches past me for the plates. "I have to agree with your mother on this. If I can guess, you want to absolve your guilt for healing a human by getting our permission."

"And you think if we just meet her," Mom adds, "we'll understand why you're throwing away your reputation as a Gyan."

I look at Dad. "You suggested she come over here. I didn't ask for this. You offered to help me figure her out."

Dad chuckles. "Son, forget ever trying to figure a woman out. Human or Elemental."

Mom sighs and steps back to open the oven, bringing out the toasted garlic bread with gloved hands.

When I reach for a piece of bread, Mom slaps my hand. "Not until dinner." She takes off the hot gloves and says, "Drew, we want to help you figure this out. We don't want you ever to feel like you're in this world alone. But this is a decision you're going to have to make on your own."

I sigh, but my attention whips to the front door when I hear a knock. "Just tell me if she's as amazing as I think she is."

Mom looks at me with a soft frown on her face, shaking her head slowly. "We can't tell your heart what to feel, Drew. That's all up to you."

I walk backwards out of the kitchen. "I just need to know that I'm not going crazy. Give me your impression of her after you meet her, okay?"

Mom turns around, transferring the bread carefully into a basket. She mutters, "He's crazy in love, and I'm supposed to talk him out of it?"

I leave the kitchen and answer that question under my breath, "Yes, she is supposed to talk me out of falling in love with a human." As far as being in love, I have no idea if that's what this is. I've never been in love before. I don't know whether that's my problem or not.

Jogging to the front door, I open it to reveal Jewels waving goodbye to her mom, who's pulling out of the driveway. She turns, and I smile at her, waving while I watch her approach with a much easier stride than she had before. She's not lurching to the right and left like she was, and her walk looks more comfortable. It makes my head swim with happiness.

She's smiling too, and I look down at her legs that are peeking out of the bottom of her coat. She's wearing a skirt or dress, and I lick my lips in anticipation of seeing which one it is. I wish she weren't wearing that coat, but we still have some cold spring nights, so it's a necessary evil.

Jewels is painfully beautiful to me, but to see her in a pretty dress might tear out the last threads of my resistance.

Before she can see me checking out her legs, I pull my eyes away.

Too late.

Her blush shows that she saw my wandering eyes only too well as she makes her way to me.

"Hi, come in, please," I say awkwardly.

Way to make a creepy impression.

She's slower than before, but she's almost walking in a natural, smooth motion.

My mouth drops open in my surprise. She stops next to me, laughing, and says, "I'm as shocked as you are. Is this improvement supposed to be permanent? I really hope so."

I'm studying her legs and planning my next healing with her to include her leg muscles. They've been through a lot of trauma too. I'm sure they could use a healing.

"Hey, Doc. Eyes up here."

I jerk my head up and meet her smiling eyes. "Sorry. I'm just as surprised at your hea-, I mean, that your treatment went so well today."

Her eyes twinkle. "I'm thrilled, believe me. But I think I was more surprised to get your invitation than for my back to work right for the first time."

I laugh. "You were *more* surprised at that, really?"

She colors prettily. "Well, yes. I don't know what I did to warrant an invitation to dinner with your parents."

I stuff my hands in my pockets. "Well, it's like I said in messages. They had heard so much about you, they really wanted to meet you."

Shoot, I forgot to tell them to emphasize that they wanted to meet her.

Thinking over in my mind how I can get them to say that, she surprises me when she says, "You must really think a lot of me to give your parents the impression I'm someone special."

If only she knew how special I think she is.

Running my hand on the back of my neck, I say, "Well, I do. That's not a secret. I told you today that you're pretty incredible."

She blushes and says, "Drew, please don't think I'm any different from the thousands of other people who have spina bifida. Plenty of people struggle with this; I'm just one of them."

"Yes, but do they all have your positive attitude? Do they all tackle life like you do? You don't let anything stop you from achieving your goals."

This time, she's blushing so hard she looks away. "You think I do that all on my own. I don't," she says in a firm tone. "If it weren't for my relationship with Jesus, I'd be a pretty pitiful person. I'm not afraid to say I'm just as human as anyone else. I struggle, believe me. I wish for a life all the time where I can do things, go places I will never see, because I can't get there."

"Maybe that will change," I whisper, feeling so full of emotion, I have to walk away.

I'm not sure if she heard me, but she follows.

"Come on in," I say in a louder voice. "I don't want you to think that the entryway is the only part of our house. Come meet my parents."

I desperately need them to get my head on straight because if it were up to me, I'd heal her right here and right now. I want to give her the life she's dying to live, full of adventure and places she's only dreamed about. Maybe that won't be with me, but at least I could have the satisfaction that she'll be able to...with someone.

Wrenching my heart back to the present, I walk into the kitchen, keeping my pace slow, and find my mom and dad waiting for us. Mom smiles warmly.

"Hello," Jewels says, glancing at my parents, then tucks her head down as her cheeks go rosy.

I want them to see her full beauty, so to have her look up, I say, "Jewels, meet my mom, Whitney, and my dad, David. They've been dying to meet you."

I catch my mom swiftly giving me a look, like she'll talk to me later before she approaches Jewels, holding her arms out. "I'm so happy to meet you. I'm a hugger. Is that okay?"

Jewels smiles and accepts a warm hug from my mom. Mom steps back and, holding her shoulders, says, "We hope you're comfortable here. We are so happy to have you."

Dad walks up and holds out his hand. "I won't accost you like my wife here, but I'm happy to have you. Please let's go and sit down in the dining room. Dinner's ready. Hope you're hungry." He stoops to capture her small hand in his, and he shakes it lightly.

Jewels looks at me with wide eyes, and I smile gently at her. It feels so natural to have her here with my parents; I don't question it, just enjoy the sensation.

"Where's Kane?" I ask as Mom and Dad lead us into the next room. The large table is set to the hilt with Mom's best dishes and the lasagna steaming in the center.

I pull Jewels's chair out and wait for her to sit before I help her push it in. I hold in an amused chuckle when she gives me a startled look. She must not be used to having someone push her chair in, but I've been raised a gentleman, so I wouldn't have it any other way. She takes off her crutches and sets them carefully next to her. I hold in my excitement that she won't need them for long.

I sit next to Jewels and prepare to have a meal with the person monopolizing my thoughts for days.

"Kane'll be a little late. He's doing something with Elia," Mom answers.

At Elia's name, Jewels's face brightens. "She told me today she was going to move her art supplies into the other room? Do you know if she did?" she asks.

Mom's face opens in surprise, but then she catches herself. "So, you're friends with Elia, too?"

Jewels nods vigorously. "Vela introduced us, and after she left, Elia and I have gotten close."

"Huh," Mom looks at me with a question in her eyes.

I interject, "I didn't know you and Elia were close."

"Mm, hmmm," she says, smoothing her napkin in her lap. "We have weekly movie nights. She forces her sappy love stories on me."

I laugh just as Kane walks in. "We're talking about Elia, aren't we?" he asks, smiling at Jewels.

She returns his smile and turns a questioning look at me.

"Oh, sorry. Jewels, this is my younger brother, Kane. Kane, meet Jewels."

He gives her a smile and reaches to shake her hand. "It's nice to finally meet you. Elia has told me a lot about you."

Jewels blushes. "Elia has been a good friend to me. I'm crazy about her."

Kane smiles softly. "You and me both."

At that, I ask, "Mom, can we please start this delicious dinner?"

Let's just hope this meal is what I need: my parents' bird's-eye view to make sure I'm making a potentially life-changing decision for a very good reason.

And that reason is sitting next to me looking like a scared rabbit.

Time to change that.

17. Jewels

♥

D rew looks at me with bright eyes and asks, "So, Jewels, tell my parents about your aspirations to help people who struggle with insurance companies denying claims for expensive treatments."

I search his eyes, wondering how he knew I was starting to feel completely lost in this big, beautiful home with his wonderful family.

I love talking about my goal of tackling big companies that keep people like me from getting the treatments they so desperately need. I go into detail by explaining my motivations and feelings on the subject.

"So," I say, finishing my spiel, "I have every ambition to be like a bulldog when it comes to going after companies that take our monthly premiums but try to deny the life-changing, life-sustaining treatments we deserve."

Whitney dishes me up a generous slice of lasagna, then offers me the basket of garlic bread. I catch Drew licking his lips in anticipation of getting a slice, so I laugh softly, then offer him the bread first.

"See?" he says to his parents with a grin after grabbing three large slices. "I knew she was a sympathetic soul. Mom wouldn't let me have a sample before dinner."

My eyes widen, and I watch him devour a slice in two bites. Kane, too, reaches and grabs two slices and then shoves one directly into his mouth.

Whitney scolds them, "Drew! Kane! We haven't said grace yet. Stop that."

Happy to participate in a prayer, I fold my hands and close my eyes. David prays, "Heavenly Father, we thank You for the wonderful company we have in our home this evening. We pray You bless dear Jewels and her endeavors and future plans, Lord. We ask that You bless this food and allow it to nourish our bodies. In Jesus's name we pray, Amen."

Opening my eyes, I try to hide my blush caused by being mentioned in the prayer.

"Hey," Drew says softly, using his finger to gently guide my chin back up. "He didn't mean to embarrass you."

I look at him with wide eyes, glancing at his parents to see if they heard what he said, but they're talking softly to each other and don't seem to have noticed.

"I know," I whisper. "It's just that I'm not used to that."

"What aren't you used to?" he whispers back, his eyes twinkling.

I lean toward him. "People I don't know praying for me. Now, be quiet before they hear us."

He snorts but obeys and holds his plate out to his mom for a helping of lasagna.

In the meantime, I enjoy my first bite of a lasagna so delicious it requires concentrated effort to avoid moaning in appreciation. When my mouth is empty again, I say, "Mrs. Ashcroft, you are a wonderful cook. This is the best lasagna I've ever had."

David looks hurt and says, holding his heart, "How do you know I didn't make dinner?"

I look at him in horror as I hold my hand to my mouth. "Oh, my gosh, I'm so sorry."

He booms a laugh while Whitney smacks his shoulder. "David, honestly, stop harassing the poor girl. You couldn't cook this if your life depended on it."

"Yeah, Dad, that's the most ridiculous thing I've heard you say in a long time," Kane says with a loud laugh.

David finally stops chuckling. "I'm sorry. I couldn't resist making a harmless joke. It was harmless, wasn't it? You weren't too offended?"

"Me offended?" I squeak. "I was afraid I offended you! No, I'm fine. I can take a joke. But be prepared for me getting you back."

David's eyes twinkle merrily. "I look forward to retribution. If you need justice, I can take a joke, too." He smiles warmly at me, and I smile back, tucking into my food, intending to polish my plate.

"I'm all about righting wrongs, so count me in for this battle," I say with a smile.

"And Jewels, call me Whitney, not Mrs. Ashcroft, please. I'm too young to feel like my mother-in-law."

I look up and nod, agreeing, but I'm not sure I'll ever be able to call her by her given name. She smiles at me so warmly that I can't refuse her, though.

We eat in comfortable silence for a minute when Whitney puts her fork down. "So, Jewels, please tell us how you met Drew."

I choke on my food, thinking of the first time I actually met their son. Drew pounds on my back as I clear my airway of errant food. When I can breathe, I look up with watering eyes and apologize.

"Oh, honey, I'm sorry. Did I catch you by surprise?" Whitney looks at me with a certain guilt I can't interpret.

She must know when I actually met Drew. But she's referring to when I met him at the clinic, of course. Or is she suspicious that I remember what I shouldn't?

"Um, well, we met at the clinic," I say, holding my scratchy throat.

"Oh, I know. I meant to ask, what do you think of his treatment plan? Are you happy with it?"

I feel myself getting warm. How do I explain his healing without mentioning it? I put my fork down so I can concentrate. I'm not going to try attempting to speak while chewing again. "Well, I can say with all honesty that Drew is incredibly gifted. He's got me walking better than I ever have before. It's like a miracle."

I twist my hands in my lap. Everything I said is true. She smiles at me to continue, and I look at Drew asking for help.

He interprets my request correctly and says, "Mom, Jewels is responding to all the protocols beautifully. She's a perfect patient. I feel she's going to do really well with our program. I can already see a difference."

Whitney and David give him a smile, but they look guarded and a little strained.

Of course. They know exactly why I'm doing better. And they must not agree with his methods.

I hide my look of utter confusion.

Do they know about his magic? Do they have magic, too? I assume he must have inherited it from them. But I could be wrong.

Drew misinterprets my look, and he puts his hand over mine where it rests on the table. "Hey, they don't need you to give me glowing reviews. They know I'm pretty amazing. You don't have to feed my ego by praising me."

"No, that's not it," I say quickly to his parents. "I'm more than happy to sing Drew's praises. I've never had such a good therapist. It's like he's got magic in him the way he knows the human body." I blush at that statement. It just fell out of my mouth before I could think better of it.

No one seems to blink at my statement, though. They all nod. I breathe a little easier and vow not to mis-speak again.

Curious, I ask, "So, are you both in the medical field, too? Is that where Drew gets his natural gift?"

They smile at each other, but David answers, "No, we aren't in the medical field. Well, not officially. You can say we have an interest in it, but Drew comes by his propensity for the medical sciences all on his own merit. He's always been fascinated by everything medical. Even as a little boy."

Wanting to hear more about Drew's childhood, I ask, "Oh, in what way?"

Whitney laughs and wipes her mouth with her cloth napkin. "Drew used to bring me every hurt thing he could get his little hands on. We had quite a menagerie at one point."

I smile widely at Drew, who's coloring slightly. "Is that true? Please tell me more about this, Drew."

He shrugs and puts a big bite of lasagna in his mouth, then motions like he can't talk because his mouth is full.

"Oh, no, you're not getting away with this so easily," I say with a laugh. "I'll wait until you've chewed your food to hear all about it."

He finishes chewing and gives his mom a look that says he will speak with her later. "It wasn't that many animals. Mainly bugs," he says under his breath.

I bark a laugh and hold my stomach when I say in between breaths, "How on earth did you collect wounded bugs?"

He looks at me with mock-hurt eyes. "Hey, don't judge. I rescue everything that needs help. Bugs, at one point, came under my protection."

Kane laughs and says, "I tried many times to squish them all to Heaven, but Drew was fiercely protective of the little critters."

Drew scowls at him. "You were a pest! You knew how much I cared about all my patients."

"Bro," Kane says, wiping his mouth with his napkin. "You went way overboard. There was nothing wrong with those things in the first place, except maybe old age. They lived way longer than they should have under your eagle eyes."

Drew looks so adorably vulnerable that I can't help but squeeze his hand encouragingly.

"All of God's creatures deserve to be healthy," I say. "Do you still rescue bugs?"

He glances at me and then studies his plate. "No, I've decided my efforts are better spent elsewhere."

I blush because he's clearly talking about me. When I'm fairly positive my face has returned to its usual shade, I say, "Now I know why you bother with me. You truly have a bleeding heart when it comes to hurting creatures."

This time, his eyes do look wounded.

I say quickly, putting my hand back on his arm, "I've benefited from it, believe me. I thank God for you every day. I meant what I said in a really good way, Drew."

Looking slightly mollified, he says, "Thank you, I think."

"No, I mean it. Look at me after only three treatments from you. I'm walking better than I ever have before. You're amazing!"

He glances at me and then looks down at his plate. "I only do what I'm trained to do. I'm just a guy who wants to help."

"I know that. But you're an exceptionally gifted caregiver," I say with meaning.

"Hear, hear," David says, picking up his water glass and holding it up. "Here's to two very special people, who are both going to go far in their prospective fields. I propose a toast to you both."

His announcement seems to cool the air significantly.

When I've gotten my heart to stop pounding in my throat, I pick up my glass and mimic David. Drew, Whitney, and Kane do the same.

"To two spectacular people. May their days be full of blessing others with their talents," David says in a proud tone.

We click glasses, and I turn my head to hide my blush from Drew.

I can't stop blushing tonight! Stop it Jewels!

Unfortunately, by turning my face away from Drew, it's in clear view for Kane. Smirking, he says, "Drew, you've always had a way of making girls turn all sorts of pretty colors."

My eyes widen in shock.

Drew doesn't let that comment slide. "Brother, you have no room to talk. The number of times you've made Elia blush is in the six digits. So, enough with embarrassing poor Jewels."

Kane has the decency to look apologetically at me. "I'm sorry, Jewels. For the record, I think pink is a very attractive color on you. So, don't take my teasing the wrong way."

I can't help but smile. Especially thinking of all the times I've heard that he's subjected poor Elia to his merciless joking. "It's okay. I'm made of strong stuff. I can take it."

Drew looks warmly at me. "You certainly are."

The dinner continues, and I find I'm really feeling comfortable at this table. Drew was right. His mom is really easy to talk to, and I find myself having several conversations with her. I find her work interesting and enjoy that she loves gushing on and on about her landscape projects.

Hearing about gorgeous water features she's crafted around stunning views of trees and plants is amazing. I wish I had her mobility so I could work outside like she does. Restraining a sigh, I push that thought back.

No sense wishing for something I can't have. But then, maybe I can with Drew's help. Could he heal me to the point where I can reach for things far out of my normal grasp?

I'm looking at Drew contemplatively when the table goes quiet. Drew turns to me and raises his eyebrows in question.

My mouth goes dry. *What did I miss?*

Whitney clears her throat. "We were wondering what law schools you are interested in?"

"Oh! Um, well, I really only have one on my list. I'd like to stay as close to home as I can. I don't really want to move."

"That's understandable. That can be a stressful thing, for sure," Whitney says with an understanding smile.

Drew speaks up. "When I was attending the university here, I was happy I stayed close to home. Classes are demanding enough. It's nice to know you have a hot meal waiting at home anytime you need one."

I squirm in my seat and give him a pained smile. "Well, it's not really that. I have so many doctors here. It would be a big undertaking to find all new ones in a different city."

He gives me a sympathetic look. "Honestly, I don't know how you manage your personal life with your school schedule."

I give him a chagrined look. "Well, my mom helps me. Scheduling isn't one of my best qualities. I'm learning, though."

He nods and smiles at me, which I can't help but grin back. I appreciate his concern, but his eyes are so warm, I get lost looking into them. They almost look silver in the dining room lighting.

David coughs and interrupts our moment. I jump, feeling guilty for checking out his son. "So, when will you graduate?"

Furrowing my forehead, I say, "I'm hoping I can keep up with my classes enough to finish my Bachelor's in the usual four years, but I've learned to have reasonable expectations. I have...certain limitations, and they can delay things." I absolutely hate admitting this, but it's true. There's no sense in hiding facts. "But so far this year, I've kept up with my classes, and I'm on track to do well."

"What year are you in?" Whitney asks.

"Finishing up my freshman year." I turn to Drew. "So, you're studying for the MCAT's?"

He nods. "Just working on my clinical hours now. I'm hoping I can rack up enough to attract the notice of good medical schools."

"I'm sure you will," I say with a smile. I turn to Kane. "And you? Are you in school?"

I figure since he's younger, he's in college now. Turns out I'm right.

"Yep," he says good-naturedly. "I'm in my third year, getting a business degree."

I smile at him, which he returns, and the meal continues for another half hour before Whitney and David collect all the plates and take them into the kitchen.

I'm standing, looking at the table, wondering what I can help with when Drew takes my elbow. "Hey, how about I show you our garden? It's pretty great. I'd love for you to see it."

"I'm sure it's wonderful if your mom had anything to do with it."

"We all help. You could say we all have a bit of her horticultural tendencies."

I turn to him fully, surprised. "Is there anything you can't do, Drew Ashcroft?"

He chuckles. "Plenty. Come on, it's prettiest at sunset."

I look guiltily at the table, feeling I should help clean up, but follow him like he asks. When I step onto the porch, I look up at the detailed woodwork and stop to admire it. Beautiful curls and vines trail the edges and fill the corners.

Drew looks sheepish as he notices what I'm studying. Curious about his expression, I ask, "Don't tell me you helped build this?"

This time he laughs nervously, stuffing his hands in his pockets.

I laugh in astonishment. My mouth drops open. "Drew! You really can do everything."

"My dad did most of it. My brother, Kane and I only helped."

"Tell me more about the rest of your family. Vela didn't really talk about them."

"But you've heard of me?"

I nod, abashed. "Vela always gushed about one of her brothers as a doctor, so it caught my attention."

"Glad I could get your notice before I even met you." He studies me in the falling light. The sun is finishing its descent, and I avoid his piercing gaze by looking at the reds and oranges that paint the sky in streaks of color.

Clenching my crutches for comfort, because it's not easy being the sole thing Drew Ashcroft studies, I say, biting my lip. "Well, my life has been full of doctors, so it's always interested me how they get their start. I suppose I followed your path out of curiosity."

My face blooms when his eyes drop to my lips.

"I don't mind piquing your curiosity."

Heat rips through my middle at his words, and he gazes at me so intently, I swallow to moisten my suddenly dry throat. I'm completely speechless. Keeping my eyes glued to the dropping sun, I jump when Drew talks again.

"Do you want to walk in the garden while we still have a little light?"

I nod and follow him into the twilight.

18. Jewels

♥

Desperate to do something besides stand like a statue, I follow Drew carefully down the steps. Once we're on the garden path, I absorb the multitude of colors. Between the pink and yellow roses, bright orange flowers on the bushes, and blue and purple azaleas, I'm struck dumb at the beauty.

"You work out here?" I ask, following the meandering path.

He nods as he leads me down the flagstone walkway. "I enjoy it. It's cathartic to put your hands into the earth and watch things grow from the fruit of your labors."

Wait, can he grow things, too? Is that what he's not saying? Does he have nature magic? And is it tied to his healing magic?

I'm so full of questions, I force myself to stay silent as he points out the different plants and flowers we pass. Vegetables lay in rows along the back fence, hot pink and baby blue hydrangeas grow in profusion with more flowers than I've ever seen on those bushes near the vegetables. To my right are different pathways promising other beautiful sights, but he takes me to the back of the garden until we reach the white gazebo I saw from the porch. It's so elegant, with its spire and black iron benches in a circle just waiting for someone to sit and chat.

After climbing the steps, much easier than I would have yesterday, I sink down onto one. I breathe deeply, enjoying the atmosphere and company. It's strange that I'm comfortable with

Drew, even with all my unanswered questions. I wish I could speak openly with him. I take off my crutches.

"So, you like it here?" Drew asks, leaning against one of the posts, his feet crossed. He looks like he's perfectly at home, and I'm glad to see him in his element.

"I do. You know," I say, braving some honesty, "it feels like I've known you a lot longer than I have. It's hard to explain."

He studies me as the sky darkens further, and my head twists when I see lights blink on all around us. I'm thrilled by the twinkle lights shining above our heads.

"They turn on automatically at sunset," he explains.

I smile, looking around. Lampposts glow around the garden. I can't wait to see what it looks like in the true darkness. "It's beautiful."

"It really is," he says, but he's not looking at anything else but me.

I blink, no knowing what to do with a compliment like that. I'm clueless. Do I flirt back? Is that even what he's doing? Flirting? It certainly feels like it.

I laugh nervously and look down at my dress. My head pops up when I see Drew taking the seat next to me.

"Do you mind if I sit here?" he asks, sounding nervous.

Why would he be nervous? "No, of course not." Before I can think twice, I ask, "Why did you invite me here, Drew?"

He looks down. Then he looks back up, his gaze suddenly bright and *intense.* "Honestly?"

"Of course. I always want honesty between us." *Even though he has magic he hasn't officially told me about.*

"I needed a second opinion," he admits.

I swallow. "Of me?"

He nods, his eyes never leaving mine.

I try to ask why, when he reaches up and tucks a stray piece of hair behind my ear. The air is suddenly full of expectation, and my eyes drop to his lips. He seems to have gotten the same message because he's looking at my lips, too.

"Jewels?" he asks.

I cock my head, waiting. *He could ask me anything, and I'd answer honestly.*

"I really want to do something that's going to cross a lot of lines. I need you to say that I can." He starts to lean toward me, and I hold my breath.

I can only nod fervently when he leans further, this time looking me between in the eyes, asking for permission.

In answer, I lean forward and press my lips to his. I think I shocked him, because his lips are firm against mine, but just for a second. He gets over his surprise and angles his head so our lips fit together better. He brings up his hands and cups my cheek like he's holding a prize. *Me.*

He kisses me so softly that I wrap my arms around his neck, feeling my way down his arms, appreciating the contours of muscle. A swarm of emotions rushes through me at this perfect moment. He angles his head and moves his lips against mine, transfixing me in boneless bliss.

It's my first kiss. And it's perfect.

He pulls back and searches my eyes.

I smile widely, leaning toward him to kiss him again when he turns his head, cutting me off. I lean back, trying to understand what's wrong.

He lets go of me and puts his hands on his knees, hunching over. His face contorts in a grimace.

"Drew?" My heart is kicking itself in my chest. "Did I do something wrong? Did I bite your lip or something?"

He shakes his head. "Are you kidding?"

I turn my head. "That was my first kiss," I whisper, humiliation slamming into me. "So, I might not have done it right."

"Your *first* kiss? That was your first kiss?" He puts his head in his hands. "I shouldn't have done that. You're my patient. It was wrong of me. I'm sorry."

"Please don't apologize," I say in a whisper. "I said you could. I knew the risks."

Standing up, he says, "You don't understand. I could lose my place at the clinic if a word of this is breathed there. And if I had known it was your first..."

Swallowing down bile that emerged when I realized he *regrets* our kiss, I say, "You don't have to worry. I won't say anything." I'm surprised my voice is as strong and as clear as it is. This will just be another of his secrets I will keep.

"That's the thing. You shouldn't have to keep this a secret. I should have kept things friendly. Onyx, you should have had a better first kiss than that."

My eyes widen. I thought it was pretty good. Can a kiss get *better*? "We're friends, right, Drew?"

He stops and looks at me, frowning. "Yes, but even that's crossing the line."

"Why did you bring me here?" I ask as heat and anger surge higher, making my tone hard. "You said you needed another opinion of me, but *why*?"

"Isn't it obvious? I can't get you out of my head, no matter what I do. I needed my parents' impression of you to get my head on straight."

"Did it help?" I ask, piercing him with my gaze. Suddenly, I'm *angry*.

He throws his arms out. "They love you. *Of course* they do. You're nothing if not perfect."

I scoff, turning my head. "Besides my back and legs."

He sits down next to me. "Don't say that."

I look at him. "It's the truth, isn't it?"

He presses his lips together. "You might have been born with a condition that makes your life harder, but I think you're perfect just as you are."

Fisting my dress, I say, looking down, "I've never been depressed about my condition, but please be honest with me. It complicates things for us, doesn't it?"

"Not for me," he says in a firm tone. His eyes look at me with such confidence, I'm momentarily speechless.

Finally, I cry, "How?"

"Because I'm sure our clinic can help you. You're going to start feeling much better, better even than you are today."

"How can you be so sure?"

He smiles softly. "Let's just say I know."

He means his magic.

Hope soars in my chest. Not just because he's promising I'm going to walk better, but because of this, *the promise of us.*

"Can we keep things like this? Just like this? Not changing anything, just not telling anyone?" I ask.

He stands back up.

"Drew." I need him to look at me. When he grants me a look, I say gently, "You are human. You'll make mistakes, but please don't think this is one of them. I'm an adult. I have a say in whether there can be anything more between us."

He turns away, looking more frustrated than I've ever seen him. "Jewels, we have to be only friends until I'm done with your treatment." He turns. "Can I ask you to wait until your treatment is finished before we deepen our relationship?"

I look down at my lap. "What if I don't want to wait? Why can't we just keep this a secret?"

He sits down beside me again and picks up my hands, holding them carefully. "Because I won't be able to do what I'm supposed to do if I know you're just a kiss away. Until you're hea... I mean, helped by the clinic and are no longer my patient, we need to keep our relationship strictly professional. I'm sorry, Jewels. I never should have crossed that line with you, even with your permission."

I push up from my seat, my limbs trembling. I try to keep my voice from warbling, but it's useless. "You regret kissing me?"

He turns his head in answer.

Inhaling deeply, I say, "Well, I'm sorry I'm such a mistake. I promise it won't happen again." I shove my crutches onto my arms and hurry down the gazebo steps and onto the garden path.

Drew stops me by saying, "This isn't over between us. I'm just asking you to be patient. Wait until..."

"Until I can walk again?" I ask over my shoulder. "Well, Drew, I hate to break it to you, but this is as good as it's going to get for me. It will only get worse as I get older."

"That's not true," he says in a frustrated tone. "If you only knew…"

"Knew what? What aren't you telling me?" I spin around. "What do you know about my condition that I don't?" I beg him with my eyes to be honest with me. I need him to open up about his abilities. *Will he?*

He looks between my eyes, seeming to war with himself. Biting his lip, he releases a shuddering breath and shakes his head. "I only know that we can help you at the clinic."

"You mean you. You can help me." *Please just be honest with me. Let me in.*

"I *can* help, like anyone else there. The machines and the therapy are state-of-the art and top-notch. You won't find better care anywhere else."

My heart drops to my feet. *He won't tell me. He's going to keep me in the dark.*

"Okay, Drew. I'll continue at the clinic. And I won't breathe a word about what happened tonight to anyone. You know you can trust me, right?" I look deeply into his eyes, wordlessly asking for honesty.

He nods but stays silent as he motions for us to return to the house. With a sinking heart, I follow him as he leads the way back inside.

19. Drew

♥

*W*hat have I done?

I have never been so stupid. Jewels is my patient. She's off limits. It was a complete breach of professionalism to kiss her like I did.

But it was so perfect. I've never felt this way about anyone.

The setting sun shone on her hair, turning her skin translucent. She literally glowed while she smiled at me. I couldn't resist. And her soft lips tasted better than I could have imagined. I growl and shake off the memory.

Jewels's offer of secrecy about it only makes what I did worse.

As we walk back to the house, my heart is heavy as I mentally berate myself. I'd like to see Jewels *romantically*. But that's out of the question right now.

I can only hope that when I'm finished healing her, because *I will heal her,* she'll forgive me in time to be mine. Resolve fills me to accomplish that. I wish I could offer her everything — a friendship, a relationship, but I can't ask for any of that today.

Give me two, maybe three weeks. Three more healings at the most, and she won't need the clinic anymore.

I can't make that promise to her, though. Her healing must appear to be a fluke. A miracle of science. If I tell her she'll be healed in three weeks, she'll be suspicious.

Will I always have to hide who I am from her?

My steps slow as my mind spins. She's amazing, the perfect complement to me. But can I let her into the Elemental world? It's forbidden for a human to know about us.

Can I let her go, though?

Jewels turns to me once she's climbed the steps to the porch. She gives me a stiff smile and says, not quite meeting my eye, "I will see myself out. Please tell your parents I had a wonderful time."

"Jewels, I..."

She stops me with her hand. "I know when to make my case and when to concede. Until you tell me...you know what? Never mind. Let's just say I understand my position. I just wish you'd trust me more."

"I do trust you," I assure her.

Her eyes drill into mine. "Enough to tell me *everything*?"

I pause. *What does she mean by that? She doesn't remember our first meeting, so what does she think I'm hiding?*

Her face smooths into a terribly cool mask. "That's what I thought. Goodbye, Drew. I'll see you at the clinic. I'll be your patient and nothing more."

My throat dries as I reach for her, but she's already turned and stepped inside.

I stay on the porch, fighting the hardest battle I've ever fought. *I can't tell her about my world. But I can tell her I care about her. What good would that do, though?*

I've already said in no uncertain terms there's not a possibility of us getting together while she's at the clinic. How I wish I were the break-the-rules kind of guy. But my conscience won't allow me to even bend them.

Or continue to. I've already bent my code of ethics past its breaking point by bringing her home to meet my parents...and starting her healing...and that kiss.

Mom walks onto the patio, looking behind her at Jewels's retreating form. "I just said bye to Jewels. She's leaving?"

I hang my head and nod miserably.

She puts her hand on my shoulder. "Son, I understand why you brought her here. She's absolutely wonderful. But really, how could she be in your life?"

My heart hammers painfully in my chest. I remain silent.

She continues, "Drew, you are my smartest, most talented child. But right now, you're not thinking straight. That young lady can never know the truth about us, so why pursue her?" Her eyes study mine when I bring my head up.

"Mom, I can't explain it. I just know she's right for me. I feel at peace when she's with me. It's an incredible feeling." I look down, shaking my head. "But I'll be surprised if she ever gives me another chance. I've hurt her. Badly."

"Drew," Mom says softly. "Maybe it's for the best."

"I'm not giving up, Mom. Not on her." I give her a hard stare. "I think you know what my plan is."

She looks alarmed. "Drew, what are you going to do?"

"What I have to." I walk past her into the house, clenching my fists.

I hear her footsteps following me. "Drew, get to know her a little better before you make that kind of decision. You can't go back once you've healed her."

Spinning around, I say, "What I already started? Do you know how good it felt seeing her walk better afterward, knowing I helped her? Someone I care about?" Then I ask, "How long did it take you to know that Dad was the one for you?"

She looks at me stunned, and she falters. "Drew, that's not the same at all. Your dad is my Intended. We share a once-in-a-lifetime bond."

"I don't need that kind of bond with her to feel this way, Mom. I'm going to heal her, and then I'm going to beg for her forgiveness."

She looks skeptically at me. "What exactly did you do to that girl? Why do you have to beg for forgiveness?"

"I did something I should have waited to do. I'm a professional. I can't have a relationship with one of my patients."

She arches an eyebrow at me. "And you didn't think of that when you invited her over here?"

"I admit I rushed into that decision. I just needed to know I wasn't alone in thinking how amazing she is."

"You're not. She *is* amazing. But, son, she's not one of us. How are you going to get past that?"

"I don't know. I haven't figured that part of it out yet. I'm going to see if she can forgive me before I cross that bridge."

She sighs heavily. "I hope you know what you're doing."

I look at her sadly and walk away, thinking, *So do I.*

Time moves slowly until Jewels's appointment with me on Thursday. I'm so on edge anticipating seeing her that I've imagined every kind of reception I'd get: chilly, indifferent, or, worse, ice cold. What I get is far beyond my wildest expectations.

"Drew!" she exclaims, walking into the exam room. "How are you? It's so good to see you." Her bright smile makes me freeze.

I close the door behind her and can't help the look of confusion on my face.

She holds her hands up, chuckling. "I know. I've been thinking. I haven't been appreciative enough of all you're doing. You've really been patient with me, and all I've shown you are my bad moods. Can you forgive me? I really do think that what you're doing here is nothing short of amazing."

My mouth opens, but nothing comes out.

"I know I've been all over the place. But the fact is, I have never walked so well in my life. And I have you to thank for that. So, please know that I'm making a promise to act the adoring patient." Nothing on her countenance says she's kidding, but still, I study her face.

"And my bad decisions?" I ask quietly.

She inhales deeply, a pained look crossing her face. "Those are yours to be upset about, not mine. I'm still thankful for your treatment. So, you can rest assured, I'll be the model patient starting today." She nods decisively.

I nod and pretend I'm studying her paperwork. I need to get my emotions under control. This girl has done nothing but surprise me from day one. Hope rises in my chest that after three weeks, she'll allow me into her life.

But can I allow her into mine?

I shove that thought away and put down my clipboard. "Well, you've always been cooperative, and I expect nothing less today. Shall we get started?"

She nods enthusiastically and sits on the bed. The paper crinkles as she adjusts, and I marvel at how much better she's moving since my last healing.

I've only healed her back once. Maybe it won't take three more times.

I direct her to lie down, and I test her range of motion. She beams as she obediently follows my directions. Her muscles are much more cooperative and not as stiff. She has a range that was not there the first time I examined her. I can't contain my smile.

She catches it and laughs. "I know. It's great, isn't it? I have you to thank for this."

My smile slips. "Jewels, I want to be sure you know it's the clinic and its specialized treatments that are responsible for this achievement. Not me."

Her eyes twinkle. "Sure, Doc. I get that."

I turn to wash my hands.

"Sorry, I won't accuse you of healing me again."

Since my back is to her, I can't see her expression. But I freeze. *Healing her? Does she know?* I turn back slowly, wiping my hands off with a towel.

She's sitting up, which makes me inordinately happy since she couldn't get up like that so easily last week. Her face is pleasant, with a small smile in place.

"Okay," I say slowly, "I'm confused. You acknowledge I'm not solely responsible for your success here, but now you think *I* healed you? How can you make both of those assertions?"

Her smile grows wider. "I don't know, Doc, maybe you can answer that." She cocks her head, waiting for my response.

I'm missing something here.

I clear my throat. "Well, let's just get on with your treatment since it's clearly working wonders."

She laughs softly. "Okay, let's go with that." She gets off the table and waits for me.

"Of course," I say, thoroughly confused. I lead the way to the room where we'll hook her up to the machine. After I've briefly spoken to the tech, I realize I was so distracted by her sunny attitude I didn't have her change into her gown. I go to retrieve one and leave the room so she can change.

Once she's on the table receiving the treatment, I monitor the machine's progress, knowing it will prepare her body for what I'll do later in her massage. I think about what she said in the exam room, studying it from different angles. It's almost like she *knows*. But that's *impossible*. The poppy seed formula is foolproof. A failure has never been documented.

Is it possible she remembers? But why would she wait until now to clue me in?

I'm fidgeting anxiously, questions jumping in my mind, but when I return to the treatment room once she's finished, all of them turn to stone in my throat.

I can't outright ask her. It might jog her memory. Maybe though, I could ask some loosely related questions.

I need to be very careful here. But then it occurs to me: *if I do want her in my life, truly, it would be better if she does remember.*

She's looking up at me sympathetically. "You okay, Doc?"

I give her a gentle smile. "Yeah, I'm fine. Let's get to the massage table." Either way, she's going to be healed. My hands are itching to get started. I know just where I left off and where to continue my special treatment. I leave and give her time to get situated under the sheet.

Once she's covered, I reenter the room, my hands ready to make a difference in her life. I feel freer than I've ever felt before. I've always felt guilty that I couldn't use my gift to heal humans, but I'm changing that with Jewels. I didn't know if I could break the Elementals' rule again, but this feels right. It's Jewels, of course it's right. She's going to be free of pain, and nothing thrills me more.

Without pausing, I get right to work.

20. Jewels

A s Drew starts the massage, I notice immediately he's using his magic. Last time, his hands didn't emit that strange warmth until he got to my back. Now he's using it as he works on my legs.

I can't help but be thrilled, but a sense of sadness lingers in my chest.

How can I get him to admit what's really happening?

When I was at his house and he kissed me in the garden, every atom in my body was ready to make a commitment to this man. I've never felt more alive than in his presence. I've always been proud of my independent spirit, but all of that changed after meeting Drew.

I don't want to fight life alone; I want him to fight with me.

He's magnetic on his own merit, but together, the two of us just connect. But how can we have a life together if he won't tell me about his true talents?

And I meant what I said about being sorry he's seen all my bad moods because I am incredibly appreciative of what he's doing. I need to be sure he knows that. And I'm pretty sure he's taking a big risk in healing me.

How will that affect him?

Hopefully not badly. So, I'm going to be such a great patient, he won't think twice about what he's doing. He can give all the credit he wants to the clinic, but I know who's responsible: Drew Ashcroft.

I'm going to get him to admit it, too.

Thinking over the clues I already gave him. I think I did a good job. He seems suspicious. Which is right where I want him.

If I know anything about someone hiding something, it's that body language tells you everything you need to know. I've studied non-verbal communication and every move he makes screams guilt. He's hiding his gift from the world...and from me.

That's going to change.

I'm in a blissful state as Drew moves his healing hands from my legs to my back. I marvel at how professional and talented he is. He's an excellent masseur in his own right. I completely relax under his hands. He's proven his commitment to professionalism after the night at his parents' house and our kiss. Every touch is designed to heal, nothing more.

His hands are on my lower back, and I notice he's taking his time on my spine. His hands are hotter than ever, but they don't burn me. In fact, it's incredible how pleasant it is. I can feel myself getting better, the stiffness melting away.

Thirty minutes go by, and I hardly feel any strain on my back at all. *Has he done it? Has he healed me completely?* My mind spins at the thought. My whole world will change if he's actually corrected my condition.

He slows down, the warmth fades, and that's when I notice his breathing has gotten labored. I strain to hear, so I turn my head, but there's only so much I can see while lying on my stomach.

"Drew? Are you okay?"

"I'm fine," he says in a strained voice. "Almost done, hold still."

Yep, he's definitely exhausted.

That's when I hear a commotion in the hallway. I hear raised voices and then suddenly light streams into the dark room as a man wearing a suit storms in.

"Drew? What are you doing?" he barks.

"*Mr. Colbourn*?" Drew asks, spinning around, his hands leaving my back.

"Sir, you have no right to barge into an exam room. You need to leave!" Mary yells, trying to move around him.

Colbourn won't allow her to come near. In fact, it's like he's shielding her from seeing Drew and me.

"Drew, you've done it, haven't you? You've broken our law," Colbourn spits at Drew, his face a mottled red.

"What law?" Mary cries. "Drew, do you know this man?"

Drew doesn't acknowledge Mary as he stares stonily at the man, hands clenched at his sides.

Colbourn turns to Mary, saying, "You need to leave. This is between Drew and me. I have every right to be here."

That's when I see three big men come into the room, crowding Mary into the corner. She squeaks in terror, and then they do to her what Drew did to my mom and me over a year ago. They blow powder into her face, and she slumps to the floor, unconscious.

"This isn't necessary," Drew grits out. His face looks strained. I watch him worriedly, knowing he's exhausted after my healing.

"You've made it necessary, young man," Colbourn says in a cold tone.

"What's going on?" I cry, covering myself up with my blanket as I sit up.

Colbourn points at me, yelling at Drew, "You've healed a human. That's against our laws. You know the repercussions."

"A human?" I ask, "So what does that make all of you?"

I'm ignored as Drew stands tall and moves in front of me. "She is more than just a human to me. She should be healed as much as any of us."

"That's not for you to decide, and you know it. This is the last time you will see her. You will not heal this young woman again." He motions for the man who blew the strange powder into Mary's face to come to me.

Before the man can get too close, Drew shoves his way in front of him. He blocks me with his body and says to the irate Colbourn, "I want this woman in my life. Which means she'll know everything, anyway. Don't give her the poppy seed formula. She doesn't need it."

Colbourn splutters in rage while the three men who came with him all frown deeply.

Ignoring Drew's statement, Colbourn nods at the other two men, who have left Mary spasming in the corner and walk toward Drew. Taking Drew by the arms, they forcibly move him away from me and hold him against the wall. Drew struggles, but he's no match against the two stronger men, especially in his tired state.

The man with the powder moves into position in front of me again.

Unwilling to face the painful convulsions again, I cry out, "That doesn't work on me! I'm immune to that powder. Drew," I say, looking at him with tears swimming in my eyes, "I remember everything from when we first met. I'm sorry, I didn't know how to tell you. I wanted you to tell me about this world yourself." Turning to Colbourn, I beseech him, "Please, sir, don't make me go through that again." Looking down at poor Mary. I feel terrible for her but know I don't want to experience the effects of that drug again.

He turns to Drew. "What is she talking about? I thought you successfully administered that powder."

Drew's face is a picture of surprise. "I thought it did. I had no idea she remembered everything." He looks at me. "Why didn't you tell me?"

"I didn't know how. I didn't want you to give me that stuff again. But I'm telling you, all of you," I say, looking each of them in the eye. "That powder doesn't work on me. I don't know why; I only know that I remember everything that happened that day. I can tell you word for word what happened."

They all looked astonished. The man with the powder is staring at me with wide eyes. Colbourn has an awed, distrustful look.

I speak up, my voice bolder than I expected. "I'm being honest with you. Now, please be honest with me. Who are you people? How do you have magic? Do you all have it? And why do you have different kinds?"

Colbourn looks at Drew. "How does she know all of that?"

Drew's eyes are tired as he responds, "I have no idea. She's smart. She must have figured it out after remembering what I did to her."

Colbourn turns to me. "Young lady, you will get dressed and come with us. We have some questions for you."

"Why should I go anywhere with you? And let him go!" I yell at the men holding Drew, shocking myself when I get down off the table, wrap the sheet around me and *run* toward them. "He's done nothing but help me." I beat at the arm of one of the men holding Drew.

Drew's face is one of shock and happiness as he struggles to free himself. "Jewels, you're walking," he says in an awed tone.

"Running," I correct him, but I can't help but look down at my legs. They're holding me up without my crutches!

"Young lady, let him go. There's nothing you can do," Colbourn says grimly. He turns to give instructions to the man with the powder, who goes to Mary, laying hands on her, helping her through her seizures.

He turns to Drew. "You will come with us. Both of you will. We'll convene at your parents' house."

"How did you find out about all of this?" Drew asks him, his eyes flashing.

"There are responsible Elementals out there who care about our way of life being hidden. They called my office with a suspicion."

I look at Drew with sympathy but am focused on the two men who crowd Drew and push him toward the door. Apparently, we're leaving now.

"Get dressed, young lady," Colbourn fires at me.

I nod and once they leave, I go to the adjoining room to change away from the eyes of the man who's helping Mary. Even though he's not paying any attention to me, I still don't want to drop my blanket with him in the room.

Even with the shock of those men bursting in, I'm more amazed at the easy way I move. Drew has worked a true miracle on me. I take several steps without my crutches again. I laugh hysterically, walking across the room again. I jump with excitement for the first time in my life, laughing loudly.

I want to push myself and see everything I can now do. But I hurry to finish dressing, since Colbourn has Drew. I don't want them to hurt Drew.

As my head swims with the sheer miracle of me *walking, no, running,* I wonder, *Who is that guy?*

He must be someone important. Drew acts deferentially toward him, treating him with respect. That doesn't even count the men who jump to do his bidding.

Not wanting to tempt fate, I put my crutches on. Even though I feel stronger than ever before, I adopt the same position I've had my entire life and leave the room, barely using the walking aids. I want to run and laugh at the same time, but I restrain myself.

Later. I'll save my celebration for when I can share it with Drew.

I walk toward the men and my uncertain future. I don't know what their plans are for a "human" who remembers what she's not supposed to.

21. Drew

♥

How am I going to get Jewels out of this?

The two goons and Alex Colbourn, the Gyan Grand Elder, leader of the entire clan of Earth Elementals, flank me, and I know I am pitifully outmatched. Especially with the way I feel. That healing took everything out of me. I want to get Jewels away from these men, but there's absolutely no way I can accomplish that.

Why would someone call and tell him about Jewels?

I can't help but feel betrayed. They must have felt a duty to tell the Grand Elder what I was doing.

But to interrupt my healing? I put everything I had into that healing. And from the way she ran toward me, I finished it completely.

I get my chance to confirm when she emerges from the room. She's walking with her crutches, but it's clear she doesn't need them. She's steady on her feet and walking perfectly.

As exhausted as I am, I realize I did it. I healed Jewels. Her eyes immediately seek mine, and she smiles tenderly at me. The constant look of pain in her eyes before is gone. Her face is bright with health, but her eyes are strained because of the threat of the Grand Elder and his men.

It's clear she's communicating to me that she's doing great. More than great, she's fully healed. My heart soars at that thought, and everything I risked to help her is suddenly worth it.

I grimace at the thought that I might be sent away to a faraway clan for this. It's how they punish Elementals for things like revealing ourselves to humans. The only exception I know of is the indigenous Elementals who live in a community with some non-elementals. But they keep the Elemental world a secret. So, we let them be.

I didn't know I had revealed myself when I was tasked with removing her memory. I thought she had no clue. Guess it doesn't matter either way. I've healed a human, a punishable offense in my world. A world I've just brought Jewels into.

How could she remember anything after I gave her the poppy seed formula?

I marvel over that as Alex's henchmen shadow me as we leave the building. They let go of my arms, but it's clear they won't let me get far if I try. I give a hasty explanation to the girls at the front, saying a family emergency has come up.

If they can't force Jewels to forget our world, maybe they'll allow her into it. I hold that hope close to my chest as the men push me into their SUV. They direct Jewels to another car, with Alex. I want to be with her to explain myself to Alex. But I honestly don't know anything other than that I've healed her.

Why, then, is she still walking with her crutches?

Questions rage through my skull, firing one after another.

I sit obediently in the car, impatient to get to my parents' home. We arrive in about ten minutes, and I'm out of the car as soon as they open the door. They march me inside, even though I want to wait for Jewels to arrive. I want to see her walk again. I could drink in that sight all day long.

With grim faces, my parents are waiting for us in the living room. I search for any hint of what's going to happen. They give me nothing as Alex leads Jewels into the room.

It must be clear to my parents what I did today for Jewels, because their faces look even grimmer after watching her walk.

"So, it's true, you healed her," Mom says.

"It appears so, except we got to him before he completed the process," Alex says, pressing lips in a thin line, clearly displeased.

"I wouldn't say he didn't finish," Jewels says in a strong voice.

To my astonishment, she slides her crutches off and walks easily across the room to me. She puts her hands on my shoulders and leans in to hug me, whispering, "I can never thank you enough, Drew Ashcroft. You've changed my life."

I return her hug, careful with her as usual, unable to believe I finished the healing.

Alex interrupts our moment by saying, "We need to discuss this. Apparently, Whitney and David, this young woman has not forgotten witnessing our gifts the first time. She remembers everything. Your poppyseed formula did not work."

Jewels pulls away from me, giving me a guilty look. I lean toward her, whispering, "We'll figure this out. Don't worry."

She smiles at me and turns around, folding her arms across her chest. "So, it's not unusual for someone with your powers to heal an incurable condition?"

Alex scowls and says, "Do not interrupt us."

"I have a right to know!" she cries.

With obvious irritation, he says, "To answer your question, no, we aren't surprised Drew was able to heal you. He's an exceptional healer, one of our best. But his healing powers are only to be used on Gyans and *not* humans."

Jewels's mouth opens in shock, and I place my hand on her arm, giving her a shake of my head, asking her to be quiet.

Mom speaks up, "So, if the poppy seed formula didn't work, it's obvious we need to try again. Maybe it will make her forget her entire experience with my son."

I don't miss the hurt look Jewels gives my mom before she turns her head.

I announce in a hard tone, "We will not give her the formula again. If it didn't work the first time, it won't the second. There was nothing wrong with it. There's no reason to put her through that again."

"That is for us to decide, young man, not you," Alex says coldly. "There are no documented cases of the formula failing. However, I happen to agree with you. If you administered the formula correctly, it should have worked." He lifts his eyebrows, waiting for me to admit to giving Jewels the formula wrong.

Jewels surprises everyone when she speaks up. "It worked on my mom. Drew gave me just as much as he gave my mother. She doesn't remember a thing, so I know it worked. The powder wasn't faulty. It's just me. Have you thought that maybe all the prescriptions I take could have counteracted the success of your formula?"

Again, her quick mind impresses me. "She's right," I say. "It's possible that because of the medications, it rendered the formula useless. We need to find out what she's taking and consider that the next time we encounter someone who uses the same prescriptions as Jewels."

Alex waves a hand in the air. "That would be nearly impossible. We can't research every medication a human takes to see if the formula is going to work on them. In all the years we've given it to humans, how is it that only one human fought off the effects?"

My dad answers, "You're right. There is no way to investigate someone's medications. We'll just have to take further precautions and check to make sure humans have forgotten their experiences. We need to alert all the clans to this incident."

"That's all well and fine," I growl. "But what's going to happen to Jewels? We can't force her to forget, so now what?"

This time, Alex doesn't have a quick answer. He folds his arms and studies Jewels with a puzzled frown. "Well," he finally says, "she's been healed, so an explanation will have to be issued on how such a miracle occurred."

"I've thought of that," I volunteer. "All credit can go to the clinic where you burst in. Their methods are groundbreaking, so they can be heralded with her success."

"And when they can't reproduce such a miracle?" Alex asks dryly.

I shrug. "Jewels is a special case. It worked favorably for her. It doesn't mean it would on everyone."

Alex straightens, a cold look coming into his eyes. "You both need to disappear. No one can know about her "miracle" as you call it," he says using hand quotes. "She will be removed from everyone who knows her, to hide her recent condition."

"What?" Jewels cries, coming to my side, holding my arm. "I'm going to college. You can't take my life away just because Drew gave me a new one!"

My parents look at her with sympathetic faces, and my mind races with what I can do. I hold Jewels's trembling body to my side. They could make an exception. They've done similar things before with extreme cases.

"Young lady, you knew what Drew was doing the entire time he was doing it. You should have known there would be repercussions."

"Repercussions? I don't know what I've done wrong!" she yells.

I take one look at my parents and make up my mind. Pushing Jewels gently away from me, I take her hand, squeezing it tightly. She turns anguished eyes to me, and I give her a hard glare, trying to communicate my thoughts. Her eyes become determined, and she turns with pursed lips to glare at Alex.

Hoping my parents will help, I yell, "Run!" I'm desperately hoping I healed Jewels enough to do this, but I pull her with me as I race out of the room. She cries out in shock but follows.

Our path out the front door is blocked by Alex's goons, so I cut into the hallway and race out the back. I hear screams and a skirmish behind me, and I know my parents are blocking Alex from chasing us.

Pulling Jewels with me, I shove open the back door and bound down the steps, praying Jewels's newly healed back and legs can support her through this. I race through the garden, but a wall of dirt forms in front of us.

I look behind me, and one guy is holding out his hand. Glaring at him, I wave my arm, and the dirt crashes down into the hole I opened underneath it. I pull a shocked Jewels over the mound of earth and run to the gate in the fence. Before I can unlatch it, a root wraps around the handle, and I can't get the root from the guy's mind. I have to mentally overpower him, and I realize I can't. I'm too tired, and I have no time to replenish from the plants around us.

I turn to face him, putting Jewels behind me. One glance at her white face tells me she's more shocked than ever before.

I wave my arms and unearth a rose bush, throwing it at the man's head. He screams at the pain of the thorns that wrap around him, and I turn around to see if it's successfully distracted him from the root on the gate's handle.

It did. I rip off the root and open the gate, pulling a stumbling Jewels behind me. I ask over my shoulder, "Are you okay? Can you do this?"

"Yes," she answers in a shaky voice. "It's a miracle, but I can follow you. I don't know how long, though."

I run to my parents' car before I realize I don't have their keys.

"Drew!" Mom yells at me. She throws her keys in my direction, and I catch them mid-air.

My heart soars at my parents' support, and I let Jewels's hand go so she can climb in the passenger seat. I'm in the driver's seat in a flash, and once I'm sure Jewels is inside, I start the car and slam on the gas, backing up into the yard to get around the two cars parked behind me.

The guys are racing toward the car, but I put it in drive and race away, going as fast as I dare.

22. Jewels

♥

I start laughing as soon as we're away from the house. We'll be followed, of that much I'm sure, but for now, we're safe. I cannot believe I just ran. The thrill of that alone got me laughing, not the absurdity of what had just happened.

Drew's focus is completely on driving as he maneuvers out of the neighborhood and onto the road.

"Where are we going?" I ask after I get my breath back.

"I don't know yet. We need to hide, that's all I know."

"Where can we hide from them?"

"I know of a place that should be safe. First, we have to get there." His hands clench the wheel in a white-knuckled grip as he makes fast turns meant to confuse anyone following us.

I look behind us but don't see Colbourn's car and SUV.

As if in response to my look, he says, "They're not behind us yet, but they'll catch up soon. Hopefully, my parents stalled them for a bit."

"Will your parents be in trouble for helping us?" I ask, looking at Drew, worried for them.

"In time, they'll be forgiven. If we make ourselves scarce, we'll accomplish what they want, anyway." He sighs heavily. "It's hard to believe they found out about you in the first place."

"I'm sorry, Drew. Why did you heal me and risk it all, anyway?"

He gives me a loaded glance. "Let's discuss that another time. My reasons were sound, just so you know."

"Okay," I say slowly, my feelings ricocheting all around my chest. "Are we going to disappear then?" My heart lurches in my chest at the thought of leaving my mother. There's always a time for a person to leave the nest, but I didn't expect this.

"If we find a place to hide, we can make our life our own, not what they would force us to do. But we need to be smart about it."

"Will I have to leave my university? Can I say goodbye to my mom?" Stress makes my voice squeak at the end.

He glances at me and then resumes driving, making erratic turns just in case they've picked up our trail. "We'll have to call your mom and explain what we can. She can't know about my world. They'll just give her the formula again. Then you'll have to come up with an explanation for your absence."

"Drew, is this really necessary?" I ask in a tired voice, suddenly exhausted from the weight of what had just happened. Today has been a momentous day. First, Drew healed me, in a way I never imagined possible. Then I was taken and learned about a magical world I only dreamed of. Now we are on the run. "Can't I promise that *I* won't say anything? And continue to live my life keeping your world secret?"

"I can't promise that, Jewels. My world punishes those who break our most sacred law. My mom warned me about this, but I didn't want to believe her. They would send you and me to some clan in the middle of nowhere, just to be sure we're quiet about all of this. Unfortunately, your promises mean nothing to the Grand Elder."

"Is that who that man was? A Grand Elder?" I say the strange words, knowing I'm going to learn a lot of new terms in the coming days.

"Yes, he's like a king among us Gyans."

"Guy-ans?" I ask, saying the word slowly.

"We're Earth Elementals. God has given us gifts to take care of the earth by feeding it."

I furrow my eyebrows. "I thought your gift was healing."

He glances at me, then says, "That's one of them. Remember when you saw that man push aside the hedge with just a thought? We can do things like that, but much more."

I think back to the fight in the garden. A root had come out of nowhere to wrap around the handle of the gate. And Drew threw a rose bush at that man's head without even a touch.

Sitting back, I look behind us again and see that Drew has successfully evaded the Grand Elder and his men. I don't see their cars anywhere. "Drew," I say in a shaking voice, fear crowding my thoughts. "I can't just leave. I have a life. It might not be much, but it is for me."

"Jewels, I'm sorry to say this. I'm sorry I dragged you into my life. But now that my world knows about you, you will never have the same life again."

"But why?" I ask, tears spilling onto my cheeks. "You healed me. Fine. Why can't I just go on with my life?"

Drew presses his lips together. "Because that's not how it works. We've been hidden from humans for centuries. They're not about to leave you alone. I have to protect you and take you where no one will look for you."

I turn to face him. "Drew, what about you? You were going to go to medical school. You have plans too. What? Do we just abandon your dreams and mine?"

"No," he says, clenching his jaw. "We just need to change our identities. Start a new life somewhere they can't find us."

My chest grows cold. "How can we hide from your own people? Don't your kind live everywhere?"

"There's a lot to explain. Let me concentrate on getting us to a safe place, and I promise to go over everything."

I sink into my seat, feeling defeated. I want to fight for my life, but I have a feeling that everything from this point forward will be different.

And I have no control over it.

I watch with detachment as Drew drives. After about an hour of driving, we arrive at a red-brick two-story home on the outskirts of town.

Drew puts his hand on my arm, preventing me from getting out, and looks all around us carefully. Once he's satisfied no one is watching or has followed us, he removes his hand and motions for us to get out of the car.

I can't believe I can get out of a car without my crutches. My whole life I've relied on them, and now...I can walk on my own. Marveling at each step I take, Drew smiles down tenderly at me as we approach the house.

"I can't tell you how good it is to see you walking. On your own, I mean."

I smile up at him. "I can't put into words what this means to me, Drew." But then my face falls. "But at what expense?"

I've stopped on the sidewalk leading up to the front porch, and Drew takes my hand, pulling me to the door. He silently moves a potted plant and grabs a key, then stands up and unlocks the door.

We walk inside, and Drew immediately ensures all the curtains are closed and the downstairs doors locked.

Since he's left me alone, I look around and then hold my middle, trying to absorb what's happened to my life.

I'm healed. I can walk.

But now I have to start a whole new life. Shaking my head, I can't believe how my future's changed. It happened so fast my head is spinning.

Then, I think *I could get out of here. Now that I'm able to run, maybe that's what I should do.*

I look over my shoulder at the door, but Drew steps back into the room.

"Okay," he says, brushing off his hands. "I've secured the house. It should be safe here. No one knows about this place."

"How do you know about this house?" I question, trying not to be too upset I missed my chance to run.

Looking around, he says, "I know the professor who owns this house. He's gone half the year, so we're lucky this is the part of the year he's not here."

"He wouldn't mind our breaking in?" I ask, not convinced we won't be arrested for trespassing.

He huffs a laugh. "No, in fact, he told me I'm welcome to use it as long as I don't have a raging party. Since that's not going to happen, no, he won't mind."

I'm feeling lost and conflicted about my feelings for Drew, so I withdraw into the next room, running my hand over the books I find on a tall bookshelf. Drew follows me and asks softly, "Are you okay? I'm sure you have a lot of questions."

I nod but remain quiet, running my eyes over the book titles to distract me from my situation. Drew's voice behind me makes me turn around. "If it would make you feel better, you can hit me."

"Why would I do that?"

He heaves a big sigh and runs his hand over the back of his neck. "Oh, I don't know. Because I've basically ripped your life away from you. I know you're angry, so just take it out on me. I promise I can handle it."

"I'm not angry," I say softly, looking over his features. His eyebrows are furrowed, and a deep crease of worry mars his forehead. He's frowning, but there's a lightness in his expression I can't read. "Are you angry?"

He turns and puts his hands on his hips. "I don't know what I'm feeling, actually." He turns again, and the look in his eyes when he stares into mine is nothing short of intense. "I'm ecstatic to see you walking so well. I can't help but want to celebrate it. But then when I think of all I took by healing you... I'm ashamed at my selfishness."

I bark a laugh, my heart pounding in my chest. "How were *you* selfish to heal *me*? Shouldn't I be saying that? I knew, Drew. The whole time I *knew* you could heal me. I *hoped and prayed* you would. So, really, this is on me. If I had told you the truth about my memories, you wouldn't have gone so far and healed me. You would have left me alone."

He cups my cheek with his hand. "No, I wouldn't have. It would have only made me want to help you even more. Emerald, you've come to mean a lot to me in such a short time. I can't explain my feelings. I'm not a writer who can come up with a fancy explanation, but I can say, I care about you. You've made time stop in my life. I haven't been able to get you out of my mind since the first time I met you."

I smile softly. "Don't say you don't have a way with words. I think that was pretty good." My chest swarms with heat and affection for this man who threw away his entire life so I could walk on my own. Granted, he didn't know it would work out this way, but still, he knew the risks that came with healing me.

"If you knew the dangers, why did you do it? I'm not worth all of this, believe me."

He steps so close to me; I place my hands on his chest. Looking up at him, I'm lost in his warm gray eyes as they drink me in. "You *are* worth it, Jewels. I knew I wanted you in my life; I just didn't know how to manage it. Everything that happened today worked out perfectly for me."

I swallow to ease my dry throat. "And what about all the clinical hours you racked up in the clinic? What about medical school?"

"All replaceable. You aren't," he says. He leans toward me and, when he's a whisper from my lips, says, "Please tell me I can kiss you, Jewels. I don't want to take advantage of you right now, but if I don't get to ki—"

I interrupt him by stepping on my toes and pressing my more than willing mouth onto his. He groans and wraps his arms around enfolding me in such a warm embrace; I don't think I'll want to move from the spot for hours, maybe days.

Moving his mouth on mine, his kisses turn demanding, and before I know it, he's spun my back to the wall, and presses me to it, picking me up to reach my mouth better. I moan when he extracts feelings from me I didn't know I could feel. The noise seems to do something to Drew because he stiffens and breaks our kiss, rubbing his nose on my lips as he breathes hard and sets me on my feet. "I need to stop," he says in a strangled voice.

"Why?" I ask, needing him to come back.

"Because I don't trust myself. I'm not the kind of guy to break down your defenses only to...do more."

Oh. My cheeks flame red, and I put my hands on them to cover them up. But there's no hiding from a comment like that. "Okay, I'll just go and check out the rest of the house." I flee the room, hoping I can be the wholesome girl he needs me to be.

Because if my hormones are any indication, I was more than willing to go further with this man now that we're alone. I happen to agree with Drew that I don't really want that. I've always wanted to save myself for marriage, if God ever blessed me with a husband.

And Drew seems to feel the same way. Plus, he liked me despite my condition. And then healed me to give me a better life. I'm in dangerous waters. *God, please help.*

23. Drew

I pray more fervently than I ever have. If God doesn't get a hold of me and nail my feet to the floor, I'm in danger of chasing Jewels up the stairs and carrying her into one of the bedrooms.

God, please help me.

I clench my fists and breathe through my nose, repeating my prayer over and over until my body cools down. After several minutes of praying and deep breathing, I open my eyes and am glad to see I'm still alone.

She does something to me. Our lives have intertwined without any effort on her part.

What am I supposed to do with that?

I must protect her, for one. I am now solely responsible for her future and her well-being. She has no idea what my world could do to her. She's not in danger of losing her life, just her dreams and hopes. The Elementals who run our world are not forgiving, and she knows far too much.

I make a vow that she will be safe and have the life she wants. It will just have to look a little different now that we're hiding from the Elementals. She'll finish her degree at another school where no one knows her.

My heart twists at the thought of pulling Jewels away from everyone and everything she knows. Who are her close friends besides Elia and Vela?

It's possible I know them since she was friends with Vela, too. Are any of them Elementals? If so, that makes all this easier. They'd understand immediately the need for us to leave this town and hide.

Realizing that she will have at least a few people who can still be part of her life helps my blood stop racing. I won't have to completely isolate Jewels from everyone she knows. I plan our escape instead. It'll have to be another Gyan community, but far from here.

How far is far enough from the Gyan Grand Elder? He's in charge of my entire clan in the US, so he has eyes and ears everywhere. It'll have to be inconspicuous enough that he won't think to look. Running the Gyan-controlled territories through my mind, I consider my options.

California is the first place I think of but dismiss it just as quickly. It's a battleground of two clans: Festans, the Fire Elementals, to the North, and the Gyans to the south. I don't want Jewels to be part of these hotly contested boundary disputes.

I consider Indiana and Kentucky, but I rule those out, too. There's too much friction right now between the neighboring Wind and Water Elementals, the Boreans and Neronians.

So, that leaves the east. Arkansas is an option; that's still Gyan territory. That's not a bad option, as I think it over critically, examining it from every angle. It borders the Water clan on the right in Florida, but to the left are Gyans. To the south are the Festans, but I'm so accustomed to dealing with Fire Elementals, I almost choose Arkansas for that reason alone.

Give me something I'm used to, as much change as this will bring. My next thoughts are about changing our identities. I'll need my parents' assistance on that one. Knowing they helped us escape makes me certain they'll come through for me with this.

I pull out my phone and search for universities in Arkansas that Jewels could apply to. I'll have to figure out how to transfer her college credits to a new name, which doesn't sound easy.

Since she's only in her freshman year, would she consider starting over with a new name?

I file that question away for later as I find several good options for law schools. One is in a town called Fayetteville. It's about three hours away from Little Rock, which I've visited. I pull up the website, having a good feeling it will be the perfect place. Call it instinct, but I've learned to trust my gut. Often, God points me toward things immediately, and since I trust His guidance, I read through the program that the University of Arkansas School of Law offers that she'll eventually want to get into.

Smiling down at my phone, my head whips up when Jewels speaks from the doorway, "I've found some food in the kitchen, so I thought we could talk over dinner."

I raise my eyebrows. "You made dinner?"

She shakes her head. "No. I found options for dinner. It's not much. But I could use some help to get it ready."

Bracing myself to be in close quarters with someone who's starred in my dreams lately, I pocket my phone and follow her into the kitchen.

I can't stop a smile from spreading across my face. Seeing the ease with which she walks will never get old. She moves like a queen and that she's been walking unassisted her whole life.

I see that she's pulled out macaroni and cheese and a package of shelf-ready Pepperidge Farm links. It makes sense those are here, even with my professor away. They last forever.

"How can I help?"

She turns an adorable shade of red, and looking at the food and not at me, she says, "I'm not much of a cook. Can you help me make the macaroni and cheese and I'll make the links?"

I hunt for a pot and pan and set them on the stove. Reaching for the pot, I turn and go to fill it up with water. Once it's back on the stove and I set it on high, I sweep my arms out. "See? I'm an excellent assistant. You're all ready to make this a four-star meal."

"*Four* stars? Why not five?" she asks over her shoulder as she works on cutting the links.

I chuckle. "Sorry, five."

She moves into position, and I notice right away that she's moving slower and a bit more stiffly as she puts the links in the pan with some oil. Alarm fills me that I've pushed her too hard. She's using muscles she hasn't used this much in her whole life. "Hey, are you too tired to do this?" I move to her side and see that her eyes are drawn and look a little pained, too.

She leans against the stove, her shoulders hunched. "I've always had far too little stamina. But," she says adamantly, pushing herself up. "I can do it." She stirs the links, and I back up, giving her space.

"You know that's all in the past. You'll only grow stronger. Just give it time. Rome wasn't built in a day, and you just got your legs and back working perfectly. It will take a while to build up your under-used muscles."

She nods but keeps her back to me as she stirs the packet of noodles into the now boiling water.

Blowing out a breath, I hope she'll open up to me. I move to hunt down some candles and a lighter. I want there to be a good ambiance for our first dinner alone. I wish more than anything I could get my hands in my parents' vegetable garden. I want to help Jewels make a delicious meal she would never forget.

When I look at our dismal options, I sigh internally. Our only option is to be grateful there's food at all. She's silent as she turns the sausage links over. I don't mind that she's silent as she works. There's a lot on her mind, problems I don't know about.

But when she picks up the pot of boiling water and carries it over to the sink where a colander waits, I can't help but notice her trembling arms. I move behind her to help if she needs it. She makes it to the sink, and then pauses, gathering her strength. When she leans to pour the water, she cries out when her knee buckles and her side falls into the counter.

Alarmed, I'm at her back in one step. I reach around her, gently taking the handle from her. I ignore the burn of the hot water as a small amount sloshes over my hand. When I've got the pot secure, I say, "Jewels, you're exhausted. Let me help you." When she presses her lips together in a thin line, I ask, "Please? Let me do this for you."

She finally agrees, releasing the pot handle. She limps to the chair at the small wooden table in the kitchen, easing into it slowly. I watch her for signs that she needs to lie down, but her color seems to return once she sits down.

Turning around, I drain the water out of the pasta, put the pan back on the stove, and get the colander out of the sink. Once I pour the pasta back into the pot, I look around for the cheese packet. I'm happy to see it's the sauce kind and not the powder cheese some macaroni and cheese boxes have. That way I don't need butter or milk, but I would kill for some fresh cheese to add to this.

Instead, I hunt in the spice cabinet for some garlic powder and parsley. Finding both, I shake some into the pot and stir the pasta. The sausage looks nice and crispy on the edges, so I take that off the burner.

Retrieving the plates, I dish the food up and bring them over. After setting one at both our places, I sit down and look up at Jewels. She's looking at me with shining, tear-filled eyes.

"What's wrong?" I ask, half rising.

She shakes her head. "You healed me, Drew. You actually did it," she whispers. "I mean, my legs can do things they've never been able to before. I can walk by myself. Why did you risk everything to help me?" She's clenching her hands together, like she's restraining herself from jumping out of her seat.

If she wants to jump into my arms, I won't stop her. Instead, I smile and look down. My mind whirs as I try to find the words to explain myself.

I look up and say, "First of all, God granted me the ability to heal. This whole miracle of you walking is because of Him." I blow out a breath as I work up the nerve to be vulnerable. "And second, from the first moment I met you, I was blown away by your absolute passion for life. Despite the enormous difficulty and pain you faced every day, you still had a zeal, a love for God and life that I pitifully couldn't say I had." I smile tenderly at her. "I found myself looking forward to spending even a moment with you. I drink in your positivity and *shine*. I can't think of one person more deserving of a pain-free life than you. I wish I could help everyone, but I'm limited to healing Elementals. But how could I resist healing you?"

Tears spill down her cheeks, and she impatiently wipes them away. "Drew. You barely know me. *Why* choose me? Why take that risk?"

Our dinner forgotten, I inhale deeply, thinking of how to explain the connection I've always felt. The bone-deep need to help her, protect her. Finally, I say, looking down at the table. "I just couldn't do nothing. I've come to care for you...deeply."

She sits back, with a stunned look on her face. Her breath quickens, and she sniffs and covers her face with her hands, looking away.

I lean toward her, reaching out with my hand. "Jewels? Are you okay? What did I say wrong?"

She turns stricken eyes toward me. "Are you really asking me that? You left your entire life, your family, all so I could walk without crutches."

"I didn't expect this to happen. I thought I could chalk it up to the center's treatments healing your back and fly under the radar in the Elemental community. Then you could have gotten your happily ever after with no one the wiser."

"That was a *big* risk to take."

I blow out a breath, running my hand across the back of my neck. "I know it was. But I'd do it again."

Her eyes fill with tears again. Her voice gathers strength, and her eyes are pained determination. "You think I deserve this, but nothing I've done or will do will measure up to ruining your life, giving up your dreams for me. Drew, if I could have you take it all back, I'd do it."

I sit back, frustration rising through me. "Don't you know your own value? See your own strength? Even what you just said...no one would turn away healing like yours. And my life isn't ruined." I lean forward and try to temper my voice. "I can go to any medical school; I'll just need to change locations. Did I expect this to happen? No. But now that it has, it frees us to pursue whatever we have together. Just with different names."

She looks away, wiping her cheeks with one hand. She sits thinking, and I give her time. Her whole life has been turned upside down. I can't expect her to just go with it, like I have. She's made of different stuff than I am. She requires stability, normalcy, and nothing that happened today can be called that. Then, a very sobering thought hits me.

Does she want to pursue a future with me?

She huffs, sighing deeply. She pauses. "What will happen with your parents? How will they find us? I'm sure they're worried."

Glad she seems to have accepted my reasons for healing her for now, I clear my throat as I gather my thoughts. "They can text me. Don't worry about me. It's you we need to figure out. Do you want to tell your mother the truth?"

"Won't your higher-ups assume she knows now that I've gone missing? Wait, do you think they've gone looking for me at my house?" She was about to put a bite in her mouth when she puts her fork down and half rises from her seat.

I put a hand out to stop her from leaving, wanting to soothe the panicked look in her eyes. "They would have gone to your house, but we are very skilled at keeping our questions discreet. They would not have raised any alarms with your mother. She doesn't, in fact, know anything, and that only works in her and our favor."

Jewels breathes a heavy sigh of relief and is almost sitting down when she pops up again, her face red with alarm. "Can they access my phone? What about your phone? How connect-ed are these people, anyway? Are we talking FBI material or just normal stalker-level creeps?"

She's leaning heavily on the table, and I can see the tops of her legs trembling. I made her run for her life when she had just gotten her legs. I get up and move to gently hold her shoulders, guiding her back to her seat.

Once she's sitting, I lean and whisper in her ear. "Shhh, it's alright. Don't worry, please. You're safe. No, they don't have access to our phones. They have no idea where we are. Unless they have laser eyes that can see through walls, they don't know we're here."

She stiffens and says, "But what if they see your parents' car? Won't they be looking for it?" She's clutching the table, and my heart goes out to her to how alien our world seems to her.

I move to my seat, too tempted to continue breathing in her scent, a soft lavender. "No, there's no chance they'll find us. This place is completely off their radar. They won't know I mentored under this professor, and it's so far outside the city, they won't think of looking here. Hey," I say in a soft voice, "You're safe. Your mom is safe. Don't worry, it's okay."

Her eyes flick around as if she's searching the room for hidden microphones. She's breathing erratically, and I can't stand it any longer. I get up and in one stride, I'm at her side. I grab her from her seat and pull her into a hug. It's the only thing that helped my sister when she got like this, and after a moment, Jewels relaxes in my arms.

I say into her hair, "You have nothing to worry about. We are *safe* here. I promise you. I wouldn't take you somewhere you'd have to worry. My parents will find me when the smoke clears, so that means we'll hole up here for a few days. So, let's enjoy some time off from our responsibilities."

I lean back and look into her eyes to transfer some of my positivity to her.

But to my horror, more tears spill down her cheeks. She speaks, but it's between hiccups. "I have work due in my classes. And now I can't go back to them. My life is over, Drew. What's going to happen to us?" She puts a hand over her mouth and sobs quietly, turning her head so I can't see her.

Putting my arms around her again, I hold her as she cries. I hate myself for being responsible for this mess. If I really think about it, yes, it's a miracle the poppy seed formula didn't work on her. But I should be ashamed at how glad I was to hear she already knew something about the existence of my world. Selfishly, I wanted her in my life, and now I've gotten my wish. But at a very high cost. I pray that one day she will be able to forgive me.

Holding her is easy. It's letting her go that's hard. I force myself to step away from her tear-filled expression. I just want to hold her forever and never let go. But I refuse to be more selfish than I've already been. I've destroyed her life. I won't sacrifice her dreams. Those will happen, I promise silently.

"Why don't you go relax upstairs? Take a bath, read a book. Get your mind off all this, huh? Let's talk about everything tomorrow morning. It'll be easier to see the possibilities when you've had time to let it sink in. But do me a favor?"

When she lifts her wet face up to me, I almost cave and take her home. But there's no use in doing that. Alex Colbourn will have eyes on her house and will snatch her up so fast, it'd make my head spin. She looks at me with watery eyes and waits for me to finish. I take a deep breath. "I promise you will achieve your dreams. It will just take a little sidestep to get there. I vow to do everything in my power to help make it happen. I've already started researching schools in other areas."

I wipe her tears with my thumbs and press a kiss to her forehead. I won't overwhelm her with a real kiss. That's the last thing she needs right now. I release her, pushing her softly towards the stairs. "Go."

She looks at me, still sniffing, but obeys, walking slowly to the stairs and then climbing them. She keeps her eyes on mine the entire time. It's not until she disappears upstairs that I breathe normally.

I'll need a miracle even to start making things right. So, I pick up the phone and call Vela.

24. Jewels

♥

I watch Drew as I walk upstairs. *Walk upstairs. I'm walking up the stairs without my crutches or even the railing! What world am I in?*

Drew holds my eyes until I've disappeared up to the second floor. When I lose sight of his thoughtful gray stare, I almost turn and go back. He keeps me grounded when I'm liable to fly off the handle.

I'm feeling the stress of the price of being healed. I *love* that I can walk. But at what cost did I pay for this priceless gift?

Blowing out a breath, I think, *Maybe he's right.* A bath sounds like just what I need right now. Taking a long hot bath is one of my favorite ways to destress after a long, painful day. It always feels so good to my beat-up muscles after a hard day of lugging myself around. Of course, at home we have a modified bathtub that allows me to use it more easily. I would have had trouble getting in and out of a regular tub before my miraculous healing.

Examining the state of my muscles, I realize I might not need piping hot water tonight. I'm tired but not hurting like usual. I just feel achiness in my muscles. This is better than I'm used to feeling on a normal day. Not when I've been running for my life.

As I hunt down the bathroom, I stop. *I ran for my life.* That sentence makes the breath in my throat freeze. Then another thought hits me. *I ran from Elementals. Another species of beings.* My head swims. How is this my life right now? I put a shaking hand on the wall and lean my hot forehead on the cool surface.

Lord, please...calm me. Help me not to panic.

With that desperate prayer, cool air flows into my lungs. I gulp it in greedily. I give myself a moment to collect myself.

Pulling back, I walk down the hall. When I turn the corner, I'm pleased to find a huge bathroom. I walk inside and smile as I see the claw-foot tub that sits on display in the corner of the spacious room. Relieved, I walk over to it, sit on the edge, and spin the handles. I plug in the stopper.

As it fills, I find a fluffy towel and set it on the floor. A variety of bath soaps, shampoo, and conditioner sit on a shelf beside the tub, and I'm grateful to not need to search for them.

I reach up and peel off my shirt and marvel that I don't need to lean against the tub to accomplish that. I've never been able to depend on my back and legs to hold myself up. I stop in the middle of changing and think for a minute. *My life is forever changed.* I'm going to be able to do a lot of things that I couldn't before.

I should be jumping, leaping for joy. Instead, I'm left with a huge sense of loss. I already miss my mom. Will I be able to see her again? How will I tell her I'm okay? She's going to start looking for me if I don't contact her soon. I was going to find my own way home today, so she's not there to pick me up at the clinic. It's easily been two hours since my appointment; she'll expect me home by now. *Have the Elementals already gone to my house and questioned her?* I can't call her, according to Drew, since her innocence is what will save her from that horrible poppyseed formula.

Sighing heavily, I peel off the rest of my clothes and ease into the hot water. Getting used to the temperature, I find some bath bubbles and add a generous amount. I lean my head on a padded headrest and watch the soapy water fill up the tub. I pray that my mom didn't panic when I didn't come home at the expected time.

No matter what Drew says, I'm going to have to contact her to tell her *something*.

What though, I have no idea.

Drew says I can still go to college, but I'll have to change my name. I'll have to move and change everything about my life. My heart pounds in my chest with this impossible checklist.

After a while, the water threatens to overflow the tub, so I reach over and turn it off. Taking a deep breath, I hold my aching chest and sink under the bubbles. I stay under as long as I can, then I sit up quickly, sloshing water over the sides of the tub.

Resting my arms on the tub, I rub the soap off my eyes and just sit back and think.

If I could disappear with anyone, it would be with Drew Ashcroft. He's grown to be very important to me. I just never imagined I would have to leave my life here and be with him *alone*. After what we shared when we first got here, it's apparent he likes being here with me, too.

No. We're not alone. We have God on our side. Every step we take has been preordained by Him.

Still, my nerves threaten to overwhelm me. I should be feeling better after remembering that God is in control, but terror at leaving my world behind is climbing my chest.

Tears fill my eyes and slide down my cheeks. *Why did this happen? Who could have turned Drew in?* I'm not ready to just up and leave. I want to be near my mother, at least until I choose to leave and I don't want to be forced into a life of hiding.

I've learned at a very young age that we don't always get what we want in life. Sometimes we're given a huge basket of lemons and instead of being left with just the bitter rind, we're expected to make lemonade.

I tuck my chin into my chest and allow my tears to continue. I've learned not to bottle up my hard emotions. Mom always says, "You can't heal what you don't feel."

So, I give myself permission to cry. Cry for the loss I'm going to experience, the work it will take to disappear, for a whole new life. I attempt to keep my sobs quiet, but it's no use, so I give in and ugly cry.

After a good ten minutes of my pity party, I pick my head up, sniff loudly, and wipe my face clean. I splash my face, scrub my cheeks, wishing I could wash away my problems just as easily.

I soak in the hot water, glad I made it steaming. I'll be in this bath for a while as I think over my situation. Drew believes our only choice is to run. I don't want to, but I acknowledge that he's probably right and resolve to accept the process.

Deciding to get the bath done, I make short work of it, using the handheld sprayer for my hair. My chest feels lighter after releasing some of my emotions, but it's still heavy with all the decisions I'm facing.

I'm healed. I could run away, even from Drew.

But what would I do then? I'd be chased down and ripped from my life, anyway. At least this way, I can still maintain contact with a few people, and I will be safe with Drew. I don't understand everything that's going on, but I know Drew will do everything he can to protect and help me.

Then a thought hits me. What makes these Elementals so important that they think they can just take control of my life? Suddenly I'm fighting mad.

I rip myself out of the tub, ignoring the water that spills everywhere. I grab another towel from the rack and furiously wipe myself off. I'm going to find out more about these people. And I'm not stopping until I get some answers.

25. Drew

♥

After my talk with Vela, I anxiously wait for Jewels to come back downstairs. Surely, it's too early for her to go to bed? I pace while my mind races with all the questions Jewels must have about my world. If I'm freaking out, she must be losing it. My chest squeezes at the thought of her suffering alone upstairs.

I have half a mind to knock on the bathroom door. I heard the water turn on a while ago, so I know she took my advice and took a bath. But she's been up there *forever*.

Running my hand on the back of neck, I rub my muscles, trying to ease some of the tension. I look at the ceiling, fruitlessly searching for her.

I've worn a path on the carpet by the time I hear stomping on the stairs. Looking up, my heart lurches when I see Jewels with her hair wet, fresh from the bath. She looks glorious... and furious.

"When are you going to tell me about your people? Am I going to have to guess everything?" she asks, fists clenched on her hips, her pretty face set in a scowl.

My smile dies on my lips. "What do you want to know?"

"Everything. Now." She stomps over to the armchair in the living room and plops into it. She leans her elbows on her knees and looks at me expectantly.

Ignoring the thrill of watching her stomp to the chair, I blow out a breath and say, "Okay, let me start from the beginning. But first, I have some news."

She waits for me to continue, and I say, "I've called Vela and asked her to be our go-between with my parents."

She nods for me to continue.

I hesitate. "Unfortunately, that's all she can do for us. She's too mixed up in her own affairs to really help us. I have some money saved up, but she's offered to lend me more if we need it. Apparently, her Intended is *loaded*."

"Intended? What are you talking about?"

I laugh and rub my neck, some of my stiffness gone now that Jewels is back downstairs, but the tension is still there.

"Elementals all have what you call an Intended. Someone who is like their soulmate. They have unique scents that only they can sense, and being near each other enhances their abilities."

Jewels eyes me. "So, you have a soulmate? An Intended?" she asks in a soft voice. She looks guarded. I want to erase that look in her eyes.

"Yes, technically I have an Intended somewhere. But it's a one in a million chance I'll ever meet her."

"Why?" she whips at me.

"Because it could be any Elemental in the world. Really, the odds are even higher."

"So, you have an Intended girl somewhere who is your other half, and you're doing all this for *me*?" She shakes her head and looks away. "You know what? It's none of my business. So, what else did Vela say?"

I pause before I answer because I need to have this conversation with her, but we have more pressing issues to discuss right now. "She didn't say much. She can't really with what she's got going on, but she can help us get in touch with my parents."

"Why would she have to help get you in touch with your parents? You're telling me you can't be in contact with them directly?"

"Not yet. It's too dangerous. We have a lot of connections, and it wouldn't surprise me if the Grand Elder gets hold of their cell phones. Vela will have to talk to them in code with any news or requests."

"Code?" Jewel's face screws up in a cute, confused expression.

"My family has a code we've developed over the years. It's not really a big deal, but it will help her to hide information about us and our location."

Jewel's eyes are wide as she absorbs this strange information. "Why would you want to be a part of an organization like this, one that would chase you down for using your abilities as you see fit?"

I frown. "My people are amazing. I've never had reason to go against them before. Though the Grand Elder has gone to the extreme trying to send us away to God knows where."

"But a secret code?"

I wave my hand. "It's just a secret language my family's had fun with over the years. We've never used it like this before."

Jewels folds her hands. "Well, I guess that's good then. Now, can you tell me more about your people?"

I smile. "I'm happy to. It's surreal talking openly to a human, but I'm glad I can, especially with you." I spear her with a gaze full of admiration. She looks brighter, fresher after her bath. Whatever she did up there has put a new fire into her veins and color on her cheeks. And it looks good on her.

She blushes but then glares at me. "Start talking, Romeo."

I smile widely and launch into the history of how God created our people to take care of the Earth with all the gifts of the elements: earth, wind, water, and fire. We were meant to live together in harmony, but because of greed, jealousy, and other vices, we separated into clans.

When I explain disputes about boundary lines, she interrupts me. "You mean to tell me that some seemingly natural disasters that have *ruined* lives were caused by Elementals fighting about trespassing?"

"That can contribute to disputes, but there's usually more to it. Most Elementals try not to harm any human's land or do too much damage."

She scoffs. "I highly doubt that in the heat of the moment, Elementals will stop fighting to avoid damaging property."

I nod, understanding how she could think this way. "We really try, Jewels. Most of us are not heartless. Some have terrible prejudices against each other, but most do everything we can to keep humans out of our battles."

She huffs in irritation. "If my experience with Elementals so far is any indication, I don't think I can see your point."

"I understand your thoughts. I do. We haven't forgotten why God gave us these gifts: to help the earth, not destroy it. And that definitely includes protecting humans."

She sighs and then asks, "Tell me about this Grand Elder. Why is he so angry with us?"

I rake my hand through my hair. "It's not you he's angry with. It's me. I've broken a very strict code, and he wants to punish me for it."

"Healing me? Why is that so wrong?"

"The one thing all Elementals can agree on is the need to keep our identities a secret from humans. Witch hunts might sound archaic, but believe me, a worldwide hunt would be a reality if humans ever found out about us."

"Your kind don't want to be exploited." She nods with a twist of her lips.

"That's one thing. But also, we don't want to be persecuted."

She looks away and bites her lip in thought. I divert my gaze to avoid being distracted by the quickening of my pulse.

"So, you think that the government will what? Exterminate your kind or force you to use your gifts for their agenda?"

"If the world found out about our powers, we would never live in peace again. We'd be put away until we agreed to use our gifts for others' gain. God's purpose for us would be perverted to fit their plan, not His."

"But are you really using your gifts for His plan now?" she asks softly.

I whip my head around to study her expression, thankful to see it's not one of incrimination or reproach, but deep thought.

"We're definitely not fulfilling God's intention by living apart. It's why so few of us have found our Intended, a gift God bestows to bless our kind. We've lost that blessing. We don't want to lose any more."

She cocks her head. "You mean, you think God will take away your gifts completely if you don't do what you're created for?"

I nod. "I'm sure of it. We've all been hoping for a unifier to come and unite us like we should be. There's a prophecy of Connection that says one will come."

"Who is it?" she asks, getting more comfortable in her chair. I'm glad to see she has relaxed a little. She doesn't look like she's on the warpath anymore.

"We call this person the Chosen Child. The prophecy states the Child's parents and their birthdates. But there's a lot of speculation about who it could be."

She sniffs. "I would imagine the Elementals would be desperate to find out who this person is."

"We really have been." I rub my neck and decide to share Vela's secret. "I, uh, actually think someone very close to me is that person."

She whips her head at me. "Really? Who?"

I blush for some strange reason. "It's my sister. She's the Chosen Child. It's crazy, I know, but..."

Jewels shrugs. "If she fits the prophecy, then why couldn't she be the one?"

I look at her fondly. "If you knew more about my people, you'd understand that's like saying she's Santa Claus."

This time, she laughs. "Really? You guys really hang a lot on this person?"

I nod seriously.

"Well, then, I hope it is Vela. She could do it."

I can only shake my head in amazement. This conversation is the first she's heard of my people, my world, and nothing I've told her has diminished her fierce loyalty to my sister.

"It's true," she says with conviction. "Vela is amazing. She probably doesn't think of herself as a hero, but she's strong enough to carry a job like that out."

I lean back on the couch and put my hands behind my head. "You really are a good friend to advocate for her like that."

She shrugs. "I call it like I see it." She gives me a direct look, and I feel a zing race through my bloodstream. I love it when I hold her focus like this. I could carry her gaze all day long and be a happy man.

"She was one of the first people to befriend me at our high school. She has something not everyone has: generosity of spirit. I would think the Chosen Child will need that in spades."

I could kiss this girl right now. Not only did she not laugh at me, but she supports and champions my sister better than I do. I restrain myself from walking over and pulling her into a kiss.

Looking away, I say, "Yeah, well. Vela's got a lot going on right now. She's so busy attempting to unite our world, she won't even tell me what's going on. She has a nearly impossible task of convincing Elementals to believe it's her."

"Hmmm, well, she will share more when she's ready," Jewels says helpfully.

"We won't be around here, though."

At this, Jewels's face goes pale. "Drew?"

I give her my full attention. "Yes?"

"Do we really have to go?"

I frown. "We do. I've been a Gyan my whole life and believe me when I say that this is not going to blow over in a little while. We need to disappear."

Her hands tremble, and she looks down at them and squeezes them together. "I need to talk to my mom. Soon. That is non-negotiable. I can't just disappear. She's probably freaking out right now about why I'm not home." She gives me a fierce glare, daring me to contradict her.

I nod grimly. "I know. I'm trying to figure that out. Let them question your mom first. That will give us a chance to figure out how to leave without them tracking us."

She frowns deeply. "You don't understand. I need to talk to her right now. She will call the National Guard, the FBI, anyone she can if she doesn't know where I am." She looks intently at me then voices my greatest concern, "And she needs to know the truth."

My stomach plummets. I've been trying to come up with an acceptable explanation for Jewels's sudden disappearance that doesn't include cluing another human in about Elementals. That certainly wouldn't win us any points with the Grand Elder. "Jewels..."

"No," she says fiercely. She whips her hand through the air. "I can trust my mom not to give anything about your people away. *You* need to trust her, too."

I hold my hand to my chest. "It's not about me trusting her, believe me. It's my clan. If they find out we told her about us, they would put her through that awful poppy seed formula again, and she'd still not know where you went. Because no matter how they try to make her forget, she won't forget you."

Jewels's face drops. She clenches her hands together. "Drew, I can't lie to my mother. I need to tell her something. Why couldn't we tell her and make her promise she would never say a word about it to anyone but us?"

I give her a hard look. "Listen to me. They will suspect something like that. If they think for one moment that she knows something of our world, they won't hesitate. They will give her the formula."

When Jewels drops her head onto her hands and her shoulders start shaking, my will crumbles to pieces. I rise and go to her, crouching in front of her and take her hands in mine. She looks up at me, tears streaming down her face. "Please, Drew? Please, can we tell her?" Her voice breaks, and I feel my resolve breaking, too.

Gripping her shaking hands, I turn my face and think for a minute. After a few agonizing moments of listening to her sniffles and sobs that tear my heart out, I turn and say, "How good an actress is your mom?"

Jewels's eyes instantly brighten, and she straightens. "She's excellent. I promise you."

And so, with a deep sigh, I say, "Okay, we'll tell her."

26. Jewels

I squeal and wrap my arms around Drew's neck. "Thank you,
thank you. I just can't see myself lying to my mom about
this. She won't breathe a word to anyone, I promise you." I
squeeze him hard, but when I belatedly realize what I'm doing,
I stiffen.

It was such a knee-jerk reaction that I didn't think twice. I
can't help but breathe in his delicious musky cologne. If I just
turn my head a fraction, my lips would meet his neck. *What
would he do if I kissed him right now?*

Lurching back, I let my arms fall and look at Drew with wide
eyes, as he studies me with an intense, heat-filled gaze.

It seems I'm not the only one who reacted to our proximity.
I swallow thickly, my throat suddenly dry. We are alone in this
big house with no chaperone to hold us accountable for our
actions. Our heat-seared kiss from earlier comes to mind, and
I frown. I don't trust myself not to jump into his arms.

When he sees the unsure expression on my face, his eyes lose
the heat, and he stands up in one sure movement.

My stomach clenches at the lost moment, but I have no
choice but to accept it for what it is. As I watch him walk away,
I think that I used to be so jealous of smooth movements like
his, but now *I* can do the same. I stand up just because *I can*.
Leaning against the wall, I watch him carefully as he walks over
to the window and peers out of the drawn curtain.

"Anyone out there?" I ask.

He shakes his head. I approach him and rest my hand on his arm. "Thank you, Drew. You don't know what it means to me I can tell my mom what's really going on."

He turns to me slowly. "She has to promise not to fly off the handle and call someone. She has to understand this is literally out of our hands. That she has no choice but to allow you to leave the state. Do you think she can do that?"

I swallow. "Yes," I say as certainly as I can. The truth is, I'm really not sure what my mom will do. She constantly surprises me with her erratic personality. But I can't keep my mom in the dark about something that affects my life so much. I'd rather do anything but that. I'll have to risk her wrath, tell her the truth, and impress on her how important secrecy is. "She'll keep this a secret. But, Drew, are you *sure* we have to disappear? You're asking a lot. Not just from my mom, but from me, too."

Drew's eyebrows draw down, and his deep frown does nothing for the hope coursing through me. He shakes his head. "I'm sorry, Jewels. If I could protect you from this and stay here, I would. But the minute someone told the Grand Elder about us, our fates were sealed. We have to hide to keep you out of his grasp. I'm sorry. I would have done things differently if we could have kept your healing a secret."

Dejected, I walk over to the stuffed chair and say in a whoosh of breath as I sit down, "Okay, so what happens? You said we have to stay here a few days?"

Adopting a businesslike persona, Drew rubs his hands together. "Yes. I've already started a search of where we can go. The time spent here will help us finalize our plans."

Looking around with downcast eyes, I ask, "What am I supposed to do for clothes? What about all my things? I have just the clothes I wore today."

He sighs heavily. "I know. I'm sorry, but you won't be able to get your things for a while. When it's safe, we'll have your mom mail packages."

Resolve filling me, I look over at Drew with piercing eyes. "I want to call my mom. Now."

Resignation crosses his expression, and he nods.

I jump up, thrilled at a seemingly simple thing, and whip my phone out of my back pocket, noticing all the missed calls. Dialing my mom's number, I hold my breath while I wait for her to answer.

She answers in a breathless tone, "Julia Patterson, where *are* you?"

"Mom, I'm going to need you to sit down. I have something important I need to talk to you about."

"What? Julia, I've been freaking out here not knowing where you are. And you wouldn't answer your phone."

"I'm sorry; it was on silent."

"Julia, you know how I feel about you checking your phone regularly. Hold on, someone's at the door."

Because I have her call on speakerphone, Drew's able to hear everything. He whips his hands in the air, telling me to stop her.

"Mom, don't tell anyone that I'm on the phone. It's important. You haven't heard from me since I left for my appointment."

"What? Julia, is this some kind of joke?"

"Mom, don't answer the door until you promise you'll say you haven't heard from me. Are you at the door yet?"

"Julia, are you in some kind of trouble?" she asks in a low voice.

"No, well, yes, but," I huff a breath, "Mom, I can't explain this in two seconds. Just answer the door, and if anyone asks about me, you haven't heard from me. It's really important that you agree to that."

She hesitates and then whispers, "Okay, I trust you. I'll call you right back. Answer the phone, you hear me?"

"Yes, ma'am," I promise, and the line goes dead.

I look up, and sweat breaks out all over my body. I turn my ringer on. "Drew, is she safe? Will they give her that poppy seed stuff? She doesn't know anything!"

I'm pacing back and forth, and Drew takes me by the shoulders. "Exactly, she doesn't know anything. That will be in her favor. The Grand Elder's people won't tell her anything about our world, believe me. She's only going to wonder what you have to do with them."

"And she has to pretend like she didn't just hear from me," I add, wringing my hands.

"Right. Give them time to question her, and when she calls you, we can answer her questions."

My heart is in my throat, and fear for my mom almost overwhelms me. I must look a mess, because Drew gives me a look and wraps me in his arms. I'm stiff at first, then I accept his support and wrap my arms around his waist.

Every time I get this close to Drew, it makes my head swim. His presence is so comforting, I can't help but melt in his arms. But the fear remains lodged in my chest. This is all too much.

Fear, confusion, self-pity all rise up, ready to burst out of my chest. I rest my head on his shoulder and say, "Drew, I'm scared. This is crazy. How did this all happen? How is this my life right now?"

He squeezes me gently and says into my hair, "I'm sorry, Jewels, I really am. If I could change it, I would. I wish we weren't reported, but it is what it is."

I pull back slightly, and look into his eyes. I need to see his face as he answers my next question. "My mom will be safe, right?"

He nods firmly, his eyes a serious dark gray.

Satisfied with his promise, I step back. Thankful I've regained my composure, I don't have a reason to continue our embrace. "Thanks," I mumble. "Sorry I'm so needy."

"Jewels, you will never stop surprising me with what you can handle. Your reaction to all of this has been amazing. I'm impressed, really."

Blushing under his praise, I walk over to the window, but before I can peek outside, Drew's hand on my shoulder stops me.

"Wait," he orders. "Stay away from the windows, just in case."

Pulling away, I ask, "Am I in danger, Drew?"

"Physically, no. They won't harm you. But if they find you, they will exile you to a community somewhere so far away you'll never hear from your mother again." Drew's eyes are sad as he shakes his head. "The only humans I know who are part of our world are the indigenous clans. They've lived with and intermarried with humans for years. But they have strict codes to keep our way of life a secret."

My phone rings in my back pocket.

Jumping in response, I fumble to answer when I see it's my mom.

"Mom? Is everything okay?"

"Julia? Maybe you need to answer that question," she says in a hard voice.

I put the phone on speaker and walk back to Drew.

"I'm okay, Mom." I laugh. "I'm better than okay. Mom, I'm healed. I can walk perfectly. I won't ever need my crutches again."

A stunned silence follows. When I'm about to say something, she says, "Julia, are you on drugs? And who were those men who came just now? They weren't the police, but you said you were in trouble."

"Did they ask about me?"

"Kind of. They asked if you had seen anything."

I look at Drew in desperation for help in explaining all of this. He nods at me and extends his hand for the phone. "Mom. I'm going to give you over to Drew. He'll explain everything."

"Drew? Your therapist? What does he have to do with this?" she shrieks.

Drew speaks, "Ma'am?" When she answers yes, he says, "Clarissa, before I explain what's going on, I need to know everything those men asked you."

Mom sounds flustered when she says, "They just asked if I had seen any suspicious activity in the neighborhood. I think they're part of the Concerned Citizens Group or something. They asked about Julia and whether she had seen anything suspicious, but I told them that I haven't heard anything from her since her appointment four hours ago. Now," she says in a hard voice. "Explain right now, young man. Where is my daughter and why is she in some sort of trouble?"

Drew breathes out heavily. "Okay, this is going to sound very strange, but the men who came to your house were asking if you've seen or heard anything about my kind."

"Your kind? What are you talking about?"

Her confusion further cements that my mom remembers nothing of what happened over a year ago.

Drew says calmly. "I'm part of a group of people who have existed among your kind, humans, for over two thousand years. We are Elementals and are gifted by God to take care of the Earth."

A pregnant pause follows, then my mom asks in an even harder voice, "Where is my daughter? What are you doing with her? What nonsense are you spewing at me? Are you on drugs? Are you giving drugs to my daughter?"

Needing to get a handle on this situation, I take the phone from Drew. "Mom? I'm right here. I'm fine. I'm perfectly fine. It's like I said, I'm healed. I'm cured, Mom. Please believe me when I say I'm not on drugs; Drew isn't either. He's telling the truth."

"Julia Emily Patterson, you get your butt home this instant. I need to lay eyes on you, and if I don't within ten minutes, I'm calling the police."

"No! Mom, you can't..."

Drew peels the phone out of my clenched hand. "Clarissa, Jewels does not need the police. She's safe. I need you to trust me."

"Why should I trust you?" she asks in a loud voice. "What is this nonsense about Julia not needing her crutches? *What is going on?*"

"Ma'am, what I said earlier is true. I'm part of a special group of people bestowed with abilities. My gift is healing, and I healed Jewels this afternoon. She can walk. She can live a pain-free life."

I hear a sob on the phone, and I rip it from his hand. "Mom? Mom, are you okay?"

She cries for a minute, then she asks in a soft voice, "Baby, is this true? What is he talking about? Are you really healed? Facetime me, *show me.*"

I take the phone, press a button, and hand the phone to Drew to show me walking across the room perfectly. My mom is in tears when I come back to the phone.

"Mom, he's not lying. He is telling the truth. And well, his people are kind of mad that he healed me, so we're hiding from them."

"Oh, Julia, honey. You really can walk. I can't believe it," she says between sobs, her tear-tracked face joyful. "I can't believe...wait, that's the trouble you're talking about? Why are they mad? What will they do to you?" Her expression immediately morphs into concerned anger.

This time Drew leans in and answers, "Because I'm not supposed to heal humans with my gift. And to answer your second question, they don't want to harm Jewels, but they would take her away to some remote place so she couldn't leak the secret of my people."

"Why would you do something to put my daughter in that kind of danger?" she asks, her forehead furrowed. "She was perfectly safe before all of this, and now...Now what? I can't see her ever again?"

"You'll see her again. But you need to give us time to lie low and for them to give up looking for us. I'm sorry, but she needs to start a new life with a new identity somewhere else. Until we're sure of her safety, you can only talk to her over the phone."

"Who is we?" she whips out. "Who else have you involved in my daughter's life?"

"Only my parents. We all want her safe."

"She's only in danger because of you. Why don't they just take you away and be happy with that?"

"Because Jewels is human. She is not supposed to know about my world. And," he continues in a firm voice, "you'll need to pretend like she's run away and you have no idea where she went. Jewels has assured me you are an excellent actress when you want to be. It's the only way."

Mom blows out her breath and with soft eyes asks, "Julia, is this all okay with you? Besides being healed, which is an absolute miracle, how are you?"

Tears fill my eyes at her question. She doesn't ask about my new ability to walk unaided; she wants to know about my emotional wellbeing. I get out, "I'm okay, Mom. It's been a lot to take in, but I'm okay. I'm better now that I've told you about all of this."

"Honey, did you know about these people?"

I hedge, "Kind of. I wasn't supposed to, but I first suspected something about their existence over a year ago."

My mom doesn't explode in temper at my keeping this from her, but her voice sounds disappointed. "You couldn't tell me about it?"

"I did tell you about it, but D—, I mean an Elemental came over and blew this powder in our faces, which made you forget the entire day."

Drew gives me a curious look as to why I didn't mention his presence. I hold up my hand, asking him not to say anything.

I'm impressed when she takes my news calmly. Mom is pretty well known for her temper. "But you didn't forget?"

"No, I think all the meds I take counteracted the effect of the powder. I remember everything."

"And you didn't want me to remember because?"

"The formula they gave us was hard on our bodies. It makes you convulse and spasm for a while. I was terrified if I said anything they would make you and me take it again."

"You're telling me you had the same reaction I did? Honey, were you okay after that?"

I know what she's talking about. I've had medication-induced seizures in the past, and I suffered for weeks after. It was difficult on my body to deal with that kind of trauma on top of the daily pain. "No, I was fine. But it was because..."

This is where I'll have to mention Drew's name, explain he healed me that day. But I hesitate.

Drew gives me a sympathetic look of understanding. "Clarissa, it was me who came over that day. I'm the one who gave you that formula. It's one of my jobs to administer it and to ease the complications. I could see that Jewels was having an especially difficult time, so I healed her through the convulsions so she wouldn't suffer later."

"Put Julia on the phone," she orders.

When I comply, I say, "Yes?"

"Why wouldn't you want me to know it was Drew who did such a terrible thing?"

"You're understandably upset to find out. The higher-ups told him to do that, and he tried everything he could to make it easier for me and you. Mom, I'd like you to go easy on him."

She sniffs. "Sounds like, wait...Julia, you *knew him* at the clinic. You recognized him, but you hid it from us?"

I knew I got my excellent memory from my mom. I laugh, surprised I can at this point in the conversation. "Yeah, of course I recognized him. But I was terrified they would give us that awful stuff again if I said anything. In fact, Drew didn't know I remembered everything until a few hours ago."

"Well, why is it so bad that you remember, anyway? Why can't he just explain everything to them and let you come home?" She sounds desperate, and my chest squeezes to have to deny her this.

When I look at Drew imploringly, he answers for me, "Clarissa, we will be in touch with you as often as we can, but it's imperative Jewels and I get away from here and hide, or my people will grab her and put her in some far off place. If you'd like to be in touch with your daughter at all, you have to let her leave."

"Let her leave?" she cries, "I don't even know where she is!"

"And that's the way it must be for now. I'm sorry. She's going to turn off her location to feed the story that she ran away from home. But," he promises when my mom gasps, "we will be in touch every step of the way. We'll tell you where she is and when it's safe, you can come join her."

"Wait, I can't even see my daughter before you spirit her away goodness knows where?" she asks, her expression anguished.

"I'm afraid that's impossible," he says softly, giving me an apologetic glance. "You'll both have to make do with a phone call goodbye for now."

Everything inside me squeezes at the thought of leaving without giving my mom a last hug. Who knows how long it will be before I see her again? Tears fill my eyes and escape down my cheeks — rivers of grief I just can't control anymore.

Drew notices my reaction and tells my mom, "Here, talk to your daughter. She needs you right now." He hands me the phone and leans his shoulder into mine.

"Mom?" My voice cracks, and I instantly see her bowed head. I blindly find a seat as we both cry.

"Julia, how did this all happen? I can't even believe it," she whispers.

After a few painful minutes, I collect my breath and stop my sobs. "Mom, I'm going to be okay. I'm not as fragile as I once was, remember?"

She inhales deeply and says, sniffing loudly, "I still can't believe you don't need your crutches anymore. I thought I would have given anything for you to be healed, but I'm not sure I would have accepted the expense of not seeing you. At the first opportunity, I'm moving to wherever you are, Julia. Do you hear me? You will not be alone in this."

A thought suddenly comes to me. "How is anyone going to believe I ran away from home without any of my things? They're going to think I was kidnapped, Drew. Which I practically was," I mutter darkly under my breath.

"I don't know how they're going to spin that," he admits. "They might just allow it to become a missing person's case. It's too important for everyone not to know about us."

Since the call is still on Facetime, Mom hears all of that. She cries even harder, and I wish so much I could reach through the phone and hug her fiercely.

Just then, a rapid knocking at the door makes mine and Drew's heads whip over to it. My heart freezes.

"Who's that?" I whisper. Cold fingers grab my lungs, and I can hardly breathe through my fear.

Drew's face becomes stone, and he strides over to the door.

"Mom, I have to go. I'll call when I can," I whisper into the phone.

"Julia...what..."

"Mom, I have to go," I say and hang up on my poor mom, who's probably going into shock right now. I'm in no better condition, and I hold my breath to see who's at the door, knowing the answer could change my entire future.

27. Jewels

I jump up and hide behind my chair. Peeking over the back of it, I see Drew open the door a crack, curse, and yank a small feminine body inside. All I can see is that she's wearing a black hoodie and jeans, and the hood is pulled over her face. I can see her curves well enough, so I know it's a young woman. "Drew!" I whisper harshly. "What are you doing? Who is that?"

My heart is in my throat, and I wildly look around for an object I can throw or use as a weapon.

"Jewels Patterson, where are you?" Elia screeches. She turns so I can see her face hidden under the hoodie and yanks her arm away from Drew, who's scowling darkly at her.

"Elia?" I ask, my muscles frozen in pure shock.

When she sees me crouching behind the chair, she whoops and jumps into action. She runs over to me and pulls me into the tightest hug I think I've ever gotten.

"Elia?" I squeak. "How on earth did you find us?"

She pulls back, and a fierce scowl takes over her entire face. "What do you think you're doing hiding out like this? Are you guys crazy?"

I'm shaken out of my shock when she grabs my shoulders and gives me a good push. When I resist and step back on my own, she looks down at my legs, her eyes wide with disbelief. "So, it's true," she whispers. She turns to Drew. "You did it. You actually healed her!" She spins back to me.

"What are you doing here?" I ask weakly, putting my hand out on the chair to stop myself from falling.

He says in a dark voice, "She's here because she can't keep her freaking big nose out of *anything*."

She whips her head at him. "I certainly can, but not when it comes to my *best friend*."

He frowns at her before looking outside again. "I thought Vela was your *best friend*."

Elia pouts. Only Elia can make a pout look adorable; even in my shocked state, I can think that. "I will have you know I can have *more* than one best friend. I have *two*." She holds up two fingers, which he ignores, so she turns to me. "So," she says, her eyes bright with excitement. "You know all about us now?"

My mouth hangs open. "You? You *are* one of them!"

She giggles. "Yep. I'm an Elemental. It's going to be so nice now that I don't have to hide that from you."

Drew, satisfied no one followed her to our hideout, comes over to us in two long strides. He folds his arms over his chest and towers over Elia, his eyes twin orbs of fury. "How did you find us?"

She laughs and holds up her phone. "I tracked her through Snapchat. You haven't turned off her location yet, so I took advantage."

Drew scowls and holds out his hand, palm up to me. He looks at me with both eyebrows raised, waiting.

"What?" I ask.

He blows out a breath. "Give me your phone. We need to take care of that right now, before more people end up over here."

Elia giggles again. "No other Elemental will be able to do what I did. I'm the only Elemental friend she has. So, she's safe enough. But yeah," she says, popping her gum, "you should probably turn it off just in case."

I hand over my phone, my spirits surprisingly buoyed by seeing Elia. She's like a ray of sunshine spilling over into this entire sordid mess, brightening up our dire situation.

In a move that surprises even me, I jump over to Elia and wrap her in my arms. "Elia, it's so good to see you. I can't believe you've hidden that you're an Elemental this whole time." I squeeze her neck, and she pats my back, wheezing.

"Uh, Jewels, calm down with the hug, girl. I'm not going anywhere. And I couldn't tell you."

I pull back. "Which kind of Elemental are you?"

She looks between me and Drew. "You haven't gotten the whole story yet? You'll only find one kind of Elemental in whatever area you live. Well, right now, anyway. This is Gyan territory. So, yeah, I'm a Gyan. I can rock out in nature any day."

I really look at her, like I can see inside her head. "And you can heal, too?"

At that question, she literally stumbles away from me. "Uh, Jewels, please don't give me that look. To answer your question, yes, I can heal, but I'm not half as good as Drew. He's the only Gyan I know who could have possibly healed you."

When she mentions my healing, I look down at my legs, still in a state of shock that I can use them fully. She looks me over, too.

"Girl, it's so good to see you looking like this. You're pain-free now?" She looks at me with such hope and expectancy, I can only nod.

At my answer, she spins around and wraps Drew in a hug that looks as tight as mine was. "Drew Ashcroft, you are the absolute best to defy every law we have to heal my bestie!"

Drew allows the hug for a moment before he disentangles himself. "How did you find us, Elia?" he asks in a resigned voice. "Or should I ask, who told you?"

She settles back on her feet, puts her finger to her lip and looks up in thought. "I thought I already told you how I found you guys. But, as far as who told me, I don't think I should tell you."

Drew's face somehow gets darker and more furious. "Why not?"

"Because I don't want you to beat him up." She slaps her hand over her mouth. "Oops," she whispers.

"Kane," Drew says like a curse and puts his hands on his hips, looking over to the door like he's tempted to go find his flappy-lipped brother.

"What? My boyfriend can't tell me when his brother is about to move away and take my best friend with him?" She puts her fists on her hips and glares fiercely at him.

Drew turns his dark gray gaze to hers. "Not when it could endanger Jewels's life," he growls.

"Pshaw," Elia gushes, waving her hand. "No one has any idea I'm involved. *No one* is watching my movements."

"And when they find out you're friends with Jewels? What then, Elia?"

Elia's face turns pale. "They'll know we're friends?"

"Aren't you on her social media?" he continues to grill. "Making comments publicly? You don't think they'll look there?"

"Oh," she says in a deflated tone, sinking down onto an ottoman that's conveniently right under her. "I didn't think of that."

"Clearly," Drew mutters and looks away again in deep thought.

"Elia," I say in a rush, "you're going to have to go home, like right now, and pretend you never went anywhere tonight."

She looks up at me with stricken eyes. "What? No, I want to be able to say goodbye."

I give her a sad look. "I can't even say goodbye to my own mom, Leelee. This is going to be the only goodbye I get. At least I get that, thanks to your coming here."

"Really?" She looks over at Drew in question, and he nods his head soberly. Seeing that, she jumps up and wraps me in another hug, squeezing tightly. "Oh my gosh, I can't believe this. You guys are leaving? When? Where?" Pulling back, her eyes tighten. "You know what? Don't tell me, just call me when you get to wherever you're going, and I'll talk you through whatever you'll be feeling. I'm here for you," she says fiercely, gripping my shoulders. "No matter what, I will *always* be here for you." Her eyes flash before they fill with tears.

Mine do the same as we hold each other tightly and weep for our shared loss.

"Oh my gosh, it is so good to see you. Thank you for finding me, Leelee. But," I say, sniffing, pushing her away, "you have to go. It's not safe for you here."

She frowns deeply before she finally nods and, with one last hug, she turns away and walks briskly over to the door.

"Wait!" Drew calls.

She looks over with a hopeful expression, but he only says, "Go out the back way. Try not to be too obvious."

Her face falls, but she nods, giving me one last sad look. Drew takes her to the back door and, just like that, she's gone.

My heart, which is already in a bad state, falls even further, and trying to hold a sob in my throat, I run upstairs to completely lose it.

28. Drew

♥

I could both hug and kill Elia right now.

She shows up completely out of the blue and surprises the heck out of us, which really shouldn't have surprised me at all. I should have turned off Jewel's location on her Snapchat first thing.

But Jewels, at least, was able to see her best friend before we flee. For that, I'm grateful. But if we get caught because Elia couldn't keep her little nose out of my business, I'm going to kill her.

When I let Elia out the back door, I turn around and see Jewels flying up the stairs, choking on tears.

It's the most gut-wrenching sound, and I barely keep myself from following her upstairs. I have a feeling she needs time to unravel all of this.

Wrestling with whether to be a shoulder to cry on or not, I finally can't take it and run upstairs to find her. I don't want her to think she has to go through any of this alone.

If I'm stepping over the line of friendship by doing this, then that's what I'm going to have to do.

Listening intently, it's not hard to follow the muffled sobs coming from one of the bedrooms. Knocking softly, I open the door, happy she didn't lock me out.

Jewels is sitting on the bed, her face in her hands. Her shoulders shake, and the heart-wrenching sound of her tears hits me unmuted. "Jewels," I sigh and go over to her, sitting next to her. I wrap my arms around her and hold her.

In one shuddering sigh, she turns to me and buries her face in my neck. I inhale the sweet vanilla and lavender scent from her still-wet hair and rock her gently as she cries big, ugly sobs. "It's okay. You're going to be okay." Smoothing her hair with my hand, I can only hope to comfort her.

I whisper encouraging words to her over and over, not being able to help but relish holding her in my arms. I just hate that my decision to heal her caused all this pain.

What was I thinking?

I could punch myself for doing this to her. I hold in the rage I'm feeling at myself, so Jewels only feels me relaxed. She doesn't need to know that I'm completely freaking out, too. I'm just better at hiding it.

After a long while, she slumps and pulls away from me, wiping her red, blotched face with both hands. Tears continue to trickle down her face as she looks out the window in thought.

"You okay?" I ask gently, moving hair from her face. Sweat mixed with her tears covers her entire face. My heart clenches at the sight. I felt how warm she got as she fought her panic attack.

Because that's what she finally succumbed to. A full-blown panic attack, and frankly, I'm shocked it didn't happen earlier.

She sighs deeply, hiccupping and shuddering. She holds her body, trying to physically contain her grief. "Yeah, I'll be okay," she says in a broken voice.

"Jewels, I'm so sorry. Will you ever be able to forgive me?"

She raises her teary eyes to mine, and I hold my breath at the lost look she gives me. Pressing her lips together in a thin line, she's quiet for a moment before she blinks and says, "Don't think that some part of this isn't my fault. I knew what you could do. I hoped, no, I prayed for you to heal me." Shaking her head, she continues, fingering the fringes of her pant leg. "I didn't really think you would do it. I mean, I didn't think about the consequences." She blows out a breath in a long sigh.

"I should have considered that you would be in trouble for exposing your secret world. Drew, really you should accept an apology from *me*. If I had been smart, I would have taken one look at you that first time in the clinic and run the other direction. Well," she says, huffing a laugh, "not run, but gotten the heck out of there."

She looks at me with such wonder in her eyes; I wish I were a painter so I could capture the magic of it. She shines with warmth and hope, everything she should not be feeling right now considering the danger we're in. "I'm just as responsible for this new life we're about to embark on. I accept that. I'm just sorry you're stuck with me. But," she says, brightening. "I have faith that we'll be fine. We'll be safe."

She looks down, and I wish she would raise her starry eyes back to mine.

"How?" I croak, completely blown away with her resilience and bravery. "How can you put such a positive spin on this? You," I say, laughing, "are a miracle. And I don't just mean the miracle of your walking. *You*, Jewels, are a miracle of the power of the human spirit. You have caught every terrible thing thrown at you and turned it around."

She shakes her head in a self-conscious way. "No, I have fought every bad thing, believe me," she says, a fierceness coming into her eyes. "I've fought things so hard."

I try to say something, but she raises her hand to stop me. "But that's the beauty of ugly circumstances and our attitudes toward them. Every time I railed against my life, God reminded me of the beauty waiting for me if I just embraced it." She leans in with gleaming eyes, reaching out to hold my hands. "He gifted me with a peace so fragile, yet so strong, I couldn't help but accept the gift for the priceless treasure it was. He does this *every* time. I take my pain to Christ, and He answers with a comfort I can only describe as heavenly. It fills me up so full I practically burst with the..." she stops for a second before she turns her shining eyes to me. "wonder of it. I should be thanking you for so much. You healed me. I didn't thank you for that; instead, I attacked you. You changed the course of your life for the sake of mine. Drew," she says, squeezing my cold fingers. "if you want to go the other direction, accept the punishment of your people and leave me to my fate, I'll accept that. In fact, I urge you to do so. You shouldn't have to leave your job, your family, your life…"

Unable to contain myself, I cup her face in my hands and silence the next ridiculous statement from her lips. I kiss her so soundly, I only hope it communicates what I feel for her. I revel in how amazing and pure she is. It's thrilling when she wraps her arms around my neck and angles her head so she can kiss me the way I've dreamed she would. There's no hesitancy, nothing unsure about her movements. She runs her hands through my hair, and I shudder at the feel of her soft lips and kiss her deeply. I pull away when I start to want more than I should. Resting my forehead on hers, my chest heaves. "You are both my kryptonite and rarest diamond. Jewels, tell me to stop."

She inhales shakily and bites her lip.

"That is not helping," I growl before I claim her lips again. After several blissful moments, I break away and tear myself off the bed, striding to the door in two long steps. I can't look at my temptation anymore. Putting my hand on the doorframe, I say without turning around, "I'm going to do some research on our new location. Goodnight."

And as hard as it is, I leave her and head downstairs. I intend to do whatever it takes to keep our relationship innocent. It's only then that I realize we never ate our hastily thrown together dinner.

29. Jewels

W hen Drew practically runs from the room, I sit in stunned silence for several minutes. Then I put my fingertips to my lips and remember what just happened. Drew kissed me when I told him he should leave and live his life.

He wants to live his life with me. That much is obvious. *But why?*

What makes me worth that gift? I've given him nothing except my optimism, which he seems to love so much. I sit back, thinking over that statement. It's such a simple thing to think positively about something. What's the alternative? Crash into dark places you'll never find your way out of?

Been there and done that.

No more, though. I've experienced enough dark days to know it's not worth the aftermath of sludging through crushing depression and negativity. Instead, I raise my chin high after I've spent time in prayer. That's what happens after I take my issues to God. He uplifts me to such a degree that I can find the beauty in any situation.

Even when there's not much to look at, there's always beauty to be discovered in God's love. He gives me peace and comfort only He can offer.

I wrap my arms around my waist and hug my middle. Despite my fierce intention to stay positive, I feel terror and uncertainty creep into my thoughts.

Shaking my head, I banish them with a prayer.

God, give me Your assurance that You're here, right here, right now. I am not alone. You knew this day would come, and You're holding me tight.

Touching my fingers to my lips that still feel the imprint of Drew's, I add, *And help me to resist Drew Ashcroft.* I raise my hand and raise my pinky, forefinger and thumb, holding up my hand. *Thank you, Lord. For so much.*

I fall back onto the pillows and relive the last five minutes. Drew is the most tempting and delicious addiction I've ever had. He could talk about quantum physics, and I would still hang on every word. I can't even help myself. I've fallen so hard for this man, I don't think I'll ever recover from the way he's taken over my world.

I put my hand on the butterflies that haven't left my stomach since he came into this room. But then I remember my mom. She's devastated I'm leaving, and I should be, too, but I can't help but want to follow Drew anywhere. I shoot her a text assuring her I'm fine.

Once I get a response acknowledging my message, I roll over onto my stomach. *What happened to my independent spirit? The one who wants to become a lawyer?*

Drew's promise, though, that I won't have to abandon that dream; will take some careful planning and an identity change. *What has happened to my world? An identity change?*

I went from being a patient of ten different doctors to living a spy thriller mixed with a Marvel movie. Living undercover and hiding from a group of Elementals with superpowers has become my life.

I'm supposed to do all of this with a man who is so gorgeous he literally takes my breath away every time he walks into a room. All while I maintain a pure lifestyle and keep my hands to myself.

Well, I think. Maybe I don't have to keep my hands all to myself. I can handle a kiss or two. Though after what's happened twice today, maybe even that isn't such a good idea.

I put my pillow over my head and scream into it. That releases some of my tension, but it doesn't take care of all of it.

The only thing I can do for myself is try to go to sleep. So, crawling under the covers, I resolve to put this day behind me. I have a feeling it's going to be a long and frustrating night.

I hate when I'm right.

After what feels like hours, I finally fall into a fitful sleep. My dreams are chased by plant-wielding and fire-breathing Elementals. I don't even know if they can breathe fire, but dragons they become. Dreams are surreal at most, but when I wake up, I shudder at how real that one felt. It certainly reflected some of the truth.

I start to get up as I always have, by rolling over to get out of bed. But when I feel how smooth the movement is and how *painless* it is, I gasp. I sit up so quickly my head spins.

It's true. I'm healed. Because of Drew's God-given gifts, my back is perfect.

Swinging my legs over the bed, I jump up and run all over the room. After two laps, I laugh. I laugh like someone who, for so long, had plenty of reasons to cry. I laugh so hard, tears stream down my face.

I'm leaning over, holding my belly, when Drew bursts into my room, looking wild with worry. In two strides, he's over to me, grabbing me by the shoulders, straightening me up. He looks me all over and finally asks, "What's wrong? Are you hurting again?"

Hiccupping, I say in spurts, "No...I'm happy. Drew, I can...walk...all by myself."

He blinks. "I know."

Giggling, I lean my head into his chest and continue to snicker.

"It's just so great. Until I met you, I never thought I would be able to run around my room."

"Is that what you were doing? I heard your footsteps, and I thought you were running from someone." He blows out a breath.

Looking up at him, with tears making my eyes shine and my face a wet mess, I must look rough. But Drew only looks at me softly. Now that his worry is gone, a certain heat I've come to recognize in his eyes has returned.

I hold my breath. *Is he going to kiss me again? It looks like he's going to kiss me. I haven't brushed my teeth yet, though...*

At the horrible possibility of him kissing me without that vitally important detail done, I duck out of his arms and run to the bathroom, giggling all the way because I can run away from him like I wanted to in the coffee shop.

"I'm really starting to worry about you," he calls after me.

"I'm good, I swear!"

"I don't think I believe you," he says after following me.

I left the bathroom door open, and when I see him looking on in amusement as I put toothpaste on my finger, I shut the door in his face.

Great. Now he knows I'm embarrassed about him kissing me before I brushed my teeth.

"Hey, I need to go to the store. Do you want to go?" he calls at me through the door.

Rinsing my mouth out, I answer, "Yes, there are a few things I need."

"Great, I'll be downstairs."

I quickly finish my toiletries and find him downstairs waiting for me.

"Fresh as a daisy," he comments with appreciation.

I blush and tuck a stray hair behind my ear. Then, I run my hands down my shirt trying to get the wrinkles out from sleeping in it.

He hands me a hat and puts one on himself. After he does a visual check of the perimeter of the house, we both get in the car. I can't help but be a little nervous driving around in the Ashcroft car, knowing we can be tracked in it. I send up a quick prayer that our grocery trip is uneventful.

We make it to the store, and for the sake of time, we split up to find what we both need. Drew tells me he's going to find the fruits and vegetables, and I go down the bathroom aisle. I'm looking for the particular shampoo I like to use when someone walks behind me, slowing down considerably. Out of the corner of my eye, I see it's a burly guy with a ball cap on who looks intently at his phone, then he glances at me. He does this twice, and I turn to fully hide my face, but whatever he saw must have satisfied him because he stops and stays close, seeming to study the deodorants.

Unnerved, I inch my way away from him, but when he glances at me again, with an intent look in his eye, I fully turn and walk quickly away.

His footsteps are silent, but I can feel his presence following me. It's confirmed he's behind me when he talks low into his phone.

Looking frantically around to find the produce section, I turn left and wildly hope it's in that direction. My heart pounds violently in my chest, and I'm speed walking when I reach the end of the aisle, my hopes crashing when I find myself in the bakery.

Taking a chance that the produce section is to the left of the bakery, I look over my shoulder and see the big guy is still behind me.

Fear careening through me, I crash into a body that's like a wall of muscle. I look up into eyes black as night. The man holds onto my arms and doesn't seem like he's going to let me go. Wrenching away from him, I open my mouth to scream when he says in a low voice, "Don't."

That just makes me want to scream even more, and I back up, only to find myself wedged between the new threat and the old one.

"It's best if you come quietly," the man with the black eyes says, reaching for my arm.

"Never in a million years," I spit out.

The guy smirks. "Not sure you have much choice."

I open my mouth to scream when he reaches into his pocket with his other hand, pulling out poppyseed formula. I look with dread to see it glistening up at me. Shaking my head wildly, I peer up at him in horror.

He would give me that here?

Closing my mouth, I debate my options, and just when I'm about to risk it and yell my guts out, Drew is by my side.

"Is there a problem here?" he says, scowling.

"You know there is," the first goon at my back says.

"Why don't we continue this discussion outside?" Drew asks in a hard voice.

The guy grunts, closing his fist of toxic powder and puts Drew and me between him and the other guy as we walk outside. "Don't even think of trying anything stupid," he says, directing his attention to Drew.

"We've said the formula doesn't work on her," Drew says lowly with heat. "Why won't you listen?"

"We make our own decisions. You've lost your right to any opinions anyway," the guy with the hat says to my right.

They lead us quickly outside, and I give a frantic look to Drew, who returns it with a grim one of his own.

"Hold on to them," the guy with the dark eyes instructs the other one. "We don't want them getting away."

When a hand wraps around my arm in an iron grip, true fear chokes my throat. *What's going to happen? Where are they taking us?*

We're deep in the parking lot with no witnesses. All looks lost. Then, Drew gives me a warning look before he thrashes in the hands of the guy holding him. I'm let go so they both can contain Drew. But that seems to be what Drew wants because once both guys are wrestling with him, he places his hands over their hearts and blasts them with some kind of power. Their faces turn white, and they fall to the ground.

Drew turns to me, grabbing my hand. He yells, "I stopped their hearts, but that'll only last a second. Let's go!" He grabs my arm and races to the edge of the parking lot where a heavily wooded area waits.

"Drew, why aren't we taking the car?" I breathlessly ask as Drew leads us into the dark arms of the packed fir trees.

"That's how they found us in the first place," he says as he weaves us around the trees. I do my best to keep up with him but, in my terror, find myself tripping easily.

Noticing my issues, he turns and holds my arm as he guides me through the trees.

"How are we going to get back to the house?" I ask, appreciating his help, placing my feet better around the roots with his help.

"I have an excellent sense of direction. We'll lose them and Uber back."

We fall silent as we glide through the trees, Drew seeming to know where he's going.

Just when I have a false sense of safety, a root shoots past my head. "Duck!" I scream and Drew obeys, barely missing getting skewered with the projectile.

As the root retreats, it wraps around my ankle, taking me down. I fall hard, my breath getting knocked from me.

"Jewels!" Drew is at my side, his eyes blazing behind me as he puts his hand on the root. "I can't get you free. I'm going to have to fight."

I can only watch as Drew stands and faces off against the two men who tracked us here.

"You won't get your hands on us to try that little trick again," the guy with the ball cap says, rubbing his chest. His look is murderous.

"I won't have to," Drew growls before he sweeps his arm around and an entire small pine rips out of the ground. He barrels it straight at the men.

It's big enough to knock them both to the ground. One rolls and is on his feet in the next moment, ripping a root out of the ground.

I look down at the root around my ankle to see if I can help, but it holds strong. I curse in frustration.

The root comes down at Drew like a whip and hits him on the head, knocking him to the ground. Drew shakes his head, wraps his hand around the root from the ground and, with his arm trembling, he tries to wrest the root from his attacker.

By now the second man has come around and, with a twin set of roots, shoots them at Drew, wrapping him up like a snake.

Drew struggles, but no matter how hard he strains, he can't get free. Looking at me with desperation, he focuses all his will on the root around my ankle. Strain shows on his face until the root finally loosens.

I quickly get out of the binding and hide behind a tree while the men keep their attention on Drew, who's firing small bushes at them. He can't seem to do as much with the use of only one arm. The two guys duck under his onslaught, but they only laugh. Rage fuels me as I creep from tree to tree until I get close to the dark-eyed man.

I have an idea, but it's crazy.

It's our only option to be free, so I continue sneaking up behind the dark-eyed man, who's busy laughing at Drew's attempts to free himself. With soft steps, I'm at the man's back. Praying I remember the right one, I reach into his pocket and, when my hand finds the powder, I breathe softly in relief.

"What the..." the man says. He turns, but I've pulled out a handful. His face is right where I want it as I blow the noxious stuff directly into it. He drops his hands, coughing violently.

The other man swears, but I'm at him in the next step, doing the same thing to him I did to the first one. With his hands occupied with roots, he can't fling them to protect his face. Breathing it all in, he coughs in fits, bending over.

With them both incapacitated, I run over to Drew and rip the loosened roots off him.

Blood runs down his face, but his grin is fierce. "Great thinking, Emerald."

Pulling him up, he looks around to the background music of hoarse hacking. Both guys are on the ground, limp as rag dolls.

"How do you like it?" I fire at them before Drew pulls me away.

Drew only grins and, with seeming no problem with direction, takes me away from the nightmare scene. I certainly don't want to witness their suffering.

"That was pure brilliance, Ruby. It doesn't affect us as much as humans, but they'll experience the effects of it for a while," Drew praises.

Warmth spreads through my body. "It was the only thing I could think of doing."

"Brilliant," he says again, and squeezes my hand he's pulling.

We walk for what feels like an hour until we reach a road.

I look all around but don't recognize a thing. That doesn't seem to be Drew's concern, though. He pulls out his phone, types in something, and then after several moments, he pockets it.

"Our ride will be here in fifteen minutes." Then he's back on his phone typing when I look at him with surprise.

"That fast?"

He nods. "We're only on the outskirts of town."

I pace, not able to help myself. Drew catches me by the waist on one of my passes. "Emerald," he sighs, pulling me to him in a hug. "We're okay, and we're going to be fine. We just need to make it to the safe house."

"And then what? We have no car, Drew."

His gray eyes dive into mine. "Hey, I've got that all figured out already. That was the only way they could track us, so I'll just have my parents buy us another car, something they won't recognize."

I push him away, but he refuses to let me go. "Drew, they can't just buy a car!"

He shrugs. "Why not?"

I splutter. "Because that's a lot of money."

"They'll just sell the one we left behind."

"And pray tell, how will they get that car back?"

"Ruby, calm down. I've already texted them the address. They're on their way to pick it up. They'll take it directly to a lot, sell it, and buy a new one."

All resistance falls away, and I slump in his arms. I narrow my eyes at him. "You have this all figured out, don't you?"

"I am a quick thinker. Any more arguments?"

Shaking my head, I lay it on Drew's shoulder, the stress of the morning hitting me all of the sudden. He rubs my back in soothing circles.

When a car pulls up, Drew lets me go only to let me get in.

Facing the window, I wonder what's next on this crazy train.

30. Jewels

We make it home with no problems, thank God, and I run inside as quickly as I can. I never want to leave our safe haven again. But I know we'll have to eventually.

I curl up in an armchair, well away from the windows, and try to put this morning behind me. But we could get caught at any time. That terrifies me, and I don't know how to stop worrying. I take my wild concerns to God. It's all I can do.

Drew makes us lunch by warming up last night's dinner we didn't eat.

To destress a little, when I set the table, I tear off two paper towels and fold them in an intricate pattern. My origami skills were one of the ways I emptied my mind of what was bothering me. I make two birds and delicately place them on the table by the silverware. The paper towels are cheap and thin, but they hold up well.

As Drew heats up the sausage on the pan, he calls over his shoulder, "Are you too worked up for coffee?"

"At lunchtime?"

He shrugs. "Why not?"

I turn and hunt down the ingredients. I mutter, "Must be an Elemental thing."

He chuckles. "To have coffee at midday? I'm human enough to love coffee anytime."

I measure out the coffee grounds and set it to percolate. To take my mind off what happened this morning, I ask, "How does that work, anyway? Where did you guys come from? Elementals, I mean?"

He thinks for a moment while he shakes the pan to flip the sautéing sausages, his movements sure and confident. "The human race did start with only Adam and Eve. But as the world populated, humans weren't taking care of the land like God wanted. So, he made a race of Elementals who could."

My forehead furrows. "Did He start with two people like Adam and Eve? Or was it more on a grand scale?"

He looks over his shoulder. "The latter. He had to have the four elements represented. So, he blessed an entire village with all the gifts, commanding them to keep their new powers secret from everyone else."

"When did this happen?" I ask, fascinated with his story and also fully appreciating the scent of sausage in the air.

"We're not sure, but we think over 2,000 years ago."

"That's the time Jesus was on the Earth."

He nods. "The oldest writings we have are around that time, yes. But we think it was a remote village somewhere in Europe. That was how the first Elementals stayed secret for so long. Then, they grew in numbers and spread to other lands."

He continues, "We don't have much written down about our gifts, to keep them from falling into the wrong hands. They're heavily guarded, but we think there was a group of Elementals on the Santa Maria."

My brows raise. "Christopher Columbus's ship?"

He nods.

"Elementals have been in America that long?"

"Yes. We also think a village of indigenous people were given elemental gifts, too. Either that or a ship made its way over to America or Canada long before the Santa Maria. We're not sure."

"Are all Native Americans Elementals?"

"No, they're mixed. They're the only ones who intermarry with humans and tell them their secret. They also haven't separated into clans like we have in the United States and across the world."

My eyebrows raise. "Are you saying they have all the powers?"

"Gifts. We call them gifts. And yes, many of them are mixed Elementals."

"That's amazing," I breathe.

"It really is," he says, carrying two plates of steaming sausage and macaroni and cheese to the table.

I bring two cups of coffee over and set them down carefully.

He sits too and looks at my napkin origami with awe. "What's this?"

I shrug. "When I was little, I needed to find things I could do sitting down. Origami became one of my hobbies. It's also one of the things that calms my mind down," I add.

"From today."

I nod, quiet.

"I'm sorry that happened, Emerald. But God took care of us. And He will continue to do so."

"Drew," I argue, "we could easily get caught again."

He shakes his head. "There's no way they'll find us here."

I grip my napkin in frustration, crumpling my bird. "How can you be so sure?"

He eyes my crushed bird and says in a gentle voice. "No one else knows about this house. I promise you. They will not find us."

"What about after? You can't promise we're forever safe."

He presses his lips together. "You're right. There are no guarantees. There's a point zero five percent fluke chance we'll be found. But, Jewels, do you trust that I'll protect you?"

I bite my lip. I watched two guys defeat him just today, but I know I'm not being fair. He did everything he could to protect me. I sigh quietly. "I do trust you. I'm just worried."

He leans in, his eyes molten silver. "You are safe. Trust me."

I nod, knowing there's not much else I can do. "Although I would like to get my hands on some more of that poppyseed formula."

He cracks a smile. "I'll see what I can do." With that conversation behind us, he picks his origami bird up carefully, turning it one way and then the other. "Sapphire, this is amazing." His eyes are wide, and he gives me an awed look.

I blush. "It's nothing."

Drew places the bird back on the table like it's a piece of delicate crystal. "I can't use this napkin. I'm going to get another one."

He's up so fast I don't have time to protest before he's back in his seat with a paper towel on his lap. He pulls the bird toward him.

"You can't keep that bird, Drew."

He picks up his fork. "Watch me."

"Drew, I can make you a more durable one. Please don't try to keep that."

He forks up a mouthful of macaroni. "It's the first gift you've ever given me. So, I'm keeping it. You want to say grace?"

I nod, frowning at the floppy paper towel bird sitting next to his plate. I bow my head and say, "Lord, help us to enjoy the *appropriate things* well and help this food nourish our bodies." Drew snickers, and I breathe out and continue, "Thank you, Father, for protecting us from the Gyan men. That could have gone disastrously, but You didn't allow it. We thank You, Father. Please, God, keep us safe and hidden. Don't let the Gyans find us again. Guide us on our monumental journey and bless our next steps. Amen."

Drew says amen, and we dig into our lunch.

When the first bite hits my tongue, I moan in bliss, not realizing how hungry I was. I've taken two more bites when I realize Drew's not eating. I look up at him and he's frozen, watching me, like a hawk.

There's an intent in his eyes that makes me all gooey and boneless. Forcing myself to break his magnetic gaze, I ask, "Um, well, what are our next steps?"

After a moment, he finally starts eating and says around a mouthful of food. "We need to lie low today, but we really should think about leaving tomorrow."

My stomach clenches, this time with anxiety. "That soon? Where do you think we should go?"

"I need to be in a Gyan community, and I found one in Arkansas that has a great law school you could eventually go to."

I look up quickly, a piece of sausage halfway to my mouth. "A law school?"

He nods, spearing his food with his fork. "Yes, it shouldn't be too hard to get into, and that way we can stay there for a while. It's part of the University of Arkansas."

I nod slowly, chewing thoughtfully. "Do they have a medical program, too?"

He nods, polishing off his plate. "They do. It's perfect for us."

Us. How did that happen? I can't believe I'm even considering this.

I'm quiet as I finish my lunch. I almost have to force myself to finish because my stomach had turned.

"I don't know how my parents are going to get your credits transferred over to a new identity. You might have to start over," he says in a quiet voice. He seems to read my silence correctly. "Is that going to be okay?"

I shrug my shoulders, not looking at him.

"And we'll have to think of a new name for you."

This time, I snap my head up. I feel the blood run out of my cheeks. "Who will I be?"

He smiles gently at me. "That's completely up to you. Who do you want to be?"

I look back down at my plate. "I want to be myself."

I see Drew move his plate away from him, leaning his arms onto the table. "You *will* be. That won't change."

"Can't I still be Jewels?" Having my identity ripped from me suddenly feels very real, and it *hurts*.

He looks away thoughtfully. "Maybe. Your real name is Julia, so we could make your fake name, Jewels."

"I'd like that."

And just like that, I've agreed both to keep and to change my name. This is getting realer by the second.

31. Drew

After lunch, Jewels grows quiet, and I allow her space to think. She needs time to settle into the idea of this new life, and all that happened today. I know it's a lot to process. Nothing I can say will help her do that quicker.

So, I work with Vela, texting her while she sends coded messages to my parents, making arrangements for new licenses and social security cards. It takes most of the morning, but I comfort myself that Jewels and I will come together for dinner.

I'm thankful for my parents' help in all of this, too. They picked up the car at the grocery store and took it right to a car lot, selling it and buying another one. They're having it delivered so no one can follow them to this house.

Jewels was on the phone with her mom a good portion of the day, letting her know what to pack up that she will want when we set up in Arkansas. Elementals visited her mom two more times, checking to see if Jewels had returned.

I'm so thankful for this safe house. Who knows where the Grand Elder's people would have sent Jewels. She would have dropped off the grid.

The way she trudges around the house, downcast and slouching, I want nothing more than to fold her in my arms and comfort her, but I'm not sure it's me who she needs right now. She's mourning her life here, and I know only God can truly comfort her. She's distanced herself from me, and I respect her need for space, though I find myself following her with my eyes.

I'm grateful we found some clothes to borrow. My professor's wife had some casual clothes that fit Jewels pretty well, and I picked out some old jeans and a shirt. We tried to take things that were way in the back of the closet, so the items wouldn't be missed when the owners return.

I find a two-bedroom apartment to rent in Fayetteville, and give the address to Vela to give to my parents to send our new ID cards.

I was relieved to find phone chargers that worked for both our phones in my parents' car. We needed some charger blocks my professor had in his home, so I added those to the list of items I wrote on a note to leave for my professor, promising to repay him for his kindness.

By the time I'm satisfied with our progress, it's dinner time. I had groceries delivered, having learned my lesson the last time I went to pick up ingredients myself.

Jewels is at the sink, drinking a glass of water, when I find her. I see her profile and take a moment to enjoy the view. She's standing in a ray of soft light. The evening sun touches her cheeks just right to make her look ethereal. I think of her again as a pixie. She fits the bill for one so well. She's studying something outside the window above the sink, and I wonder what's captivated her.

"What'cha looking at?" I ask softly, not wanting to startle her.

She jumps anyway and spins to face me. Putting her hand on her chest, she says breathlessly, "You scared me."

I smile. "I would say I'm sorry, but I enjoyed the view too much."

She blushes and looks down. "I was too. I mean, not you...outside. I was enjoying the view out there."

I step toward her and look over her shoulder to see what could have gotten her interest. Seeing nothing particularly intriguing, just small pine trees and the neighbor's shed, I give her a quizzical look.

She explains, "I was just wondering how much of our world's beauty should be attributed to your people."

"We have a lot to do with the health of our world, inanimate and animate."

When she cocks her head at me, I say, "The things you see and don't see are all in our scope to heal and to maintain. What you see on the ground — the plant life, the rivers, the lakes and oceans — we take care of, but also under the layer of the earth is our terrain, too."

Her eyebrows rise, and I proudly elaborate, "When we feed our energy into the topsoil, it sinks into the Earth, blessing it. Gyans can feed direct energy to the subterrain, too. But we don't have to do it often."

"How do the natural disasters work then, if nature is supposedly so happy and content? It certainly doesn't seem that way when nature strikes out in tornadoes, floods, and earthquakes."

I give her an understanding look. "You're right." That's her way of saying we're not doing our job. "But sometimes, unfortunately, we are responsible for those disturbances."

She frowns. "Oh, right, you guys fight each other with your gifts, in huge magnitudes."

"Unfortunately, yes. We're hoping that now that Vela is the Chosen One, she will unite the clans so we can get back to our God-assigned duty of helping the Earth work as it's intended."

She smiles softly, the line between her eyes easing. "I really am so proud of her. She is amazing. Always has been. She's one of the people I've been so impressed with."

I return her smile. "Doesn't surprise me. Vela is a compassionate person. Who was the first one to impress you?" I ask, suddenly curious if it was another Elemental.

"It was Linc, actually. He came right up to me and offered to help me when I was trying to walk around something."

A sudden zing of jealousy fires through me. "Linc, huh?"

She looks at me quickly. "He was incredibly kind. He still is, I mean."

"Sounds like you have a little crush on Vela's husband." I look away. I'm not surprised. The guy was a hot commodity. When he came to Breckenridge, he made quite a splash in the Elemental and human community.

"Not at all," she says hotly. Her eyes are wide as she looks at me. "He's a friend, Drew. And that's all. Wait, are you *jealous*?"

I shrug and then look at her directly. "Should I be?"

"I just said no. Wait, are we a we?" she gestures between us.

"I hope that we will be."

At my direct admission, she snaps her lips shut and just stares at me.

I step toward her. "That really shouldn't surprise you, Onyx."

She tries to step back, but bumps into the sink.

On the prowl now, I approach slowly, giving her plenty of time to run away, like she did this morning when I was about to kiss her.

She doesn't move.

Smiling widely, I crowd her, putting my hands on either side of her on the counter, boxing her in.

She leans back, but there's nowhere for her to go. Her eyes widen when I move toward her, and just when it seems I'm about to kiss her, I lean close and whisper in her ear, "Will you be my girl, Onyx?"

She shivers, and I run my nose up along the column of her throat.

"Is that a good idea? We'll be in such close proximity, won't we?" she asks breathlessly.

I nod, kissing her throat softly.

Her throat moves as she swallows. "Then what happens when we fight?"

I kiss her smooth skin again. "Then we'll make up." I smile at the feel of goosebumps on my lips.

She gasps. "Umm, Drew, I don't think I should live in the same space as you if you're going to do things like this."

I run my nose up her throat again and say against the corner of her lips. "What if I get you your own apartment?"

She nods violently, her lips rubbing against mine with the movement.

Before I finally kiss her, I ask, "So, you'll be my girl?"

"You make a very convincing argument," she whispers.

"You won't regret it." Unable to hold myself back any longer, I mold my lips to hers. When I feel her dropping, I grip her arms, holding her up while I continue to kiss her, tasting and sealing our agreement. At that thought, I break the kiss. "Was that a yes?" I say against her lips.

She kisses me in answer.

I pull back, needing a vocal answer. "You're going to need to say it, Onyx."

"Why do you only call me Onyx when you're kissing me?"

I cock my head to look into her eyes. "Because I like to remember the color of your eyes darkening even more when I'm kissing your mouth. I like how much I affect you."

She smiles. "I like it, too."

"Onyx," I say in a deep voice. "You haven't said it yet."

She peeks up at me, giving me a teasing glance. "What?" She smiles.

I'm a breath away when I growl.

She laughs. "I'm sorry. Yes, I will be your girl. Now, can we continue?"

Needing no more encouragement, I angle my head and give her a kiss so intense, I can only moan in contentment. When she returns my kiss with just as much passion, I have to force myself to step back.

Holding up my hands, I say hoarsely, "We'll need to set some boundaries."

She nods fervently and steps forward, her eyes locked on my lips. Her own lips swollen from my attentions.

"We also need to respect each other enough to stop when the other wants to."

That freezes her. "Do you want to stop?"

I lick my lips, which only makes her gaze more tortured. "Honestly, no. And that's why I think it's wise that we do."

Her shoulders slump, but she nods. "Okay, that's probably for the best. You just bring out the worst in me."

I smile crookedly. "I disagree. I think I just found the best in you."

She frowns at me, crossing her arms. "You would say that."

I nod. "I would."

She huffs and rubs her face with both hands. "Okay, so what are we doing? Are we leaving tomorrow?"

Pulling my focus from the beautiful girl before me requires my turning away and taking deep breaths to cool my body down. "Actually, I think it's best we leave tonight."

"What?" she asks. "Tonight?"

I look over my shoulder at her. "Once we clean up from dinner and get our things together, yes. It will be safer if we leave while it's dark. I'll drive through the night. The new car's already been delivered."

A small frown shows her displeasure.

"Are you ready for this, Ruby?"

She hugs her middle. "I guess I'll have to be."

"I'll get a simple dinner made. While I'm doing that, will you go and make the beds? We don't have time to wash the sheets, unfortunately. But we can be sure to leave the house clean and tidy."

She nods, leaving the room with a troubled look on her face.

I'm tempted to chase her down and continue our previous activity, but I know I have more pressing things to do. So I stay put, surprised at my strength of will. I whip up an easy marinara and pasta, pan-frying some chicken to go with it.

By the time Jewels comes back into the kitchen, she looks a little revived, which makes me glad.

"I'm ready," she announces, then sniffs appreciatively. "Smells good in here."

"Thank you," I say, dishing up two bowls of pasta and chicken, covering them with the sauce.

When we sit down, Jewels asks, "Can I say grace?"

"Of course."

She bows her head, breathes in slowly through her nose and then says, "Lord, we come before You tonight with nerves tight and anxiety constantly trying to steal our joy. You are a God who holds no room for fear in Your mighty hands. We ask for You to go before us on our journey. Continue to keep us safe and protected. Divert any problems and gift us with a safe journey to Arkansas. And, Lord, bless our time there. We ask for favor. Thank You for all You've done, all You're doing, and all You're going to do. Amen."

A full peace settles over me like a cloak with her prayer. I keep my head bowed for one more moment as I bask in God's presence. He fills the entire room with his Holy presence. "Thank you, Lord," I whisper before I open my eyes and see Jewels's soft smile of contentment. I can only ask, "What?"

"I love that you love Jesus."

"Ditto."

We gaze at each other for a moment, then she finally breaks eye contact and digs into her meal. I wait for her response to the first taste and am not disappointed. Her eyes drift closed as she sighs in foodie bliss, which makes me tear my eyes off her and start my own dinner.

"This is possibly the best thing I've ever tasted. I'm so thankful I don't have to avoid gluten anymore. Or you." She peeks up at me.

Jewels Patterson is the biggest temptress who's ever crossed my path. I'm going to have to take precautions to protect us both from letting temptation run wild.

God, help me.

32. Jewels

After a quick dinner and cleanup, we throw our meager possessions into plastic shopping bags, hop into the car, and get on the road. I whisper prayers of protection and comfort. The further we get from home, the more my heart pulls, missing my mom. I'm in agony that I couldn't tell her goodbye in person.

Calling her is my only option, so that's what I do. She answers after two rings.

"Julia, is everything okay?"

"Yes...I'm just letting you know we left."

She's silent, but when she talks, her voice sounds upbeat. "Okay, this is the next step for you. Enjoy every moment."

It's obvious she's trying, so I do the same. "Yeah, of course. I'm looking forward to seeing my new home."

"I've already ordered some things for you. I used the new address Drew gave me. I'm glad you've each gotten your own place. That's wise."

"Thanks, Mom."

"And, Julia, I don't need to tell you to be careful with that boy. Even with your own place, you're going to have a lot of alone time. Don't forget your morals. You've always stood by them. Don't let a guy break them down."

I feel pretty awkward talking about him sitting right next to me, but I have to answer my mom. "He would never do that, Mom. He feels the same way I do."

"Good. Now, I have a blessing for you. Put me on speaker so Drew can hear it."

I switch the call to speaker mode and hold the phone between Drew and me.

"*The Lord bless you and keep you, the Lord make his face shine upon you; the Lord turn his face toward you and give you peace.*" *Numbers 6:24-26.*

I let God's Word hold in the car for a moment before I say, "Thank you, Momma."

"I love you, honey. Take care of yourself. Both of you."

Drew replies in a solemn voice, "I'll be sure to watch over her, Clarissa."

"Be sure you do, young man. I'm depending on you."

"Yes, ma'am."

"Bye, Momma, I love you."

"And I love you to the moon and back."

I smile and hang up, looking at my phone for a long moment.

"You okay?" Drew asks, reaching for my hand.

"Yeah," I say, sighing, lacing my fingers through his and holding tight.

"I love that blessing. It was apt for the moment, don't you think?"

I chuckle. "Yes, she always gave me that blessing if I ever went anywhere without her. Like a trip. Those didn't happen often, but I always felt I was under her and God's protection whenever she said that prayer."

We fall into easy conversation for hours, and I find I love knowing things about Drew he's never told anyone. Like what it feels like to heal and grow things. I thought it would feel like a burst of power, but he says it's a subtle heat that saturates whatever he touches. I also learn that his favorite color is yellow, which shouldn't surprise me, but it does. He says, "It's one of the many reasons you captivated me. You were like a ray of warm sunshine."

We talk about a million and one things, and the air is full of laughter and embarrassing moans at our early teen years. Barely halfway into the trip, though, he's forced to stop to rest at around one in the morning.

"I'm sorry I can't help with driving," I say with a frown.

He parks at a rest stop somewhere in Kansas and lays his seat all the way down. He turns to look at me. "Don't worry about it, Sapphire. It would have been difficult for you to drive before a couple of days ago."

I cross my arms. "I know. But it's hard to watch you so tired."

"It's safer if we stop. My eyes were closing against my will. At least we're halfway there."

I turn to lie on my side, curling my legs up under me in my reclined seat. "Will you teach me how to drive?"

At my question, his eyes pop open. "Of course. I'd love to teach you."

I sigh, happy for the moment. "I've always wanted to learn how. I just didn't trust my legs well enough. There are cars with hand controls in addition to the pedals, but my mom could never afford one for me."

His eyes widen. "Really? How do those work?"

"Huh? Oh, they have levers you operate with your hands. It's really cool." I yawn, and my eyes slide closed.

"You continue to surprise me, Onyx."

This time, my eyes pop open. I find him studying me with darkening gray eyes. He's giving me *that* look. Is he about to kiss me?

Sure enough, he leans toward me. "A goodnight kiss?"

I nod suddenly very warm.

Unlike our past kisses, this time his lips barely caress mine, lingering for just a moment. Breaking away, he rubs his stubbled cheek against mine, and I breathe him in. He smells clean and musky at the same time, and the result makes me weak in the knees.

"You never cease to amaze me," he breathes and then kisses me on my forehead.

Though I wish he would go back to my lips, he pulls away and lies back down, putting his arm over his eyes.

I watch him as he tries to sleep, thinking he can't see me.

"I feel your eyes on me. Stop looking at me like that, Temptress."

I laugh. "Oh, first I'm Onyx, now I'm Temptress."

"Yes," he grumbles. "That's your alter ego. And I need you to go back to being Cute Pixie Ruby."

"Pixie?" I ask, my eyes popping open.

He smiles with his eyes still closed. "Yes," he says tiredly. "I always thought you looked like one."

"Is that a good thing?"

"A very good one. Now go to sleep," he orders.

I pout but settle into my seat, obediently closing my eyes, smiling to myself.

When I drift off to sleep, I dream of nothing but gray eyes and snuggling into warm hugs. When I wake up, I'm surprised to find myself in Drew's arms.

During sleep, he had shifted himself so he's between our seats. His hip rests on the center console, and his shoulder leans into my seat. He's pulled me completely against him. It must be an uncomfortable position for him, but when I look up, he's sound asleep.

Without moving, I look out the windshield and see it's morning. I'm guessing about eight o'clock. Needing no encouragement, I snuggle into Drew's chest, perfectly happy with the situation.

At my movement, he jerks awake with a gasp. He lets go of me, looking down in confusion. "How did we end up here?"

I shrug. "I have no idea. I woke up like this."

He slides over to his side of the car, stretching as much as he can in the cramped space. His back cracks, and I gasp. "Drew, you shouldn't have held me like that."

He turns to me. "I didn't know I did." He looks away, embarrassed. "I'm sorry I accosted you in your sleep."

I put my hand on his arm. "You don't need to apologize. I loved it. I woke up very happy."

"Good." He looks around and sees we're one of only two cars parked in the parking lot. "Did you notice anything weird out here?"

I shake my head. "No, it's been totally fine."

He nods, studies the surrounding area and then opens the door. "Let's use the restroom and get going."

I grab the toothbrush and toothpaste Drew had delivered from the store and then open my door. As we walk toward the bathroom, the person from the other car passes us as he returns to his car.

Drew stiffens, and he grabs my hand. I look back alarmingly at the guy who just passed us. "Don't look at him," Drew says harshly.

I whip my head back around.

"Was he looking at us?" he asks.

"No, he was just walking."

He sets his mouth in a grim line. "That was a Festan."

"A what?"

"Festan," he says in a low voice, even though no one is around.

"What's that?"

"A Fire Elemental. It's weird he didn't even look twice at me. We've been enemies for centuries."

I force myself not to turn back around and to keep walking to the bathroom, puzzling over the guy's lack of reaction to a sworn enemy.

After using the bathroom and brushing my teeth, I emerge to find Drew leaning against the concrete block wall waiting for me.

My heart warms at the sight of him. He really takes my breath away. He's so breathtakingly beautiful. I wonder what he sees in me. I have average looks at best. But at his warm smile, I blush because he makes me feel beautiful.

He takes me by the hand, and we walk back to the car. I'm thankful to see the Festan's car is gone. We slide into our seats, and Drew maneuvers back onto the interstate.

"Why do you think that guy didn't even look twice at you?" I ask.

He frowns. "I guess it's Vela's influence as the Chosen Child. A lot of Elementals are moving into other clans. In fact, boundaries are slowly disappearing. That's just the first time I've experienced it."

I mull that over, and then the talk turns to parts of his world I could have only dreamt of before.

In the middle of his explanation of how water elementals fight, I ask, "You're telling me that a water elemental can not only shoot ice spears and ice bombs, they can freeze someone's blood inside their body?"

He quirks a smile at me. "How else would they do it if not in their bodies?"

"I don't know. Like if it were dripping down their face, I can see them freezing that easily enough, but to do it while it's in their body? That's crazy!"

"It's not easy, from what I understand. Only the Neronian Grand Elder can do it, and a handful of others."

I shake my head. "You guys are terrifying. If the military ever gets their hands on you, you'll never be used for anything else but fighting our wars."

He frowns. "That's why our gifts must stay secret. We'd be heavily exploited, not to mention experimented on."

"Yeah, I can see that happening. Absolutely. They'd want to recreate how God made you."

"They never could. That's why it's so important you stay quiet about all of this." He looks meaningfully at me.

"I will, I swear. I mean, I already have for a year, not breathing a word to anyone, not even Elia."

He laughs. "I wish you had said something to her. I would *have loved* to see her expression if you had come out and told her what you saw." He laughs so hard, he leans forward, holding his stomach with one hand.

"Watch the road, Drew!" I cry, putting one hand on the steering wheel. Not that I would know what to do if he actually let go.

His laughing eases, and he wipes his eyes with his free hand. "Oh my gosh, I haven't laughed like that in a long time."

"Would she really have freaked out?"

He chuckles. "Yes. Yes, she would have." Then, he quickly sobers. "But then she would have had to report you, and we would have given you the poppy seed formula again. Elia would have hated that."

The mood in the car is heavy as I remember that horrible experience. He must be remembering too, because he holds his hand up, and I put my hand in his. He squeezes my fingers and says, "For what it's worth, I really hated doing that to you and your mom, but especially you."

"Why do you say that? I'm sure you've had to do that lots of times."

He shakes his head. "No, not really. I had only done it a couple of times, but watching how it wrecked your body really killed me."

Then he glances at me with both sadness and admiration. "But you were so brave about it. I barely even heard a peep out of you. You must have been so confused."

"Especially when I didn't forget, like you said I would. When I woke up the next morning and my mom had no memory of the previous day, I knew something had gone wrong."

"Or right," he says softly. "It's no coincidence that God allowed you to remember."

I smile sadly. "Yes, you're right. At first, I thought I had gone crazy and hallucinated the whole thing, but then I saw an Elemental opening a hole in the ground with a wave of his hand."

"I wonder how many other humans have seen things and think they're crazy?"

"Do you think there are people out there who know and keep it secret or think you're aliens or something?"

He laughs. "Yes, you're probably right. With the millions of people out there, it makes sense for others to come up with wild explanations of what they see."

After that, he quizzes me about my life for hours, until I beg him to stop. He finally agrees. "I just want to know what other hidden talents you possess, like origami."

"I'm nothing extraordinary, believe me."

"Now, I have to disagree with that. I have never met anyone more fascinating."

I blush. "Glad you think so. But I don't see it."

He leans over and pushes hair behind my ear. "If you could see half of what I do, you would think a lot more of yourself."

"I guess."

He pauses. "Okay, one last question."

I moan.

"Just tell me what else you know how to do."

"What are my hobbies?"

He nods eagerly.

I sigh. "Well, I know sign language. And I can crochet and cross-stitch."

"Seriously? Can you teach me sign language? And what is cross-stitch?"

I laugh. "You really want to know how to sign?"

"I do. That's an awesome skill. We could have entire conversations, and no one would know what we're saying."

"Except other people who know how to sign."

He shrugs. "How many people know though?"

"Not many," I concede. "And cross-stitching is a kind of needlework where you make x's and half x's forming a beautiful picture. It's like a painting."

"I bet you know how to paint, too."

I shake my head. "No, that's my mom's domain." At the mention of her, I fall silent. Sorrow pierces my chest like a dagger. I miss her terribly, and I just left yesterday.

"Hey," Drew says softly, reaching for my hand. "You'll see her again. Let's get settled in Arkansas, and she'll come to live there when it's safe."

"Will it be safe, Drew? For us, I mean?"

He nods, his expression fierce. "I'll make sure we stay under the radar. Don't breathe a word of our world to anyone else, not even other Elementals we meet. If we keep our heads down, we'll be fine."

I nod, but I look out the window, lost in my own thoughts. I don't want to admit that I'm terrified. This whole experience has stretched me in ways I've never been stretched before. I'm way out of my comfort zone leaving my home and driving cross country to start completely over with a new name and everything.

Drew thinks I'm such a brave person, but really, I'm a big wimp. I've really fooled him if he thinks that. I'm always struggling with self-doubt and anxiety. If I've ever had peace, it's because God blessed me with it. Consumed with my disturbing thoughts, I take the matter up to God. My one constant in life.

Lord, I'm scared. Please, Father, give me courage. Help me be like Ruth in the Bible, who left her homeland to be with her mother-in-law in a strange land. She trusted You, God, and I need to do the same. You not only provided her with a secure future, but You put her in the line of Jesus. Father, if You could take care of her so well, please, Lord, take care of me. I'm so lost right now. I'm completely dependent on Drew, and I need to trust that he'll make the right decisions. Give me peace, Lord, that I'm on the path You want me to be. I don't want to take any step, literally and figuratively, that You haven't guided me to take. And give Drew wisdom as he leads us to a new place.

At that, I open my eyes to find Drew glancing at me, but leaving me to my thoughts, or rather, prayers.

I can see on the car's GPS that we're only an hour or so from Kansas City. I fidget in my seat, closing my eyes. I almost feel like I have phantom pains in my back where I used to have stiffness all the time. Reaching behind me to feel my scar, I press down on it, but with no pain, I'm assured it's only my imagination.

"Are you okay?" Drew asks, noticing where my hand is pressing.

I nod. I'm still in a state of disbelief that I'm healed. Every minute, I expect to go back to what I've felt my whole life. But then I move in a way I never could have before. That shows me I really am healed.

I lean my seat back and close my eyes, hoping to sleep until we have to stop for gas or lunch. I pray that I feel more confident when I wake up.

"Jewels?" Drew asks.

I turn my head to show I'm listening.

"If God is for you, who can be against you?" he says gently.

I take a deep breath, exhaling slowly, listening intently.

"Remember, every one of your steps was planned before it came to be," he continues.

Not trusting myself to speak, I open my eyes, watching him, continuing to listen.

"I know what you're facing is scary, terrifying even, but you have God on your side. Imagine how David felt when he was going up against a giant."

I nod, tears finally slipping down my cheeks, and I let them come. I feel like the tears are my fears showing themselves. A new life, a new town, new people, a new school, knowing no one besides Drew.

"Listen. You have a bright future. You always have, but now you have full use of your legs and back. Just because you're going somewhere new doesn't mean you're not safe, loved and protected."

"I just wish I could see into the future," I whisper. "The unknown is so scary. I prayed and asked God to let us stay in Breckenridge, but still we're going. He said no to my prayer."

"I'm sorry, Jewels. We can't know the mind of God. Sometimes He says yes, no, and sometimes He makes us wait."

"That's the hardest when He says wait."

"You know, you don't always need to see into the future. You have the might of God behind you. Guarding you, guiding you, encouraging you. You feel Him, don't you?"

I nod, wiping my face.

"Then know you're right where you're meant to be."

"I just wish it weren't so hard to trust that we're doing the right thing."

"God never promises that our path will be easy. In fact, He's constantly telling us not to fear and to have courage. He wouldn't say that if we weren't going to go through hard things. It's not His promise that life will be easy, but our wish."

"Do you have peace this is the right decision? To leave like this?" I ask, my voice trembling.

"I do. I feel with absolute certainty I am to take you away and out of the Grand Elder's hands."

"Why do I feel so scared if you're so sure? Shouldn't I have the same peace?"

He shakes his head. "We're on our own journeys. You need to come to your own realization that you are going where God wants you to go. I can't make you feel that. But I can encourage you that you have me on your side, and God has tasked me to protect you."

I sink into that statement because it feels more like a promise. It fills me up, and I bask in the feeling of contentment that saturates my veins.

"I wish I could have a heart-to-heart with God and hear His voice. I want it to be black and white," I say.

"You just did. I saw you praying. That was you communicating with Him. He'll answer, in His own way. It could be through His Word, or through someone else. It could be a whisper on the wind. Just be open to how He chooses to reach you."

The car fills with silence at his words. I suddenly recall a Scripture. It fills my mind. *Peace, I leave with you; my peace I give you. I do not give to you as the world gives. Do not let your hearts be troubled and do not be afraid. John 14:27.*

Warmth spreads through me, and I know God is feeding me His strength and comfort. Through His Word and Drew. Just like Drew said would happen. I feel joy trickle through me. A small tingle of excitement builds. I have a future, and God is with me. Fear lingers, but I banish it because only God knows what will happen. I have God's assurance that I'm right where He wants me to be. I suddenly know how Ruth felt when she told her mother-in-law Naomi she would follow her and her God anywhere. She sounded utterly confident. I recall her words, *Your people will be my people and your God my God.* That's how I feel right now. I'm going to a place with new people, and I will make a life there. Confidence races through me. I'm headed to the right place.

33. Drew

We drive for a few more hours, and all the while, Jewels is quiet. I know she's praying; I see her mouth moving as she pours her heart out to the only One who can help her.

I've done my best to encourage her, but she needs to get there on her own. She finally falls asleep, and for that, I'm glad. She's been through so much these past three days. My heart clenches at all she's lost because I healed her. So she saw Elementals use their gifts and wasn't affected by our memory formula. Are those really such punishable offenses that she has to leave everything behind and run to avoid capture?

Jewels would be miserable tucked away in some isolated community without even me as a thread from her real life. The Grand Elder would exile her. And so, we flee.

Anger rushes through me so hot, I'm glad there's nothing green around me, or it would combust in growth. Not that it matters if that happens around Jewels anymore. She knows all about my world.

At that thought, my shoulders relax, and my pounding heart slows. I wanted her to be in my world, and now that I have it, I am selfishly very happy. But then I remember what she sacrificed for that knowledge, and my warm and fuzzy feelings dissipate.

When I see the sign for Kansas City, I decide we should stop and get gas and some food. Jewels wakes as I pull into a small station just on the outskirts of the city.

Relieved that Jewels slept through the rest of the drive from Kansas City, even slept through my gas stop earlier, I breathe a sigh of relief when I see a sign indicating Tuscaloosa is just thirty miles away.

My heart lurches, looking all around. This is the area I'm going to spend time with Jewels, my Onyx. When did I start thinking of her as mine, anyway?

I'm not sure, but it feels as if the feeling were always there.

One thing is clear; it's a good thing she insisted on renting two apartments. The cost isn't ideal, but if I have her tempting self in my personal domain twenty-four hours a day, I'd have a hard time keeping my hands to myself.

My parents are happy to pay for both of our apartments as a way of apologizing for not helping more with the Grand Elder. But what they could have done, I don't know. They helped us get away and get a new car. I have a feeling Jewels won't like that they're paying again for something else, but I'm not bothering her with that detail right now.

Thinking she'll want to see our new town, I gently shake her shoulder.

She jumps and blinks several times. When her eyes adjust, she looks around in awe, her mouth open. "Is this Fayetteville?"

"Sure is. Do you like it?"

It's April, so full green trees meet the eye everywhere you turn. Lovely homes of all styles dot the neighborhoods we pass. Our apartment complex is in the downtown area, and when I notice brick pathways meandering around the garden areas, I hope Jewels and I can walk around those together. Now that she can walk easily, the options have really opened up with what we can do.

My heart warms at all the moments we could have here. I hope she feels the same. It's her next question where all those dreams crash.

"Are there Elementals here?"

I swallow. *How am I going to live a life with a human? How is she going to truly fit into my life?* "Yes, this is a Gyan area."

She looks at me curiously. "I thought you guys don't have your own territories anymore? That you all live together now that Vela united you."

I nod. *Just because we're united doesn't mean Elementals are okay with a human knowing about our world.* "That's true, but it's going to take time for people to change their entire way of life."

"It opens up areas they can move to now, doesn't it?"

"Yes," I say slowly. "But we'll see how long it will take for Elementals to truly give up the safety of their home regions. It's going to take time."

"So, I'll only see Earth Elementals?"

"Most likely. But remember, don't show in any way that you know about our world. They'll report you immediately if anyone suspects you know anything about us."

She bites her lip. "So, even though we ran away from your Grand Elder, I'm still in danger."

I hesitate. I don't want her to feel threatened, but I have to impress how important it is that she stays quiet. "You need to understand, Ruby, that Elementals have lived in hiding from humans for 2,000 years. We're not going to change anytime soon."

But then a thought comes to me so huge, so monumental, I slam on my brakes. I'm lucky no one is driving behind me because the car screeches to a stop in the middle of the road. Jewels screams.

"What's wrong, Drew?" She looks all around us for a threat to materialize, and when all looks quiet and calm, she turns to me.

I'm breathing hard, like I've just run a race. Sweat breaks out all over my body, and I stare unseeingly out the windshield as I think furiously.

"Drew? What's going on? Are you having a heart attack?"

When a car beeps at me, my head clears for a second, and I pull over to the side of the road by a closed laundromat.

By this time, Jewels is in pure panic mode. She looks me all over and puts her hand on my head. "Oh my gosh, are you going to die on me? You're sweating like crazy. You can't die, Drew. Don't leave me here all alone."

Taking her by the hand, my heart is pumping so hard with this absolutely crazy idea that I'm surprised it doesn't jump out of my chest.

Jewel's hands are shaking as she grips me back, and I realize I'm squeezing her hands to death. I ease my hold and say in a hoarse voice, "I think I've figured out the final piece of our problem."

"What problem?" She blows out a breath. "I mean, what other problem? We have a lot of them, but what has you so crazy right now?"

"Jewels, I can't say yet, but I need you to trust me. Really, really, trust me. You know I only have your best interests at heart, right?" I lick my suddenly dry lips. My head is reeling with this preposterous idea, but I'm wildly excited, too.

She looks at me askance. "Drew, I don't know what you're going on about, but if it's not obvious enough after I agreed to move across the country with you, then yes, I trust you. Why can't you tell me what's got you all fired up?"

"Because I can't yet," I say with finality that brooks no argument. "Let's get our apartment situation taken care of because I have a call to make."

I let go of her hands, suddenly more than ready to get out of this car and start a chain of events that has never been seen in this world. Pulling back into traffic, I follow my phone's directions to our new home.

We pull up to a cluster of brick buildings a few minutes later, and I jump out of the car. Jewels follows more slowly, one eyebrow raised as if she's concerned for my mental health. I laugh wildly, which probably doesn't reassure her. "Let's go. Everything is going to be great."

"Uh huh," she says uncertainly, but she follows me.

I nearly skip to the rental office, heart soaring. I try to keep my head from spinning out of control, but it's hard with every thought I have careening around it now. The sheer hope of my idea is going to give me a heart attack if I'm not careful. I force myself to calm down.

Finalizing the rental process for our apartments goes pretty quickly, and before I know it, I've signed two lease agreements in record time. I profusely thank the girl who helped us so quickly. She nods shyly at me, and Jewels gives me a dirty look. When we leave, she whispers, "You are crazy. That girl thinks you're half in love with her."

I'm riding so high, I don't even think twice when I slide my eyes to her and say, "She's not the one I'm in love with."

I realize Jewels is no longer next to me when I get to the car and turn to see her standing frozen on the sidewalk. I walk back to her.

"What did you just say?" she whispers.

I crook a smile at her. "Isn't it obvious why I've done all of this, Ruby? Why else would I leave everything behind for you?"

"Are you really proclaiming your love for me, whipping around the word love like you just told me I have nice shoes? Are you really going to do that, Drew?" Her voice finishes on a shrill note, and I squeeze my eyes shut.

When she puts it that way, I can see how bad this looks for me. When I open my eyes, I have to lower them because I can hardly think straight with how Jewels is searching my face. Hope, desire, and anger all rolled into one emanate from her dark orbs. I need to make my phone call, but it's clear we need to have this conversation first.

"I'm sorry. I'm a little crazy right now, and I guess it just slipped out. I should have chosen a better moment to tell you how I feel. I'd do anything for you. Anything. And there's only one reason why."

"Because you love me? You're in love with me?" she whispers.

I nod slowly, locking my eyes on hers.

She trembles, and I long to wrap her in my arms, but I wait, because I need to see what she thinks about my profession of love. *Why couldn't I be more romantic? What is the matter with me?*

She puts her hands over her mouth, and now I'm frozen in hopeful anticipation that she feels a quarter of what I feel for her. A love so profound has filled me for this girl, and I would give my right arm for her to love me back.

"Onyx?"

Covering her face with her hands, her shoulders shake, and I realize with horror that she's crying. Or is she laughing? I can't tell, and I'm determined to find out.

Reaching for her, I move her hands away and see tears trailing down her face, but she's smiling. She turns her face up to me, and she's so beautiful, I can't help but lean down, and softly press my lips to hers. I taste tears, and I love that they're tears of joy. She wraps her arms around my neck and molds her lips to mine, suddenly matching me kiss for kiss.

I tear my lips off hers and hug her to me fiercely, saying into her hair, "Is this okay?"

She nods hard. "I love you, too," she whispers.

At her words, we're both laughing before I lean away. "Glad to hear how I feel is reciprocated." I hug her hard again, basking in the moment. After several long minutes, I pull away and say, "Let's get you settled in your place so I can make this phone call. It's very important that I do it right away."

When I look back at her, she's in a sort of daze, so I open her car door and carefully guide her into her seat, shutting the door softly so as not to jar her. It's like she's in a dream.

I laugh. I'm in one, too. But one that could go extremely wrong if I'm not very, very careful.

34. Jewels

♥

Drew leads me back to the car, and I allow him, but my head is completely in the clouds. I have a boyfriend, my very first one. And he loves me. I buckle my seatbelt and finally look at him.

I tuck my foot under me. "When are we having our first date?"

He smirks. "We should do that, shouldn't we? I don't think we can count my parents' dinner as a first date. Or the nights at the safe house."

I smile softly at him. "I think a first date should feel like one, too. I thought I was just having dinner at your parents' house. Although, it did kind of feel like it was just the two of us in the garden."

He grins wolfishly at me. "Kissing you was the best part of my night."

"Even though you regretted it?"

He grimaces. "I'm really sorry about that. I did not for one second regret the actual kissing. It was the repercussions that concerned me."

"We don't really need to worry about that now, do we?"

"No. We have complete freedom to do whatever we want now that we're here."

After following the helpful leasing office girl's instructions, we arrive at a three-story building. "Is this one mine or yours?" I ask.

"Yours. I'll get you settled, and then I'll come and get you in an hour and a half. We'll have our first date tonight, if that's okay. Will you be alright by yourself?"

I nod, suddenly facing the prospect of living all by myself. I've never done that, and I don't know what to expect. It's always been my mom and me. Suddenly, a swarm of excitement fills me. This is a whole new chapter of my life, and I've gotten to it quicker than I intended, but why not embrace it?

I'm healed, I have complete use of my back and legs, and life is good. I kiss my three fingers and hold up the sign of I love you to the sky.

Drew looks at me curiously. "Why are you thanking God?"

I smile because he remembers me doing this in the coffee shop. "I'm just thankful for where I am. I'm about to *walk into* my new apartment. I'm dating a gorgeous guy; life is very good at this moment."

He grimaces, a sad look coming over his face. "I just had to separate you from your mom to do it."

I lay my hand on his arm. "I would have eventually moved out and lived on my own, Drew. This moment just came before..."

"You were ready," he finishes, looking down.

I lean in and kiss his stubbly cheek softly. He hasn't had the chance to shave since we ran, not able to find a razor at the house we holed up in. I actually really like this look on him.

"I'm ready now."

He faces me fully, his expression sad. "And you find this a blessing?"

I nod.

His eyes fill with wonder, and he cups my cheeks. "Are you real? How am I so lucky to have found you?"

Unable to resist, I lean in and kiss him softly to prove to him I am, in fact, real. With my lips against his, I breathe, "Do I feel like a figment of your imagination?"

"No," he growls as he cups the back of my head for a better kiss. He kisses me relentlessly, and I wrap my arms around his neck, thoroughly enjoying myself. After several moments, he pulls away, smirking. "If we're ever going to get to our date, I have to let you go."

I look down. "I don't have anything else to change into."

"Yes, you do. Wear what you were wearing when we escaped. I washed your clothes at the safehouse."

I frown. "I would like to wear a dress on our first ever date."

He cocks his head. "I didn't realize it would be that important to you. Listen, I have a call to make, but after that, I'll go find you a dress at the boutique we passed. Will that work?"

I look at him, doubt coursing through me. "You think you can pick out a dress I would like?"

He smiles. "I have a sister, remember? And I saw you in that cute little dress you wore to my parents'. So, I know your style."

"Okay," I say doubtfully. "If you really think you can do this, I'm a size four."

I would love to go shopping with him, but he seems antsy to leave and make this mysterious call, so I get out of the car without argument.

His steps are brisk as he leads me to my apartment, finding it quickly. It's on the second floor, and I marvel at my legs as I climb the steps. I still cannot believe I can do this so easily.

I'm smiling even as I'm out of breath when Drew turns around after he's opened the door. "I feel like I should carry you over the threshold."

I smack his shoulder lightly. "That's only if we're married, silly."

"Well, the moment is this big. Are you really going to make me wait to do this tradition?"

"Yes," I say firmly and brush past him to walk into my very first apartment. Then I twist to face him. "Wait, what do you mean, you need to wait?"

He looks at me slyly. "No reason. It was a slip of the tongue."

"Uh huh," I say and turn to take my first look at my living space.

Drew stuffs his hands in his pockets as he comes to my side, looking all around. "Is it okay? Do you like it?"

The front door opens right up to the living room, and I already love the bright light diffusing the room through the big window off to the left.

"Ooooo, a window seat!" I croon as I rush over to it, sitting down on its roomy ledge.

I watch as Drew walks into the apartment, checking out the bedroom and adjoining bathroom. He leaves, looking satisfied. "There's a bathtub if you like to take baths." He coughs and turns to hide his expression.

I jump up and run over to him, turning his face to me. "Are you embarrassed about that?" I ask, laughing.

His face coloring, he clears his throat. "It's not telling you that, it's imagining..." I gasp and push him away as he chuckles. "Sorry! I'm a full-blooded guy here. I'll keep my thoughts in check better."

"You'd better, Drew Ashcroft," I say as I walk into the small, but practical kitchen, feeling his eyes on me. *It's very good that we're living separately. We wouldn't have lasted five minutes alone in an apartment together without doing things we shouldn't.*

My mood sobers as I think that, because those moments can still happen even though I'm living alone. I'll have to be very careful to keep compromising situations from happening.

Suddenly, I feel Drew's hands running slowly down my upper arms to my hands. Shivering, I turn and look into the eyes of my boyfriend.

"What are you thinking about, Onyx?" he asks in a husky voice. He's tantalizingly close to my lips, but I decide to be open and honest with him.

"I'm thinking we should be very careful with how we choose to spend time together," I say, goosebumps racing up my arms as he runs his fingers lightly back up them.

He nods slowly. He cups my face with one hand. "I think that is wise." He runs his nose from my ear down my cheek.

"Like now," I say breathlessly. "You should really think about going to your own apartment."

He jerks his head up as if he's just remembered something. I feel his heart pounding under my hand.

Turning in a spin, he walks to the door and turns, pointing at me. "You, my little Jewel, are going to have to stop distracting me."

When he opens the door, I protest, "I was just standing here. If I'm a distraction, that's on you, not me."

His eyes shine with a light that I only saw when he slammed on his brakes earlier. "Well, whatever spell you cast on me needs to stop because I have something very important to do."

"Are you going to tell me what this important thing is?" I fold my arms across my chest.

He shakes his head, a wide smile taking over his face. "Not yet. I'll see you later. In an hour and a half?"

I nod, and he's gone.

I busy myself by exploring my new apartment and calling my mom. After catching her up on our trip and my new home, we browse the internet for furniture and things I'll need to make this place livable.

I find the address on the copy of the lease, and make some purchases. Before I know it, it's been an hour and a half. I jump off the window seat and rush to the bathroom to do what I can with water to calm my flyaway curls. After splashing water on my face, I pinch my cheeks but don't really need to, since my color is high with excitement over my very first date.

A knock on the door makes me turn off the water and rush from the room.

Drew is standing on the stoop in his same clothes, but he holds up a bag triumphantly.

"Is this my new dress?" I ask, excited to see what he picked out.

He smiles. "It is. Now, hurry and put it on. I think your sandals will work with it." I take the bag, peeking in to see what's in there.

I shut the door to the bathroom and pull out a sundress, so cute I gasp in pleasure. Squealing, I hurry to try on my new dress. The yellow material complements my tan skin, and I love the embroidered embellishments. Small flowers sewn with gold thread dot the dress and make it sparkle in the light. From the thin spaghetti straps to the ruffled bottom that falls just above my knees, I love it. I swish the skirt, loving the way the folds of fabric make it move perfectly. I spin in front of the mirror to get the full effect.

I stare at my reflection for a full minute, still unable to process that I can move so effortlessly, so *easily*.

Giggling, I leave the bathroom, fully ready to enjoy this time with Drew. His back is to me when I emerge, and I clear my throat.

He turns and when he sees me, he freezes, his gray eyes darkening as they look me up and down. I twirl like I did in the bathroom, and he whistles long and slow.

"Onyx, you probably shouldn't wear that. Go and change." His eyes argue with his words, however, because they twinkle and then he smiles. "I'm kidding. You, woman, are gorgeous."

At that, he lunges and catches me by the waist, lifting me while he spins. I squeal and hang onto his neck. Looking down at him, I ask shyly. "So, you like it?"

He sets me down slowly and steps away. A grave look comes over his face. "I do. Too much. Let's go before I'm tempted to enjoy myself more than I should."

Appreciating his effort to keep our relationship pure, I squeeze his hand when he grabs mine, and we walk out of the apartment and to the car.

"Do you think we should go to Walmart and get some necessities? After our dinner, of course," I ask once we settle in the car.

He nods briskly. "We're going to need a lot more than what Walmart can provide."

"I already bought some furniture and kitchen stuff with my mom."

He raises an eyebrow. "That was very industrious of you."

"If you give me a card number, I can do the same for your apartment," I offer.

"That's alright. My parents can pack up my apartment back in Colorado and send me most of what I'll need."

"We'll at least need to get a couple of air mattresses and bathroom stuff."

He nods, and then we both enjoy the quiet as he drives us to a cute little restaurant, called Antonia nestled in the center of the downtown shops.

Once we park and walk up to the quaint space, I look around in appreciation. Twinkle lights stretch across the patio, providing an ambiance that can only be described as sweet and reminds me of our stolen moment in his parents' garden.

Drew smiles at my delight in the outdoor space and asks the hostess to seat us outside. I happily follow her to our table. We're at a small table tucked against the back wall, but it's low enough that we have a great view of the shops.

Once he settles in his seat, Drew asks, "Is this what you envisioned for our first date?"

I smile widely. "It's perfect." I reach for his hand and lace my fingers through his. "How do you know me so well already?"

He studies me, his eyes twinkling. "Honestly, I'm guessing. But I had a feeling you'd like this place."

"Well, you were right." I let go of his hand and study my menu. Since this is an Italian place, there are lots of pasta choices, and I suddenly look up and beam at him. "Are you sure that graduating from my program at the clinic means I don't have to be on a gluten-free diet? I mean, I know we've eaten pasta a couple of times, but I'm just checking."

He gifts me with a beautiful smile. It's so full of warmth, I inhale sharply.

"Say that again."

I blink. "What? That I don't have to be on a gluten-free diet?"

He shakes his head. "No, that you've graduated from my clinic. That you're healed. You're not suffering anymore."

I don't know why, but I blush and look down. Maybe it's the intense look on his face, or the memory of his hands all over me during our healing sessions. He was nothing but professional, but for some reason, I'm embarrassed to think of how much he's already touched me.

"What is it?" he asks.

I force myself to look up at him, willing the blush out of my cheeks. "It's nothing," I rush to say.

He chuckles. "It's obviously something. Tell me please, Ruby."

I laugh nervously and squeeze my fingers in my lap. "I don't really want to say." My heart pounds at admitting my thoughts.

"I'm begging you, Onyx. Put me out of misery and explain why that beautiful blush is all over your cheeks."

I turn my head so he can't see my embarrassing reaction. "I'm just remembering how you healed me."

"Yes? And that makes you blush?"

I nod furtively, still not looking at him.

"Ah, you're remembering my massages." He sounds so satisfied, I look up sharply. His eyes are warm as he puts his napkin on his lap. "That's one of my best memories of our time together."

"Why?" I ask in a hoarse voice.

"Because you absolutely trusted me to treat you. As much as I loved putting my hands on you, though, I was thinking more of what was under your skin than your skin itself. So, you don't need to be embarrassed."

I blush harder and look down at my lap. "You're pretty amazing, you know that, right?" I whisper, emotions choking my voice.

"I'm only who God made me to be. There are plenty of other...people with my same gifts."

I shake my head hard and look up at him, my eyes shining with tears. "You will never understand what you've given me. I will never be able to thank you enough. There's no gift big enough to show my appreciation."

"I know of one." His eyes pierces any resistance I have left against completely giving my heart away to this man.

"What's that?" I ask.

"I need your trust. It needs to be absolute with no reservations."

"You have it," I say with no hesitation. "You have done nothing but good in my life. I know you would never hurt me."

A flicker of uncertainty crosses his eyes, and he looks away. Twisting his lips, he says, "Not intentionally, no. You're right."

"I really wish you could tell me this big secret. Do you not trust *me*?"

He looks up quickly. "Of course I do. I just don't want to say what I'm thinking. Not yet. In fact, the only person who can tell you has to get here. She'll be here in two days."

"Who?"

He grins. "Vela."

I nearly jump up. "Vela is coming here? Why?"

"She'll explain everything."

I huff a breath. "Okay. I just hope this oh so mysterious information is worth it."

"Oh, believe me, it is."

The waitress appears and takes our order, and the night passes happily. We laugh over everything and nothing. As we eat our meal, I enjoy his sense of humor. He has a funny story for every stage of Vela's life.

"I love how much you love her," I say as I sip my water.

"She is impossible not to love. Why do you think that Elementals across the world have accepted her so easily as our Chosen Child?"

"Was it really that easy?"

He grimaces. "No, not at all. But once she had the world's attention, she kept it. She is a very good leader."

"Well, she has a gold mine in Linc. He's a born leader himself."

He raises his eyebrow. "That is the second compliment you've given Linc. Should I be jealous?"

I laugh. "No. He's all Vela's. Like you're all mine."

He smiles. "Indeed." He wipes his mouth with his napkin. "Do you want anything else?"

My stomach warms. "Nothing you can offer me here." I look at him under my lashes.

His gaze heats. "Okay." He looks around and flags down our waitress. Once he pays, he guides me to the door, his hand firm on my back.

I really need to be careful with my words because, the way he's rushing me out of the restaurant, it's clear what's on his mind.

When we get to our car, I employ supreme effort to make my next request. Because I have to be honest, I'm tempted. I can say I only want to kiss Drew, but what will happen in the heat of the moment? Because I'm not sure, I say, "When we get to my apartment, I think I need to be the only one who goes up."

He's leaning down to open my car door, but he snaps his head up. He studies me. "Is that what you want?"

"No. But it's what I need. I'm sorry, but I'm not ready to do anything more than kiss you."

A wounded look comes into his eyes. "I would never ask for more than that, Jewels."

I cringe. "I'm sorry. But I think I gave you the wrong impression just now."

He inhales deeply and then takes me by the shoulders, squeezing gently. "I am a man of God first and foremost. It's as important to me as it is to you that we keep things from going too far. You do not need to worry that I would ever pressure you for more. I'm not that kind of guy."

I nod, relieved. I knew that, but hearing him say it eased a worry that had pinched my chest the past few minutes. "Even so, I think I need to go to my apartment alone. It's not you I don't trust. It's me. I have these feelings that take over all my common sense and reason. I don't want to lose myself and my hopes to save myself for marriage."

"That makes two of us. So, we'll cool our jets and be good. Does that sound okay?"

Unable to help myself, which is probably giving him mixed signals, I wrap my arms around his neck. "Thank you. For being the guy I need you to be."

He squeezes me softly and then pushes me away. "Let's get you to bed. Alone."

We make a stop at Walmart on the way home, and fill the cart with toiletries, a couple of outfits, some pajamas, two air mattresses, pillows and some sheets so we'll sleep somewhat comfortably tonight. We also grab some easy breakfast options and sandwich materials plus disposable plates and utensils.

After that, we make our way back to our apartment complex. Once we drive into the parking lot, I ask Drew to show me his apartment before he drops me off at mine. He points out his building a few away from mine before he drives me to the sidewalk that leads to my door. As I walk to my apartment, loaded down the shopping bags, I can't help but grin; my heart is full.

35. Drew

I approach my apartment slowly, my mind reeling. *Why would Jewels ever think I would ask her for more than just a kiss?* Haven't I proved to her by now that I would *never* do that?

Running our conversation over in my mind, I remember she had said it's herself she doesn't trust. That makes me feel marginally better. But there must be some mistrust for her to even have that conversation.

I have to admit, though, when she insinuated that she wanted more than just dessert after our amazing dinner, I jumped at the chance to be close to her. She gave me those come-hither eyes, and I was lost. All I could think about was getting her in my arms for a good long while.

Would we have taken things too far? That's a question that makes me think. It would be far too easy to lose control with her if we allowed it to get that far. I have never been more attracted to a girl in all my life. In the heat of the moment, it probably wouldn't have been a conscious decision to take things further, but one thing leading to another.

I've kissed a few girls, but I'm proud to say I've never taken things too far with any of them. I was serious with Jewels when I said I wanted to wait until marriage. I've come too far to mess up now, even if Jewels is far too tempting for her own good.

We need to have a very frank discussion, so I can be sure she completely trusts me. I need that more than anything else. Especially with what I have planned when Vela gets here.

At the thought of mine and Vela's plan, my heart pounds. I rub my chest to calm its frantic rhythm. I only pray it will work. Because I've run out of options. If I want Jewels in my life permanently, this Hail Mary has to work.

The next day, I work up the nerve to go over to Jewels's apartment. We need to have the conversation I vowed to have last night. Standing before her door, I inhale deeply, wondering why I'm so nervous. I take a moment to gather my thoughts before I knock.

I know she'll be on board with what we need to discuss, but if I catch a hint of fear that I'll be anything but a gentleman, I'm not sure how I will react. Knocking before I can talk myself out of it, I wait just a few seconds before Jewels opens the door. When she sees my expression, she smiles a thin smile at me and lets me in.

I take a minute to appreciate the few changes in her apartment. She's unboxed a few decorations that came in and, because she has nowhere else to put them, I see a picture frame, a vase, and a fake potted plant on the kitchen counter. These must be what her mom ordered for her.

I smirk when I see a bright orange Doberman Pinscher statue by the front door. When she catches me looking at it, she blushes and says, "That was my mom's idea. She said since I won't get a dog to protect me and I'm living alone, she'll get a representation of one." She waves her hand at it. "I put it by the door to discourage potential intruders."

I chuckle. "She should have made it look somewhat realistic if she wanted to really do the job of protecting you."

"I know! That's what I told her. But she just went on and on about making my apartment look good. How that thing will accomplish that, I have no idea, but I'm used to her artistic opinions by now."

I quirk an eyebrow. "My sister has a Doberman, and your statue surprisingly looks a lot like him, except the statue is orange and not red."

She cocks her head. "Her Doberman is a red rust, right?"

I nod. "His name is Jack. She might bring him tomorrow. He's married now."

She lifts both eyebrows. "Her dog is *married*?"

"He really is. Vela had a doggie wedding and everything."

She laughs. "Please tell me you attended."

I sigh. "Unfortunately, I was too caught up finishing up my degree to go, but you should ask her to show you pictures."

"I will," she says, giggling. Her expression sobers. "You said you needed to talk to me?"

She looks worried, and I realize she must think I want to end things. I rush to reassure her, saying, "It's nothing like what you're thinking. I just," I exhale roughly, "wanted to have an open and honest conversation with you about our...physical relationship."

"Oh," she says, her expression horrified. Then, an adorable blush covers her face. She looks down to hide it.

I nudge her chin up with my finger. "You don't need to be embarrassed. Can we sit down?"

She gestures around. "I don't have anywhere yet except my window seat."

"That's perfect." I take her by the hand and lead her to the brightly lit space. Once she sits, I say, "I'm worried about something."

Her eyebrows fly up. "About what?"

"I'm worried that you think I'm going to break my promise."

"What promise?"

"The one where I said I would never ravish you...not until we're married, if that day happens."

This time, her blush covers her whole face. She tries to pull her hand away, but I hold it tightly. "Okay, so we're having *this* conversation," she says. She blows out a breath, looking away. "I told you I trusted you."

"But there was a part of you that didn't really believe me. Right?"

She looks at me mournfully. "I can't help it. My mom has hammered it into my brain that guys want only one thing, and I guess I believed it."

My lips flatten in a thin line. "While that may be true about most guys, I am not one of them. I want what you want. I've never gone further than a kiss. So, let my track record prove that I'm genuine. And that you really can trust me."

"You've never been with a girl intimately?" she asks with doubt in her voice.

"No, I'm just as serious as you at keeping it that way until marriage. But I have all these impulses when I'm alone with you. I don't know if I can trust myself." I squeeze her fingers. "So, you can rest easy because I will *always* stop things before they get too far. Let's make a promise together."

She nods, her eyes lighting up.

"Let's promise each other that we won't put ourselves in compromising situations where we'll be tempted to fail in our vows."

In answer, she wraps her arms around my neck. I breathe in her scent, enjoying the sweet lavender scent of the body spray she bought last night at Walmart. I am only too happy she made that choice.

I pull away and kiss her on the nose. "Are we good?"

She nods happily.

"Good, because I'm hungry."

We exit the apartment to search for a good meal. One I'm happy to have now this issue is behind us.

It's been a full two days since my date with Jewels, and I can't stop my knee from bouncing up and down in anticipation of what Vela and I have planned.

Vela and Linc arrived three hours ago. She didn't want Jack boarded under the plane, so she left him with our parents. It's too bad, because I really miss that dog. It's weird, though, because normally Jack goes with Vela everywhere. This is the first time I've seen her without him in a long time.

After a lengthy conversation, we've gone over every aspect of my wild and, hopefully, not reckless plan. We're finally ready, just waiting for Jewels to get here.

A knock sounds, and I exchange a nervous look with Vela. I know why she's nervous. She's never tried this on a human, and I had to really coerce her into agreeing to do it now. Well, I begged. My pleas worked, though, and she's here and half willing.

"It's going to be fine," I say for the millionth time.

"You better be right because I do not want Jewels's death on my hands," Vela says, worrying her lip.

Linc wraps his arm around her shoulders in silent support.

Please, Lord, let this work.

I open the door and try to project a confident smile. But one look at my face and Jewels's smile drops.

"What's wrong?"

My eyes widen at how well she's come to know me. "Come in, Ruby."

She steps gingerly through the door. When she sees Vela, though, she drops her purse and launches herself at my sister.

Vela catches her but nearly falls over.

Jewels laughs. "When Drew said you were coming, I could hardly believe it! How are you? Let me look at you." She pulls away and holds Vela at arm's length, looking her up and down. "You look healthy. Wow, Vela! Marriage really suits you. You're practically glowing." She turns to Linc after letting go of Vela.

Vela looks at Jewels with astonished eyes. She turns a wide-eyed gaze to me and mouths, "Good job."

I will never tire of seeing Jewels have full use of her legs and back.

"Linc! You look good and married, too!" Jewels cries before she wraps him in a tight hug.

I give Linc a dirty look, but I remind myself he's married, and Jewels and he were friends back in high school. I never knew myself to be a jealous guy, but Jewels inspires the best and worst in me.

Linc pulls back and looks down at Jewels's legs. "Look at you, Emerald! You're walking! And without crutches, wow." He smiles widely at her. Unable to prevent myself, especially after hearing one of my nicknames for Jewels come out of his mouth, I step up and wrap my arm around her shoulders. Linc looks at me and smirks knowingly.

"Isn't she doing great?" I say with pride. I look down at her and smile.

I catch Vela eyeing me with one eyebrow raised. If I had to guess, she's watching me look at Jewels with more than a measure of friendship. I give her a half grin. Of course, I'm all in with this girl. If we're going to attempt our experiment, I'd better be. Honestly, my heart was toast after our first kiss in my parents' garden. One taste of her lips, and that sealed the deal. I'm hers if she wants me. Here's to finding out if she does.

I turn Jewels toward me and look deeply into her eyes. She returns my gaze, looking puzzled.

"Remember when I asked you to trust me totally and completely?" I ask.

She nods.

"I'm going to need to cash in on that promise right now."

"Drew, will you please tell me what this big secret is?"

I inhale deeply and look at Vela and Linc, who each nod at me.

I return to look at Jewels. "I thought about this every which way, and the problem with you and me being together is one that is too big to ignore."

"Okay?" She looks between my eyes, worry pinching her brows together.

I squeeze her shoulders. "But I came up with a solution that has never been done before in the history of the Elemental world."

"You have?" Now she really looks confused.

I nod somberly. "My sister, Vela, has an unbelievable ability now that she's the Chosen Child. She can take away an Elemental's power and hold it to give to someone else, another Elemental. She only does this to Extremists, Elementals who've committed an unforgivable act. Then she gifts the power to someone more worthy."

Jewels's eyes widen and her body stiffens under my hands. Her voice catches when she says. "Are you saying what I think you're saying?"

"Well, if you think I'm suggesting you become an Elemental, then, yes." Fear fires through me at the thought of this going horribly wrong, and I try to breathe through it.

Her eyes widen even more. She blinks rapidly. "How is that even possible?" she asks hoarsely.

"Without Vela, it's not possible. We're not positive it'll work on a human, but she's holding an Elemental gift in reserve, and she's willing to give it to you."

Jewels backs up, her head swinging between Vela and me.

My heart freezes at the thought that she's going to say no. *Does she know this is the only way for us to truly be together safely?*

Vela speaks up in a cautious voice. "Jewels, we have to know you're in complete agreement before we try this."

I clear my throat. "I've been over and over how our relationship can work. It would be so much easier if you were one of us. I'm not saying it's impossible…" *It is.* "But if we don't try this, we may as well say goodbye to living in the United States. We'd have to go to Canada and live in an indigenous community where Elementals and humans are together."

"Seriously?" she asks in a shaky voice.

"For us to be romantically involved here, it would make it so much easier if you became an Elemental."

She turns her face to Vela. "What element do you have for me?"

Vela gives her a frank look. "The first question is, do you want to be an Elemental?"

Jewels puts shaky hands up to her mouth. "I need time to think. This… this experiment could backfire, couldn't it? I mean, an Elemental gift could be too much for a human."

Vela and I exchange heavy glances. It's Vela who nods. "It could backfire, yes. I don't think you'll die, though. If I give it to you and it looks like your body is rejecting it, I will just take it back. I wouldn't allow it to harm you. If your body suffers, Drew and I are Gyans. We would heal you. And for the record, I have a Neronian gift waiting to give to you if you agree. So, if it's successful, you'd have a water gift."

Jewels nods but turns tear-filled eyes to me. "I want to be with you more than anything, but at this cost? Please give me time to think. I need to pray about this."

I nod gravely.

She turns to the door, but before she leaves, she says over her shoulder. "For the record, thank you for even considering doing this. I really am honored."

At that, she leaves. I'm not sure what to think or even how to feel when I look around the apartment and already miss her presence. *Will she reject this because I asked too much of her?*

I'm at a loss when I have no answer. I run my hands through my hair, pulling the ends.

Vela approaches me slowly. "Drew, we talked about this. She has to agree, or I'm not doing it."

"I know that, Vela. Believe me, I know. I guess I just hoped she'd jump at the chance."

Linc snorts. "Seriously? We tell her she could be in danger, and you want her to ignore it? Be real, Drew. She's not stupid. I respect her more for thinking this over."

"And praying about it," I add.

"Right. This is not an easy decision for her to make. I'm sure she wants to discuss it with her mom and come to terms with whatever decision she makes."

I nod morosely. I feel like I'm in an ocean of what-ifs and I'm about to drown in them. Running my hand over my mouth, I hold my aching chest.

"I don't really know what I'm going to do if she says no," I finally admit.

Vela and Linc both give me sympathetic looks.

"I mean, she's the only girl I've ever felt this way about. The thought that she could be one of us is so tantalizingly close, but also so far away."

My apartment has a window seat, too, and I walk over to it with heavy steps and sit down.

"Drew, you're going to have to come to peace with her decision. You made some promises just now that, frankly, I'm a little surprised you made. Are you really going to move to Canada if she chooses to stay human?"

I lean over and put my elbows on my knees. "Of course. I need her in my life if she'll have me."

I see Vela's shoes in my field of vision before I hear her say, "Brother, that's a huge move."

"I know."

Vela says as she puts her hand on my head. "I support you, whatever happens. I'm here for whatever you need."

I look up. "Can you go over to her apartment and at least tell her what it's like living as an Elemental?" I shake my head. "It shouldn't come from me. It should come from a friend."

"You're her friend, too."

I stand up, and she backs up. "I'm not the friend she needs right now. Please, Vela?"

She seems reluctant to nod. "Let me give her an hour or so before I go over there."

I agree and go get my computer that came in the mail today. I bring it to her. "Can you show her pictures of our gatherings? Just go into my iCloud account and pull them up."

Taking my computer in one hand, she puts her other hand on my arm. "Give this to the Lord, Drew. Let Him help you."

Nodding, I go to my room and shut the door, hoping with all I have that the girl I love will agree to try to join my world.

36. Jewels

I walk back to my apartment in a state of disbelief. *Is what I just heard real? Could I really become an Elemental? Should I risk my life to become someone magical or supernatural?*

Everything in me screams yes! What are you waiting for? But I force myself to listen to the voice of caution. It's like I have two angels on my shoulders, telling me opposite things.

The first thing I need to do is call my mom. I pull out my phone, and she answers in two rings. "Julia? Honey, are you okay?"

"Yes," I say in a shaky voice.

"Really?" She clearly does not believe me. She confirms it when she says, "Why do you sound so stressed, then?"

I blow out my breath. "I have some news. But, Mom, before you freak out, just know I haven't decided yet."

"What haven't you decided? What is going on, Julia Emily?"

I hesitate before I finally blurt out, "Drew has a way for me to become an Elemental."

Silence screams through the phone.

"Mom?"

"I...I don't know what to say to that."

"Yeah, I don't either. I'm thinking about it."

"You're really thinking about doing this? Why?"

"What do you mean, why? I could have an awesome ability, Mom. It's an incredible opportunity."

"Have they ever done this before? Made a human an Elemental?"

I shake my head, and when I realize she can't see me do that, I say heavily, "No. I'd be the first one."

"Well," she scoffs. "I don't know. How do they know it's even safe?"

"That's the problem. It's an experiment. But they're Gyans, Mom. They can heal me if anything goes wrong."

"If anything goes wrong?" she asks in a shrill voice. "Julia, you cannot seriously be considering this."

"I am. Drew and I would always be in danger here if we continue to date while I'm human."

"So, let me get this straight. This could kill you. And because a guy asks you're going to say yes? Haven't I raised a smarter daughter than this? Has my life not been one gigantic example of how a man can literally destroy your life?"

"Mom, you have a wonderful life," I weakly argue.

"Yes, but that's after I was broken almost past repairing. Listen, you're going to make this decision. This is your life, not mine. But I would not do this for a guy just because he asked me. Every decision in your life should be for you and then only if it's God's will." She sounds tired when she finishes, and I wish more than anything I were closer so I could wrap her in a hug.

"I wouldn't do it just to be with Drew, Mom. This gift would be from God. I would be part of his work here on earth. I'm going to pray about this. I just wanted you to know about it."

"Well, let me know what you decide before you do anything, okay?"

"Of course. I love you, Mom. Do you want to know which element I would have?"

"No," she says resolutely. "It doesn't matter to me what element it is. It could hurt you, baby. I'm not okay with that. Even if they fix you afterward."

I tell her despite her saying no. "I'd get the gift of water."

"Wonderful," she says in a deadpan voice.

"Okay, I'm going to go. I have some praying to do."

I open the door to my apartment and go over to the window seat, sitting down heavily. Immediately, I bow my head.

"Lord, I'm lost here. I've just been offered a wonderful gift. You know all, Lord. Please tell me if this is Your plan for me or man's. I don't want anything in my life that You haven't put in my path. Tell me what to choose, Lord."

I sit with my elbows on my knees, my hands together as I wait in silence, keeping my heart open for any kind of whisper from the Lord.

After a while, I hear a knock on my door. I stand up to answer it, bracing myself to see Drew on the other side. I don't want him to talk me into this decision. I'm still waiting for my answer from God.

When I peer through the peephole, it's Vela who's looking at me sheepishly. I open the door.

"Hey," she says, biting her lip. "Can I come in?"

I notice she's carrying a laptop with her. "Sure," I say, but then wonder what she wants. "Did Drew send you?"

She looks down. "I'm afraid he did. But I wanted to come. Jewels, I want to give you an idea of what you'll be getting into should you choose to accept my offer."

I hesitate for a beat and then let her in.

"So," she says after blowing hair out of her eyes. "I don't know what you know about us Elementals as a people, but you should have a complete view of our world before you, you know...?"

I nod and fold my arms across my chest. "It's always good to be well informed before you make a decision of this magnitude."

"Right. That's Drew's thought, too. But he thought it would come better from me."

"I happen to agree with him."

She looks at me with relief. "Okay, good. So, let's sit on the floor and look at some parts of my world."

"You have pictures?"

"Of course! Ever since the digital age, we take all the pictures and video we want and hide it in accounts that hackers can't access."

"Great, let's look then."

Vela gets comfortable on the floor, and I join her. After opening up the laptop, she types in the password and finds the pictures she told me about.

Before too long, she angles the computer to show me a festival of sorts. I look hungrily at happy faces in what looks like Elemental games.

I laugh when I see a video of two adorable little girls wearing matching looks of concentration as they grow flowers from a seed. "Are they competing against each other?"

Vela nods happily. "Yep, it's a way of practicing our gift from a young age. Here, look at this one." She shows me a video of two teen boys with vines like the guys who attacked Drew used. They're trying to grab cans and set them in a basket with the vines. It's a combined effort of concerted concentration and skill. The crowd behind them cheers when one of them finishes first.

I watch video after video and see more photos than I can count before I finally sigh and lean back. I realize something. "Are those Drew's pictures and videos?" Because a lot of them were selfies of him.

She nods. "Honestly, Jewels, what are you thinking? How are you feeling about all this?"

"Honestly? I don't know," I say before I rub my face hard. "This life looks amazing and everyone looks so happy with their gifts, but I just wonder if I'm meant to have one."

"Do you want me to wait until I have a Gyan gift to give you? Is it the water gift you're not sure about?"

"No," I rush to say. "It's not which gift; it's *the gift*. Being an Elemental. I'm going to be honest with you. I want to accept, to be the first human ever to have such an enormous blessing like that, but I need to know if it's God's will. Because it will completely change my life if I accept."

"Do you have any questions I can answer?"

I scrunch my face in thought. "I am wondering something. If I accept your very generous offer and the experiment works on me, will I have to report someone if they see me using my gift?"

She nods with a serious look on her face. "You'll have to swear to do it, Jewels. We have to keep our way of life secret. If someone sees you using your gift, water or any of them, they'll need to be given the poppy seed formula."

I cringe. My experience was so horrible I can't imagine being the reason someone has to endure that kind of torture. Then, I ask, "What do you mean, any of my gifts? I'd have more than just the use of water?"

"I don't know if this will happen, but if your body accepts the full Neronian gift, you should inherit the secondary gift, too. You'd be able to take away an Elemental's gift, but only temporarily. It's like it freezes in their system so they can't use it for a while. But things have really been changing lately. Because we finally have our Chosen Child, me, clans are fighting less and less. You shouldn't have to use the second gift."

I nod and then look down, my heart heavy.

"Are you worried about Drew and your moving to Canada if you say no?" she asks me gently.

I can't help but nod. "It's so far from my mom. I would hate that. But, Vela, I can't live my life on the whim of a guy. I have to live my life in what God wants. No one else."

She nods decisively and pats my knee. She gets up with the laptop and takes it and herself to my front door. "I'm going to leave you alone so you can take this up with Big Guy Himself. And, Jewels, for what it's worth, I'd love to have you in my life as an Elemental. But I'll always be your friend, no matter what you choose."

"Thank you," I say hoarsely and go to her by the front door. I wrap her in a tight hug.

She laughs as she squeezes me back. "I never thought I'd see you walking like this. It's already a miracle what's happened to you, Jewels."

"I know," I say and let her go.

After she leaves, I return to where I sat on the floor with Vela. I put my head in my hands and take this life-altering decision to God again.

Lord, what should I do? Is this the life You want for me? I need to know that I have Your permission, Father. I want to use my life to further Your gospel.

I sit for what feels like hours, and when I pick my head up, I see the sun shining — the afternoon sun. My insides are still one big, tangled mess. I realize I'm holding onto this decision without letting it go and fully giving it to God.

Breathing out slowly, I close my eyes and with all my heart, pray, "God, I give this crazy decision to you. I can't bear this burden myself. It's too big." My voice cracks, and I pause to swallow. "But what I really need is an answer, Lord. I need to know Your will. How about this? Give me peace if I'm to accept this gift. Or take away my peace if I'm to reject it?"

With that said, I sit in silence. When fear continues to plague me, I pop my eyes open. *Am I allowing fear to make my decision for me? Have I truly given this over to God? It doesn't feel like it.*

So, I close my eyes again and say again, "God, I give this to you. Please, Lord, take this burden of fear away. I will do whatever Your will is."

With that proclamation, I blow out a heavy breath and with it, release all my doubts about whether God really would answer me.

Fear flies off with my doubts, and I'm left with such a feeling of peace, one I've never experienced before. It settles deep within my soul, anchoring me and tethering my life once more to the Lord and His will for me.

When I feel nothing but a soul-deep tranquility, I open my eyes and smile.

I know what my decision is. God has given me His choice, and with that, I jump up, rejoicing once more that I can. Joy fills me, and I laugh outright. I spin in a circle, then I rush to the sink.

Popping up the handle, I let the water flow over my fingers and wonder what this will feel like once I have a water gift.

I sober quickly, shutting off the water. *This might not work. God's given me peace to do this, but that's not a promise it will be successful.*

Straightening, I wipe my hands off on my shorts. Not taking any more time to allow worry to take over, I march to the door, pulling it open. As I walk to Drew's, I call my mom.

It's time to change history.

37. Drew

I'm pacing the room, despite Vela and Linc telling me it won't make time go faster, when a knock sounds.

In one lunge, I'm at the door, yanking it open. Jewels is waiting, her face hopeful. Trying to interpret it, without having the nerve to ask what her decision is, I just stand memorizing her lovely features.

"Drew? Can I come in?"

With my throat shutting down, I'm unable to respond. I can only nod and step back. As she passes me, she lays her hand on my arm but lets me go just as quickly.

I shut the door and spin, still unable to utter a sound. I can only stare at her profile, my face one big question. *What is her decision? Or rather, God's, because she went and prayed about it?*

Vela and Linc stand from their places on the window seat. We all just watch Jewels.

"I'm at peace with a decision," she says tentatively. "It comes at a great cost because I don't know what could happen." She turns to me.

My heart is in my throat. This is a certain kind of torture meant just for me. I clench and unclench my fists at my sides. She walks toward me slowly. "Drew. I want you to know that I'm so appreciative of all you've done for me. You've sacrificed your whole way of life just so I could walk without pain. I'm incredibly grateful."

"But," I croak, my chest falling inward. A crashing disappointment threatens to overwhelm me. I hang my head, trying not to show her my grief. *She's turning us down.*

Gentle fingers lift my chin, and I pull my eyes up to Jewels, who's smiling softly. "I want to try and do it. Make me an Elemental." She nods decisively. "I'm ready."

Ignoring Vela's gasp in the back of the room, I crouch and wrap my arms around Jewels's waist, lifting her. Spinning slowly, I bury my head in her neck, breathing in her lavender scent. I have no words for several minutes before I ask hoarsely, "Are you sure?"

I feel her nod, and I hold her even tighter.

She kisses my cheek softly, trailing kisses down my jaw. "Even if it doesn't work, I want to try. This is what God wants for me." Her soft words breathe onto the side of my face.

I finally pick my head up to look at her. "Have you talked to your mom?"

She nods, tears glistening on her lashes. "She knows."

I inhale deeply, studying her face for any measure of fear or doubt. When I don't see any, I gently set her down. "When do you want to do this?"

She looks over her shoulder at Vela. "No time like the present. Vela?"

Vela's face is white, but Linc has a firm hold on her, his arm around her shoulders. She bites her lip, and then her face transforms with determination. "Drew? You remember what we've talked about?"

I nod, breathing shakily. I've already gone outside and boosted my healing gift with the surrounding trees. I rub my hands together. I just hope I won't need my healing gift today.

Vela walks over and faces Jewels. "I know you're ready, but I'm not." She takes a shaky breath. She puts her hands in front of her face like a prayer.

Jewels's face drops. "Have you changed your mind?"

I hang on to Vela's answer, because I'm wondering the same thing myself.

Vela shakes her head hard. "No, but I want all of us to pray first. In fact, Drew," she turns to face me. "I want our family to pray. Let's call everyone and have them stop what they're doing. I'm not doing this without God's overwhelming answer."

"Jewels said it's what God wants," I say, pointing at her. *Am I going to get this close to my prayer being answered and then be denied by someone in my family who doesn't have peace about this?*

Vela gives me a steely glare. "I know that. But, Drew, this has *never* been done before."

"That we know of," I mutter, rubbing the back of my neck.

"I'm not taking any chances. We need all the prayers we can get."

I nod, knowing she's right. *Please, God, don't take this from me.* Then, a wash of conviction fills me. This isn't about my happiness or even Jewels's. If it's truly God's will, then we need to verify. We need to be sure.

"Okay," I say with new determination. "I'll call Kane. Kane will tell Elia to pray."

Vela turns, reaching in her back pocket for her phone. "I'll call Mom and Dad."

Linc adds, already dialing a number, "I'll call our good friends, Hannah and Andy. They'll have everyone praying."

Jewels just stands in the middle of the room, looking lost for a moment before a light seems to shine on her and she turns to the abandoned window seat. She sits and bows her head, and her lips move in silent prayer.

Taking in the serene sight, I look down at my phone and dial Kane's number. He answers on the first ring.

"Hey, is everything alright?"

"Yeah, we're good. Except we need you to pray. In fact, we need you and Elia to stop what you're doing right now and pray."

Kane's voice is hesitant as he asks, "Drew, you said everything is alright."

"It is." I take a deep breath. "Vela is going to try to make Jewels an Elemental." The phone goes silent for so long I ask, "Kane?"

He coughs. "I'm sorry. Did you say what I think you just said?"

"I did."

"Drew," he starts.

"Look, I know it sounds insane, but Vela has a Neronian gift she's held onto, Kane, it's the only way for Jewels and me..."

"To really be together," he finishes.

"Yeah, basically. We'll be on the run our whole lives from Elementals who would never allow me to be with a human."

Kane sighs loudly. "Man, you know how to stop a heart, you know that?"

"Please, Kane. We could use all the prayers we can get."

"You've got it, brother. I'm here. I'll call Elia right now. In fact, I'll go right over and we'll pray together. When are you going to do this? Or Vela, I mean?"

"We think tonight. We're asking everyone to pray first."

"Okay. Let us know when it's...over."

"I will."

I put my phone back in my pocket and walk toward Jewels. Sitting beside her, I put my hands over hers. I bow my head and pray, *God, I can't promise I'll never ask for anything ever again if You do this, but Lord, I'm begging You. Please tell us if this is safe for Jewels. You've given her the gift of full range of motion; will You breathe new life into her? Make her an Elemental? I know I'm asking for a lot. Like the impossible. But God, You are the God of infinite possibilities. You gave Lazarus back his life after four days in the grave. Can You make Jewels one of us?*

I'm praying so earnestly, I don't realize Jewels has leaned her head on my shoulder. Vela and Linc are kneeling in front of us, their hands on Jewels's knees.

I start praying out loud, "Lord, we all come together in agreement to do this miraculous thing. But, Lord, we'll only do this if it's Your will. Please direct our steps. Allow Vela to bestow this great gift on Jewels, a human. Lord, this has never been done before, but nothing is impossible to You. We trust in You and Your will. Give us all peace if this is what You want. Father..." I can't talk more because my voice chokes.

Vela picks up, "Lord, You've gifted me with an incredible power. But never, Lord, would I do anything without Your permission. This is Your gift. I just use it. Lord, is this Your will? Please, Lord, if it is, give me the ability to share this Neronian gift with Jewels, whose body isn't used to this kind of power. I'm not foolish enough to think this will be easy, but I trust in You, God. Only You."

She goes quiet and after a moment, Linc prays, "God, I've seen some incredible things, but this is going to take the cake. But I know if it's Your plan for Jewels to become an Elemental, it will happen. Give my wife Your special peace and gifting. I pray especially for Jewels's safety, Lord. For her body to accept this great power. Please, Lord, keep her safe."

Tears trail down my face as I squeeze Jewels's hands. Fear grips me at Linc's last words. *Are we asking too much? Is this going to hurt my Jewels?*

Jewels's quiet voice rings out, clearly and without hesitation. "Father, I'm not in any doubt that You can do anything, including the miracle of making me an Elemental. I'm asking, Lord, that You give the same peace You've given me to everyone in this room and to the others praying. Whether I stay a human or become an Elemental, I have You, Lord. I don't need any special gift to tell me that I'm Yours completely. Lord, be with us here and now. I ask for a peace so infinite, nothing can question it. We won't do this without You, Father."

After her prayer, we all sit in silence, meditating in silent communication with God. It's after some time that I feel a Presence in the room with us. I don't have to open my eyes to know it's not a physical being, but the Holy Spirit, moving. I can't help the joy that fills me with a total and transcendent peace. Lifting my head, I let my tears speak for me as I praise

God. I place my hands on Jewels's head, drawing her against my shoulder gently.

"Are you ready, Precious?" Opening my eyes, I see Jewels's face almost glowing with a divine light. Her eyes are still closed, but she's smiling.

Vela rises, her movements sure and ready. She takes Jewels's hand and pulls her up. Jewels follows, her eyes remaining closed. I take her other hand, and Vela leads us to the middle of the living room, "Lie down, Jewels. It's time."

Having seen videos of Vela bestowing an Elemental gift to another Elemental, I know that the experience knocks them on their back; the power is so great. So, I appreciate Vela thinking ahead and sparing Jewels a concussion.

Linc stands behind Vela, watching her carefully. I know that Vela also gets knocked back, so he's in the perfect position to help his wife.

Jewels gracefully crouches and lies down, folding her hands on her stomach. A smile still graces her mouth, and her eyes remain closed. Taking a deep breath, I kneel next to her, ready for anything to happen. Fear overwhelms me for a moment, making my throat so dry that I cough. It robs my breath, and I inhale deeply, squeezing my eyes shut. *Lord, banish this fear, I pray! I ask for peace; forgive my doubt. Forgive me, Lord.*

With those words ringing in my head, warmth washes over me, canceling out the fear that had stolen my peace. I breathe easily now, and I open my eyes to see that Jewels's countenance hasn't changed, nor has Vela's.

My sister's face is one of pure focus. She closes her eyes briefly, bringing her hands to her chest. She makes a fist, and then, as if pulling deeply from inside herself, she opens her eyes and brings her hands together, making two fists. With measured breaths, she walks carefully toward Jewels and kneels slowly next to her, like she's holding a priceless treasure, which she is.

I pray for Jewels's safety so strongly, I'm screaming in my mind.

Vela opens her hands and places them on Jewels's chest. Like a defibrillator, it's as if 800 volts of electricity fire into Jewels's body because she gasps and her chest lurches upwards. Vela runs her hands over Jewels's arms and legs, continuing to gift and empower.

Lord, is she okay?!

Jewels takes several gasping breaths, but instead of her popping her eyes open in exaltation like the other Elementals, I see the opposite. Jewels's head falls to the side. Her face is white as a sheet, and my chest clamps in total and complete fear.

"Jewels?" I lean over her and feel her pulse. My eyes bulging, I shake my head when I don't feel one. "Ruby?" I search for her heartbeat again, but still, nothing.

"No!" I blink away my teary vision and lean over her. When I still don't feel a heartbeat, I know my Gyan powers are useless. Once the heart has stopped, there's only one thing that will restart it: CPR. Clamping my hands together, I line my shoulders over hers, locking my elbows. I compress her chest the two inches needed and start counting as I continue the compressions. I don't dare lose count of them as I work on someone I can't imagine my life without. I hold in my sobs as I count to thirty. I expected seizures, convulsions, her body rejecting this power, but I didn't think of her heart stopping.

Taking a deep breath, I tilt Jewels's head back and seal my lips over hers, pinching her nose closed before I breathe two long breaths into her, carefully watching as her chest rises with each of my exhalations.

I rise to check her pulse again. "No!" I scream when I don't feel anything.

Leaning over her again, this time sobs tear free from my throat as I start the compressions all over again. After another thirty life-giving pumps, I have to hold in my sobs as I pinch Jewels's nose closed and breathe two long breaths into her.

I hear Vela weeping next to us, but all my focus and attention are on Jewels. I feel for her pulse, and when I'm met with cold skin, I cry out, "Oh, God, help!"

I give her compressions again and again, repeating the motions: pump, breathe, check for heartbeat.

I've lost count with how many times I've done this when Vela lays a cold hand on my arm. "Drew."

Scouring Jewels's face for any sign of life, I ignore her.

I lean over my Jewels again, pumping harder. I wince when I hear one of her ribs break. Easing my pressure, I continue.

This time, Linc's hand grips my shoulder, pulling me away. "Drew, man. She's gone."

I rip myself away, growling, "No! I refuse to believe that! I'm not giving up!" Finally looking up at Vela's tear-tracked face, I spit, "Take it out of her. Now. Take the gift back!"

Defeat fills her face, but with ashen skin, she nods jerkily. A cold silence fills the room.

A wild desperation fills me that when the gift is gone, Jewels will return.

Just when Vela lays shaking hands on my girl, I hear the most beautiful sound in the world. A gasp fills the air.

"Jewels?" I ask hoarsely. Tears drip off my face as I cup her head, leaning it back so she can breathe easier. Soft pink cheeks greet me, and I cradle her face, crooning to her. "Just breathe, baby. That's right; take your time. You've got this."

Loud sobbing leaves the room as Linc takes Vela away into the bedroom.

I have eyes only for the jewel of my heart, though. Jewels's eyes rove wildly at first but finally settle on me, pain lingering in her gaze.

"Drew?" she croaks. "What happ...?"

"Shhh, baby, let yourself rest. You've been through major trauma." Breathing heavily, I run my hands over her, healing her broken rib. Checking for any other injury I may have caused, I close my eyes to sense every organ and vein in her body. I slowly go over every inch of her until I breathe in complete relief. All her vital signs are good.

"You're fine, Ruby. All I sense is... Jewels, what do you feel?"

Her beautiful eyes study me as if she can find her answers with me. Her gaze moves over my whole face as a look of concentration comes over her. She licks her lips. "Umm, I feel a lot. I'm not sure what to focus on first."

I run my hands over her arms. "That's okay. Take it one thing at a time. Tell me whatever you want to tell me about first, and we'll go from there."

Her eyes snap to mine. "Do you know? What I'm feeling, I mean?"

I nod slowly. "As a Gyan, I've been trained in every Elemental gifting. I have an idea. But you tell me first, and I'll confirm if it's an Elemental feeling or not."

She barks a laugh. "Oh, I'm pretty sure it's Elemental. Well," she says, blowing out a breath. "First, I feel cold," she says, shuddering. "But it doesn't feel bad. Like the cold is a part of me now."

I nod.

"And...it's like I have a rushing river in my veins. Like I could...shoot water from my fingers if I want?"

I nod, smiling.

"Can I?"

"What?"

"Shoot water?" Her anxious eyes undo me.

"Go for it," is all I say with a wide smile.

Her grin answers mine, and holding out her hands, she does a Spiderman move. But instead of webs, two streams of water, one from each hand, shoot out of her. I let her delighted laugh wash over me as I sit back and enjoy watching her spray water all the way over to the window seat.

"Careful," I warn.

"Of what?" she says, laughing as she keeps going, thoroughly enjoying using her new gift until finally she slumps back, her body limp.

Having expected this, I catch her before she hits her head on the carpeted floor. I cradle her in my arms as she sighs while I adjust and move her onto my lap. Pushing hair out of her eyes, I gaze down at her, saying softly, "Careful you don't use too much energy. You'll burn out fast like that."

"But I just got started," she moans. Her head slumps to the side.

Moving her so her head will rest comfortably on my shoulder, I say, "You just got your gifts; give yourself time to get used to them. Which reminds me, do you feel another power? Particularly mine? It'll feel differently than yours."

She scrunches her nose at me and opens her eyes sleepily, looking up at me. "I do feel a kind of adrenaline that's just out of reach. I thought I could use it to make more water, but then it was just gone."

Trailing my finger down her cheek, I take a moment to marvel at another of God's miracles. I look up and say, "Thank you, Lord."

She closes her eyes again. "I guess it's good I felt that?" She snuggles into my neck, and it takes everything in me not to kiss her. This is not the time.

"Uh, yes, that is a very good thing. It means you've gotten the second Neronian gift. You're feeling my power. If you had more energy, you could command my gift to be silenced."

Her eyes crack open. "Really?"

I nod, chuckling. "Really, but please don't." I say soberly.

She yawns. "Why?"

"Because you need to rest. We can try that another day."

Snuggling into my chest more, she mumbles, "Okay. Drew?"

"Yes?"

"He did it," she mumbles before she's out like a light.

I run my hands over her to make sure she's just sleeping. Relieved to find her healthy, just exhausted, I sit and hold her. I lean my head on hers and take this moment to thank our Creator. "You're right, baby. God did do it. And you're going to be just fine."

38. Jewels

♥

I wake up feeling like I'm in another body. It's such a foreign feeling, I immediately snap awake, jumping up, completely disoriented. I look down at my arms, wondering why it feels like water is rushing through my veins at a breakneck speed.

"Hey, hey, calm down," a deep voice says. "You're okay. If you stop panicking, those feelings will slow down."

I turn slowly, looking at Drew with horror. "What's wrong with me?"

He laughs, his eyes twinkling as he lies on the floor. "Wrong? Absolutely nothing. You are the picture of health."

I blink my eyes completely awake. I rub my arms, trying to feel something besides this feeling of *other*.

"You're fine, I promise. It's normal to feel your water gift."

I blink. *That's right. I have the Neronian gift.* "Last night...that wasn't a dream?" I rub my chest, wincing when I feel sore muscles and tenderness. It seems I fell asleep next to Drew last night.

"No, Baby, that was all very real." He notices my expression as I press tenderly on my chest. "Hey, are you okay? I should have healed all your bruises."

Looking at him with outrage, I ask, "What did you do that could have bruised my chest?"

He looks at me with chagrin. "That would be when I performed CPR on you. I may have broken a rib."

"Oh." I rub my chest not feeling anything broken.

His eyes search mine. "Are you in pain?"

My head spins with all this new information. Then suddenly, I remember everything that happened last night. Vela sending in a fiery power into me, losing consciousness, waking up to Drew leaning over me, the first time I used my gift, nearly passing out from the stress of it. It all flashes by in my mind.

He looks very contrite as he rises to a sitting position. "I'm so sorry, Ruby. Are you okay? Does it hurt to breathe?" He starts to raise his hands like he wants to examine me himself but lets them fall.

I smirk at him. "Do you want to check me?"

He quirks an eyebrow. "May I?"

I nod, but suddenly I'm shy. This is my chest, after all. But I completely trust Drew. He has been nothing but a gentleman to me ever since our journey began.

He stands up, focusing on me, and runs his hands over my sides, ghosting his hands over my chest. A pulsing warmth follows when he heals my bruised muscles. He breathes a sigh of relief when he's done. "You're okay. I'm sorry. I thought I healed everything."

I raise my eyebrows. "Can that happen with CPR?"

He frowns. "Frequently."

"I don't know how I feel about you breaking my bones, Drew," I tease. I give him a mock frown.

He looks alarmed. "I tried not to use too much force." He looks away. "I got desperate."

I lean in and nuzzle his nose. His eyes stare at me, intense and vulnerable. "Thank you," I whisper.

"For what?" he whispers back.

I kiss his nose. "For saving my life. I understand you are responsible for bringing me back."

He pulls his head back. "God did that."

I cock my head. "Through you."

He nods reluctantly as relief fills his eyes. "Yes, He did." Pure grief washes over his face. "I lost you, Ruby," he says in a hoarse voice. He puts his forehead to mine.

I stay there contemplating the very real fact that I had died, and Drew brought me back to life. "I'm sorry," I say softly.

I pick my head up. "Am I rested enough, Doc?"

His eyes glitter at me. "For what?"

I scoff. "Seriously? What do you think?"

He crooks a grin. "How about you practice your gift for five minutes at a time? Take it slow this time. We don't want a repeat of last night."

"I will after I've freshened up," I say, wanting the get the business of brushing my teeth out of the way before I kiss my man.

He chuckles, knowing how I feel about kissing him in the morning.

I turn to walk into the bathroom.

Before leaving the room, he calls out, "Call me when you're ready to practice your gift."

A little annoyed that he's leaving and I won't get *any* morning kisses, I call after him, "What if my gift is kissing?"

"That is definitely one of them," he calls back, but he's gone.

He's probably brushing his teeth, too, which I can't be too upset about. I sit down and slump back, landing on a pillow I hadn't noticed before. Blowing out a breath, I take stock of how I feel.

The fast pace of the blood in my veins is not what I would call normal. It's so different, I lie there and study it. First, I try to get used to it. But the feeling of power, like I could do anything with water, is a bit overwhelming. It's as if the water is straining to burst forth.

Lifting my hand, I drop my fingers down and sprinkle water onto my waiting palm. I collect the water and spin it into a ball. I laugh outright, but then quiet, wanting this moment for myself. I don't want anyone to come in just yet. With my imagination going wild, I turn the small globe of water into a square, then, feeling inspired, I squint at it and picture a horse. Taking one finger, I draw the end of the square up and curve the small line of water into a tail. Biting my lip, I focus on the other side and with a pinch of my fingers create a head. It's not much, but with practice, I'm sure I can do it. Not wanting to give up the picture I have in my head, I sweep my hand over and attempt to form the body. Giggling quietly, I pinch four legs on the bottom, then study it. It needs a mane. I'm concentrating so hard on making it, I don't notice Vela entering the room.

"What in the world is that?"

I drop the water with a splash, rubbing my hands on my shorts. "It was nothing," I say hurriedly, sitting up.

"It looked like a blob of water with lines coming out of it," she says with a chuckle.

"It was a horse," I mumble but move to get up. I stumble, and Vela is right next to me, steadying me.

"Hey, didn't Drew tell you to be careful using your gift for too long?"

"He might have mentioned it, but I just wanted to see..."

"What you can do," she finishes with a sigh.

"You understand completely, I know. Have you burned out with your gift, too?"

She snorts. "Frequently. Linc is...often concerned. He helps me know my limits. Sometimes, it's like he knows me better than I know myself." She finishes talking so softly, I peer at her.

"Our guys are very good to us, aren't they?" I smile, looking forward to seeing Drew even though we just parted.

Vela helps me walk out of the room. "Yes, they are," she agrees quietly.

"Vela, how did it feel giving a human an Elemental gift?"

She's silent for so long, I study her.

Her face pinches, like she's in pain. "It wasn't pleasant. It felt wrong somehow. When your heart stopped, I thought..." she falls quiet, hanging her head.

I put a hand on her arm. "You don't have to talk about it." I say, even though I'm burning with questions.

"No, it's fine. We've been talking this morning and wonder if you have Elemental blood somewhere in your history. That's the only thing I can figure out about why your body finally accepted the gift."

Vela helps me into the living room, and Linc and Drew look up at us from the kitchen. Drew's face draws down in concern. "Jewels? Are you okay?"

"Just a little tired, is all."

He walks toward me, shaking water off his hands. There still isn't much in his apartment, which I vow to change soon. He studies my face, looking me over for any adverse effects of the gift coursing through me. "You need to take it easy for a while. You've been through a lot."

I turn to Vela. "Do the Elementals who receive an extra gift ever complain of being exhausted after?"

She shakes her head, continuing to hold my waist to keep me steady. "No, the opposite, in fact. They're full of energy."

I frown. "Shouldn't I be feeling all kinds of energy then?"

Drew crosses his arms, like he's itching to take Vela's place next to me. "You must have enough Elemental blood to accept the powers in you, but it must be very diluted for you to have these residual effects. Plus, you would have had powers when you were little if you had more Elemental blood."

I nod. "I can't imagine who it could be, unless it goes way back. Or," I say thoughtfully, "it could be on my dad's side."

Linc walks up, mirroring Drew's stance. "Is it possible he was an Elemental?"

I look at him with wide eyes, feeling more shocked than I've ever felt. "My dad? An Elemental?" I shake my head hard. "No way. No."

"Do you remember him well?" Drew asks, his eyes gentle. He knows how sensitive this topic is for me.

"No, not really. He abandoned my mom when she was pregnant. I only met him once."

Vela, Linc and Vela exchange a look. "It's possible," Vela says.

"But then why is her body still weak?" Drew asks. "If she's half Elemental, she should be taking this much better. Plus, she definitely would have had a gift long before."

"I think her body is weak because her heart stopped last night," Vela answers. "She nearly died. Give her time."

Drew clamps his lips shut, frustration glinting in his eyes as he studies me.

"I'm actually fine. I have the gift. I'm just a little weak. And, like you said, I would have had my father's gift, right?"

"It's possible," Vela says. "From what I understand of the indigenous clans intermarrying, their children do inherit gifts, but it's not guaranteed. It depends how diluted the Elemental blood is. So, there's no telling what Jewels would or wouldn't have."

"It must be further back than your father," Linc says.

I huff. "There's no telling about my father's ancestry. I know nothing about anyone in his family."

Vela says, looking at Drew and me, "On another note, we need to sit down and figure out what the future looks like for the two of you now. As an Elemental, Jewels can't live anywhere she's lived before and would be known by humans. Among our kind, we need to be sure her human background stays secret."

Feeling the weight of such a decision and thinking of my father's mysterious roots, I sink to the ground and sit cross-legged. "Can we stay here? I kind of like this place," I ask, looking up at the rest of them.

Vela nods as Drew joins me. She sits too, pulling Linc down with her. "No one knows either one of you here, so this place would work," she says. "But we're going to have to come up with a plausible background story for Jewels. Elementals are notoriously curious about where their fellow Elementals are from. We have to make it a place they can't check."

Linc speaks up. "She could come from an off-the-grid location. That way, if someone wants to corroborate her story, they can't."

Vela's face lights up. "That's brilliant, baby!" She kisses him on the cheek and turns to me. "You can be from a hidden Elemental community in Canada. We know enough about those communities to give you enough details to make it convincing."

Drew has been quiet the whole time, and I wonder what he's thinking.

"Okay, so you're both staying here," Vela says, checking off her fingers. "And Jewels is from an off-the-grid community. What else?"

Drew looks intently at me. "I know a way to hide Jewels's name, protecting her further."

"How?" I ask, my stomach pitching at how he's looking at me.

He studies me, quiet for a moment. "I could give you my name."

The room goes quiet, and I swallow, my throat going completely dry. My vision is like a tunnel. I can only see Drew, who's looking at me like I should say something. *Wait, is he proposing right now?*

Vela clears her throat and gets up, smacking Linc's shoulder over and over. "Okay, so you guys have...stuff to talk about. So, we're going to... go." When Linc just sits gaping at Drew, finally, Vela grabs Linc's shirt, yanking him up, almost desperately. "Right, honey?" she squeaks.

When he finally gets up, shaking his head, he looks pointedly at Drew with wide eyes that clearly communicate the seriousness of the situation. He and Vela leave the apartment, shutting the door firmly behind them.

I lick my lips. "Um, Drew? What...?"

My body is practically vibrating with the whirring of my new powers, and I'm losing my composure. Water gushes out of my hand, and I hold it with my other hand, trying to stop the flow.

Drew leans into my sight, talking softly. "Calm down, Emerald. You're fine. Take deep breaths. That's it."

I do as he suggests and, with great concentration, get the faucet to stop. Brushing water out of my eyes, I ask, "Are you...are you proposing to me right now?"

He shifts and rises on his knees in front of me as he reaches slowly for my hands. Hands that are trembling with what feels like anticipation. He grasps my hands and holds them carefully in his own. The ones that have healed me, protected me, saved my life, and now this.

He pulls me until I'm on my knees too. Then, he gently guides me into a standing position. I look down at him still kneeling in front of me, my throat closing with the intensity of my emotions. I suddenly have the crazy idea that if I let loose the tears crowding my eyes, I will flood the room with my water gift.

I push those thoughts out of my mind when Drew puts one leg up, kneeling only on one knee. He says solemnly and reverently, "Jewels Patterson, Ruby, Emerald, Onyx, I want to cherish you for the rest of my life. Not as a friend, but as my wife, as my soulmate. You are everything I could ever want in a partner, as a life mate. You have the courage of a warrior, the heart of an angel, and one of the keenest minds I've ever known. You hold my heart in the palm of your hand. Will you be my wife? Jewels, marry me, please. Make my life have true purpose. I want to love you and care for you until the end of our days."

Losing all ability to stand, I drop to my knees and cup his face in my hands. "You know how to shock my heart into starting and stopping, you know that?"

He smirks, but his look is unguarded and vulnerable. "You haven't answered my question."

"The answer is I do, I will, I want to, yes! Any more agreements you want from me?" I ask, throwing my head back in a slightly crazed laugh.

He kisses a line up my throat until he reaches my lips. He whispers against them, "Look at me, please, fiancée."

It was the please that makes me bring my head down and gaze into his heated eyes. His smirk has turned into a smolder. "I love you, Onyx, and I will until I have no breath in my body, and even longer. I'll love you for the rest of forever."

"Okay, it's my turn to say very pretty things to you." Wrapping my arms around his shoulder and pulling his face to my level, I rub his nose with mine. "I think I loved you from the first moment I met you. You impressed me with your healing skills, but what I love the most about you, Drew Ashcroft, is your compassion and your ability to love. You don't love in half measures; you love with your whole self, not holding back. I love you, Drew. I don't want to imagine my life without you in it."

He leans in and kisses me so softly, it's as gentle as the old butterfly kisses I used to give. He whispers against my lips, "I love you too, Ruby. Let's start our life together. First on the agenda are wedding plans. I don't think I can wait very long to marry you. How does a month sound?"

I rear back my head. "A wedding in a month? Are you crazy?"

"Yes," he says with a smile, nodding. "For you."

"I need longer than a month, Drew Ashcroft. How about six months?"

"Two."

I huff. "Four."

He kisses me tenderly, breaking my will slowly but surely. "Two and a half, final offer."

"Or what? The offer is off the table? Three, and that's *my* final offer." I give him such a hard glare that he relents, throwing his head back and laughing deeply.

"Fine, wife. We'll get married in three months."

"I'm not your wife yet, Doc. Don't make premature statements."

He smirks. "Fine, fiancée of mine."

I nod. "That's better."

He releases me from his embrace but continues to hold my hand. "Let's go find Vela. She probably went back to your apartment."

I swing his hand up high, joy spreading through my veins faster even than my new Neronian blood does. Life has gotten very good indeed, and I cannot wait to see what is yet to come with this amazing man by my side.

39. Epilogue

Three Months Later

"Are you ready?" Vela asks softly as she peeks her head into my room.

After we'd finally finished the hours-long preparation it takes to become a bride, I retreated to my room, needing some time alone to pray. I'm ready to make this dream happen and marry my best friend. I look up and smile at my soon-to-be sister-in-law. "Yes." I've gotten much better at containing my water gift. It took all three months to control the urge to do Spiderman moves with water all the time. I trust myself to be in front of humans now.

When I don't get up from my bed, she cocks her head and asks, "So, why aren't you getting up? Anything wrong?"

"No," I say, chuckling, looking around the sparsely decorated room. I didn't get much for myself in this apartment, knowing Drew and I would be living in his. "I'm just taking in the quiet before the chaos."

"Now, why would you think a thing like that? A chaotic wedding? Pfsh, no way."

I study her to see if she's serious, but it's the smirk she's sporting that makes me know she's being entirely sarcastic.

"Come on," she says, waving me toward her. "You'll have to get it over with sooner or later."

"Over with?" I gasp. "I've been looking forward to this day my whole life!"

"Well, then what are you waiting for? Let's get this show on the road." She smiles widely at me.

I get up, following her out of the room. After that, it's a blur of action until I'm in the vestibule of the church, waiting to walk down the aisle.

Just knowing Drew is waiting for me at the other end keeps me jumping on my toes. I may not be his Intended, but I am who he's chosen, and he's mine. I'll forever be grateful that he didn't wait to find someone who's supposedly his soulmate. I didn't really understand the bond of an Intended couple until I saw what Vela and Linc have, so at first, I felt guilty I was taking that experience away from my fiancé.

When I expressed my concerns to Drew, he resolutely, and with many, many kisses to punctuate his feelings on the subject, silenced every protest off my lips. "I don't need to know who she could be," he had said in between kisses. "I have you, and you're the only one for me."

So now, with my arm tightening on Drew's dad's arm, I discreetly wipe my moist palm on my dress. I try to banish the residual anxiety that I'm robbing Drew's Intended, stealing him away.

David smiles down at me. "I know I might be a little biased in saying this, but you couldn't have picked a better guy to marry."

I smile. I had shyly asked David to walk me down the aisle since my father isn't in the picture. He's soon to be my father by marriage, so I tamped down my embarrassment at not having a father of my own and asked him. He was shocked but overjoyed and immediately agreed.

"You know, I thought I'd only get to walk one daughter down the aisle, so you're giving me an immense privilege in allowing me this honor. Thank you." He lays his hand over mine, and I beam up at him.

"I'm blessed to be marrying into your family, so it's I who should be thanking you."

"Hey," he says, chuckling. "You're taking one of my cantankerous boys off my hands. Believe me, I'm thanking you. Wholeheartedly."

I laugh softly. "If anyone is cantankerous, it's me. I don't know why Drew chose me, honestly." I say the last part so softly, I'm not sure if he heard me.

"Because you're perfect for him," he answers, gently squeezing my hand.

My heart warms, and I blink away tears. I hear the music for Elia and Vela to walk ahead of me. I'm thrilled Elia can be at my wedding. She graciously took the job of spreading rose petals for me in place of a flower girl, since I didn't know any little girls.

"I can be a flower girl," she had said with cheekiness. "I'm not old and married yet like you old fogies, so technically, I'm still a child."

I wonder about her relationship with Kane. They look very much in love, but no wedding bells have rung for her just yet. I don't know what's stopping Kane from proposing, but that's their story to tell.

Vela disappears from the room and then, with one last wink at me, Elia follows her.

Nerves crowd my throat, and I attempt to swallow them.

"Are you alright?" David asks me.

"Yes?" I squeak.

He looks down into my eyes and nods. "You need anything?"

"Water?" I croak.

"Of course." He rushes from the room and returns quickly with a bottle of water.

I could have just sprayed some water into my mouth, but I want to look like a bride not a hose. I take a long drink, and then the doors open. The water bottle is in my hand, so in a panic, I throw it in a nearby fern, straightening just in time for the doors to widen, showing me and David.

I latch my eyes onto the one person I want forever.

Drew's eyes burn into me, and I smile shyly. If his look is any indication, he loves my dress as much as I do. It's strapless and has a sweetheart neckline to a corset that tightens all my curves. The skirt flares out after hugging my hips and falls gracefully to the floor. It's a simple cut, but its elegance called to me.

I start walking, and I recall all that Drew and I went through. It's because of him that I can walk down this aisle without crutches. He sacrificed so much so I can walk normally.

My nerves flee like a horse running into the wind. I allow excitement to carry me down the rest of the aisle toward my future. At the end of the aisle, my mom steps forward to give me away.

With one last squeeze of my hand, David steps away to stand next to Whitney, Drew's mom.

Mom takes his place, tears crowding her eyes. She leans toward me, kissing me softly on the cheek, whispering, "I'm so happy for you, baby. You enjoy this life and all it holds. I'll always be here to watch life unfold for you. I'm proud of you, always." She leans back, holding my hand tightly at first, then hands it to Drew, who takes it and tucks it into his arm. I look over my shoulder at my mom, mouthing, *I love you.* She mouths the same to me, and I turn to find Drew looking at me with his mouth slightly ajar and his eyes wide. I blush deeply at the emotions his gaze elicits.

You're gorgeous, he mouths.

I look down, but the minister brings my attention back up when he speaks. The ceremony passes in a blur, much like this morning. I shake myself out of my bliss-induced stupor and have to remind myself we had to change our names. Because when the pastor asks Drew, "Do you, Andy Williams, take Jewels Lawlor to be your lawfully wedded wife in sickness and in health for as long as you both shall live?"

Drew's hands tighten around mine as he smiles at me with tears in his eyes and says, "Yes, I do."

The pastor asks me the same question, and I answer a little too loudly, much to Drew's delight, if his gleaming eyes and wide smile are any clue.

After we exchange rings, the pastor pronounces us man and wife and says, "You may now kiss your bride."

Drew takes one look at me, and sweeps me in his arms, dipping me deeply and kissing my breath away. My spine tingles with awareness of him. He brings me back up after what seems like a long time and somehow also feels way too brief. My knees are weak with the passion I see in his eyes as he puts a steadying arm around me.

I can't help but think that less than four months ago, he never could have dipped me without causing me a great deal of pain.

He kisses me again fully upright, and the small audience erupts in cheers.

Drew walks me down the aisle, my senses still spinning from such a perfect kiss. *And that's what I have to look forward to for the rest of my life?*

I smile widely at the thought.

As we walk together, one thought overshadows the others: I can't wait to spend the rest of my life with this man who healed me, brought me back to life, and loved me enough to rearrange his entire life to marry me.

I look up at Drew and find him gazing back at me. "I'll love you forever, Doc."

He kisses my hand and leans in to say quietly, "And I, you, Mrs. Ashcroft."

"For as long as we both shall live?"

He laughs, picking me up, swinging me around. "Longer, wife, much longer."

When he goes to put me down, I squeal and throw my arms around his neck so I can peer deep into his eyes. "I approve of my title."

"Good," he growls as he sits me on my feet, "because I'm getting used to saying it."

As our loved ones approach us, I continue to hold on to my husband. It's like there's no one else in the room. They all disappear. "I think I want a kiss," I whisper.

"Your wish is my command." He leans in and kisses me with a tenderness that belies the passion I can sense bubbling below the surface.

I sigh with happiness. For as long as we both shall live. And according to Drew, for much longer.

The End

Author's Note

This story is very special to me. I once knew someone with spina bifida, Ann, and her resilience and positive attitude left quite an impression on me and everyone around her. As this is a work of fiction and fantasy, I wrote that Jewels was healed of her condition, but obviously that is not reality. I wish that were different.

My dear hope is to anyone who lives with a condition that affects their lives minute by minute will know that I wrote this book for them. You are an inspiration every day to live with hope and peace despite what you're handed with in life. I admire you greatly.

How I wish there were Elementals who could actually heal and do all the wonderful things they do in my books, but since they don't, my next and biggest hope is that everyone knows there is a God above who loves you more than you can possibly imagine.

He is real. And His power is immense. He can provide comfort when it seems impossible to have it. He CAN heal, has done so many, many times and I believe He still does. Believe in our Creator, or at least open a Bible and read the stories and accounts of those who've chosen to believe in Him. Those are stories of power.

God is not in any way a fantasy, and I truly hope you can find a way to get to know Him and His powerful love.

Would you leave a Review?

I sincerely hope you enjoyed Operation Jewels!
If you loved this book, please leave a review on Amazon, Book-
bub, or Goodreads, or if you're especially generous, all three! It
means more to us authors than you know.
I thank you from the bottom of my heart!

Fill your rooms with the delicious scents of my book candles!

Vela, Honey Butter Rolls
Linc, Roasted Marshmallows
Rayne, Evergreen and Ash

Go to:

https://linktr.ee/sofiasimpsonauthor

Read the first four books in An Elemental Series!

Free Book!

Receive a free novella, Operation Kane, from the Terra, Torch, Tempest and Tidal world if you join my newsletter!

Elia will do anything to get her best friend's older brother to notice she's a woman now, even become a spy.

Dive into this world of Elementals, unrequited love, and the power of hope. Enjoy the best friend's older brother, forbidden love, fake dating, and friends-to-lovers tropes in this powerful story of faith and young love.

Go to: www.sofiasimpson.com to find this charming novella. Connect with me there if you'd like to have me on your podcast.

www.ingramcontent.com/pod-product-compliance
Lightning Source LLC
Chambersburg PA
CBHW021407110726
47901CB00008B/2090